The Following of the Star

by

Florence Barclay

The Echo Library 2007

Published by

The Echo Library

Echo Library
131 High St.
Teddington
Middlesex TW11 8HH

www.echo-library.com

Please report serious faults in the text to complaints@echo-library.com

ISBN 978-1-4068-2339-4

Contents

GOLD

GOLD

CHAPTER I

THE STILL WATERS OF BAMBLEDENE

DAVID RIVERS closed his Bible suddenly, slipped it into the inner pocket of his coat, and, leaning back in his armchair, relaxed the tension at which he had been sitting while he mentally put his thoughts into terse and forcible phraseology.

His evening sermon was ready. The final sentence had silently thrilled into the quiet study, in the very words in which it would presently resound through the half-empty little village church; and David felt as did the young David of old, when he had paused at the brook and chosen five smooth stones for his sling, on his way to meet the mighty champion of the Philistines. David now felt ready to go forward and fight the Goliath of apathy and inattention; the life-long habit of not listening to the voice of the preacher or giving any heed to the message he brought.

The congregation, in this little Hampshire village church where, during the last five weeks, David had acted as locum-tenens, consisted entirely of well-to-do farmers and their families; of labourers, who lounged into church from force of habit, or because, since the public-houses had been closed by law during the hours of divine service, it was the only warmed and lighted place to be found on a Sunday evening; of a few devout old men and women, to whom weekly church-going, while on earth, appeared the only possible preparation for an eternity of Sabbaths in the world to come; and of a fair sprinkling of village lads and lassies, who took more interest in themselves and in each other than in the divine worship in which they were supposed to be taking part.

The two churchwardens, stout, florid, and well-to-do, occupied front pews on either side of the centre; Mr. Churchwarden Jones, on the right; Mr. Churchwarden Smith, on the left. Their official position lent them a dignity which they enjoyed to the full, and which overflowed to *Mrs.* Jones and *Mrs.* Smith, seated in state beside them. When, on "collection Sundays," the churchwardens advanced up the chancel together during the final verse of the hymn, and handed the plates to the Rector, their wives experienced a sensation of pride in them which "custom could not stale." They were wont to describe at the Sunday midday dinner or at supper, afterwards, the exact effect of this "procession" up the church, an oft-told tale for which they could always be sure of at least one interested auditor.

Mr. Churchwarden Jones bowed when he delivered the plate to the Rector. Mr. Churchwarden Smith did not bow, but kept himself more erect than usual; holding that anything in the nature of a bow, while in the House of God, savoured of popery.

This provided the village with a fruitful subject for endless discussion. The congregation was pretty equally divided. One half approved the stately bow of Mr. Churchwarden Jones, and unconsciously bowed themselves, while they disregarded their hymn-books and watched him make it. The other half were for

"Smith, and no popery," and also sang of "mystic sweet communion, with those whose rest is won," without giving any thought to the words, while occupied in gazing with approval at Farmer Smith's broad back, and at the uncompromising stiffness of the red neck, appearing above his starched Sunday collar.

Mrs. Smith secretly admired Mr. Jones's bow, and felt that her man was missing his chances for a silly idea; but not for worlds would Mrs. Smith have admitted this; no, not even to her especial crony. Miss Pike the milliner, who had once been to Paris, and knew what was what.

The venerated Rector, father of his people always bowed as he received the plates from the two churchwardens. But then, that had nothing whatever to do with the question, his *back* being to the Table. Besides, the Rector, who had christened, confirmed, married, and buried them during the last fifty years, could do no wrong They would as soon have thought of trying to understand his sermons, as of questioning his soundness. "The Rector says," constituted a final judgment, from which there was no appeal.

As he slowly and carefully mounted the pulpit stairs, one hand grasping the rail, the other clasping a black silk sermon-case, the hearts of his people went with him.

The hearts of his people were with him, as his silvery hair and benign face appeared above the large red velvet cushion on the pulpit desk; and the minds of his people were with him, until he had safely laid his sermon upon the cushion, opened it, and gently flattened the manuscript with both hands; then placed his pocket-hand-kerchief in the handy receptacle specially intended to contain it, and a lozenge in a prominent position on the desk. But, this well-known routine safely accomplished, they sang a loud amen to the closing verse of "the hymn before the sermon," and gave their minds a holiday, until, at the first words of the ascription, they rose automatically with a loud and joyous clatter to their feet, to emerge in a few moments into the fresh air and sunshine.

A perplexing contretemps had once occurred. The Rector's gentle voice had paused in its onward flow. It was not the usual lozenge-pause. Their subconscious minds understood and expected that. But, as a matter of fact, the Rector had, on this particular Sunday, required a second lozenge towards the end of the sermon, and the sentence immediately following this unexpected pause chanced to begin with the words: "And now to enlarge further upon our seventh point." At the first three words the whole congregation rose joyfully to their feet; then had to sit down abashed, while the Rector hurriedly enlarged upon "our seventh point." It was the only point which had as yet penetrated their intelligence.

In all subsequent sermons, the Rector carefully avoided, at the beginning of his sentences, the words which had produced a general rising. He world smile benignly to himself, in the seclusion of his study, as he substituted, for fear of accidents, "Let us, my brethren," or "Therefore, beloved."

It never struck the good man, content with his own scholarly presentment of deep theological truths, that the accidental rising was an undoubted evidence of non-attention on the part of his congregation. He continued to mount the pulpit steps, as he had mounted them during the last fifty years; attaining thereby an elevation from which he invariably preached completely over the heads of his people.

In this they acquiesced without question. It was their obvious duty to "sit under" a preacher, not to attempt to fathom his meaning; to sit *through* a sermon, not to endeavour to understand it. So they slumbered, fidgeted, or thought of other things, according to their age or inclination, until the ascription brought them to their feet, the benediction bowed them to their knees, and the first strident blasts of the organ sent them gaily trooping out of church and home to their Sunday dinners, virtuous and content.

Into this atmosphere of pious apathy, strode David Rivers; back on sick-leave from the wilds of Central Africa; aflame with zeal for his Lord certain of the inspiration of his message; accustomed to congregations to whom every thought was news, and every word was life; men, ready and eager to listen and to believe, and willing, when once they had believed, to be buried alive, or: tied to a stake, and burned by slow fire, sooner than relinquish or deny the faith he had taught them.

But how came this young prophet of fire into the still waters of our Hampshire village? The wilds of the desert, and the rapid rushings of Jordan, are the only suitable setting for John the Baptists in all ages.

Nevertheless to Hampshire he came; and it happened thus.

Influenza, which is no respecter of persons, attacked the venerated Rector.

In the first stress of need, neighbouring clergy came to the rescue. But when six weeks of rest and change were ordered, as the only means of insuring complete recovery, the Rector advertized for a locum-tenens, offering terms which attracted David, just out of hospital, sailing for Central Africa early in the New Year, and wondering how on earth he should scrape together the funds needed for completing his outfit. He applied immediately; and, within twenty-four hours, received a telegram suggesting an interview, and asking him to spend the night at Brambledene Rectory.

Here a curious friendship began, and was speedily cemented by mutual attraction. The white-haired old man, overflowing with geniality, punctilious in old-fashioned courtesy, reminded David Rivers of a father, long dead and deeply mourned; while the young enthusiast, with white, worn face, and deep-set shining eyes, struck a long-silent chord in the heart of the easy-going old Rector, seeming to him an embodiment of that which he himself might have been, had he chosen a harder, rougher path, when standing at the cross-roads half a century before.

An ideal of his youth, long vanished, returned, and stood before him in David Rivers. It was too late, now, to sigh after a departed ideal. But, as a tribute to its memory, he doubled the remuneration he had offered, left the keys in every bookcase in the library, and recommended David to the most especial care of his faithful housekeeper, Sarah Dolman, with instructions that, should the young man seem tired on Sunday evenings, after the full day's work, the best old sherry might be produced and offered.

And here let it be recorded, that David undoubtedly did look worn and tired after the full day's work; but the best old sherry was declined with thanks. The fact that your heart has remained among the wild tribes of Central Africa has a way of making your body very abstemious, and careless of all ordinary creature comforts.

Nevertheless, David enjoyed the Rector's large armchair, upholstered in maroon leather, and delighted in the oak-panelled study, with its wealth of valuable books and its atmosphere of scholarly calm and meditation.

This last Sunday of his ministry at Brambledene chanced to fall on Christmas Eve, Also, for once, it was true Christmas weather.

As David walked to church that morning, every branch and twig, every ivy leaf and holly berry, sparkled in the sunshine; the frosty lanes were white and hard, and paved with countless glittering diamonds. An indescribable exhilaration was in the air, Limbs felt light and supple; movement was a pleasure. Church bells, near and far away, pealed joyously. The Christmas spirit was already here.

"Unto us a Child is born, unto us a Son is given," quoted David, as he swung along the lanes. It was five years since he had had a Christmas in England. Mentally he contrasted this keen frosty brightness, with the mosquito-haunted swamps of the African jungle. This unaccustomed sense of health and vigour brought, by force of contrast, a remembrance of the deathly lassitude and weakness which accompany the malarial fever. But, instantly true to the certainty of his high and holy calling, his soul leapt up crying: "Unto *them* a Child is born! Unto *them* a Son is given! And how shall they believe in Him of whom they have not heard? And how shall they hear without a preacher?"

The little church, on that morning, was bright with holly and heavy with evergreens. The united efforts of the Smith and the Jones families had, during the week, made hundreds of yards of wreathing. On Saturday, all available young men came to help; Miss Pike, whose taste was so excellent, to advise; the school-mistress, a noisy person with more energy than tact, to argue with Miss Pike, and to side with Smiths and Joneses alternately, when any controversial point was under discussion.

So a gay party carried the long evergreen wreaths from the parish-room to the church, where already were collected baskets of holly and ivy, yards of scarlet flannel and white cotton-wool; an abundance of tin-tacks and hammers; and last, but not least, the Christmas scrolls and banners, which were annually produced from their place of dusty concealment behind the organ; and of which Mrs. Smith remarked, each year, that they were "every bit as good as new, if you put 'em up in a fresh place."

During the whole of Saturday afternoon and evening the decorative process had been carried on with so much energy, that when David came out from the vestry on Sunday morning he found himself in a scene which was decidedly what the old women from the alms-houses called "Christmassy."

His surplice rasped against the holly-leaves, as he made his way into the reading-desk. The homely face of the old gilt clock, on the gallery facing him, was wreathed in yew and holly, and the wreath had slipped slightly on one side, giving the sober old clock an unwontedly rakish appearance, which belied its steady and measured "tick-tick." Also into the bottom of this wreath, beneath which the whole congregation had to pass in and out, Tom Brigg, the doctor's son, a handsome fellow and noted wag, had surreptitiously inserted a piece of mistletoe. This prank of Tom's, known to all the younger members of the congregation, caused so much nudging and whispering and amused glancing at the inebrious-looking clock, that David produced his own watch, wondering if there were any mistake in the hour.

His sermon, on this Sunday morning, had seemed to him a failure.

His text confronted him in letters of gold on crimson flock: "Emmanuel—God with us"; but not a mind seemed with him as he gave it out, read it twice, slowly and clearly, and then proceeded to explain that this wonderful name, Emmanuel, was never intended to be the world's name for Christ, nor even His people's name for Him. However, at this statement, Mrs. Smith raised her eyebrows and began turning over the leaves of her Bible.

Encouraged by this unusual sign of attention, David Rivers leaned over the pulpit and tried to drive into one mind, at least, a thought which had been a discovery to himself the evening before, and was beginning to mean much to him, as every Spirit-given new light on a well-known theme always must mean to the earnest Bible student.

"The name Emmanuel," he said, "so freely used in our church decorations at this season, occurs three times only in the Bible; twice in the Old Testament, once in the New; and the New merely quotes the more important of the two passages in the Old.

"We can dismiss at once the allusion in Isaiah viii. 8, which merely speaks of Palestine as 'Thy land, O Immanuel,' and confine our attention to the great prophecy of Isaiah vii. 14, quoted in Matthew i. 23: 'Behold a Virgin shall bear a son, and shall call His name Emmanuel.' The Hebrew of this passage reads: 'Thou, O Virgin, shalt call His name Immanuel'; and the Greek of Matthew i. bears the same meaning. I want you to realize that this was His mother's name for the new-born King, for the Babe of Bethlehem, for the little son in the village home at Nazareth. His Presence there meant to that humble pondering heart: '*God* with us.'

"If you want to find *our* name for Him," continued David, noting that Mrs. Smith, ignoring his two references, still turned the pages of her Bible, "look at the angel's message to Joseph in the 21st verse of Matthew i.: 'Thou shalt call His name Jesus, for He shall save His people from their sins.' That name is mentioned nine hundred and six times in the Bible. We cannot attempt to look them all out now,"—with an appealing glance at Mrs. Smith's rustling pages— "but let us make sure that we have appropriated to the full the gifts and blessings of that name, 'which is above every name.' It was the watchword of the early church. It is the secret of our peace and power. It will be our password into heaven.

"But Emmanuel was His mother's name for Him. As she laid Him in the manger, round which the patient cattle snuffed in silent wonder at this new use for the place where heretofore they munched their fodder, it was 'God with us' in the stable.

"As, seated on the ass, she clasped the infant to her breast through the long hours of that night ride into Egypt she whispered: 'Emmanuel, Emmanuel! God *with* us, in our flight and peril.'

"In the carpenter's home at Nazareth, where, in the midst of the many trials and vexations of a village life of poverty. He was ever patient, gentle, understanding; subject to His parents, yet giving His mother much cause for pondering, many things to treasure in her heart—often, in adoring tenderness, she would whisper: 'Emmanuel, God with *us*.'"

David paused and looked earnestly down the church, longing for some response to the thrill in his own soul.

"Ah," he said, slowly and impressively, "if only the boys in your village could be *this* to their mothers! If their loyal obedience, their gentle, loving chivalry, their thoughtful tenderness, could make it possible for their own mothers to say: 'I see the Christ-life in my little boy. When he is at home, the love of God is here. Truly it is Emmanuel, God with us.'"

"What did that young man mean," remarked Mrs. Smith at the dinner-table at Appledore Farm, "by trying to take from us the name 'Emmanuel'? Seems to me, if he stays here much longer we shall have no Bible left!"

Mr. Churchwarden Smith had been carving the Sunday beef for his numerous family. He had only, that moment, fallen to upon his own portion. Otherwise Mrs. Smith would not have been allowed to complete her sentence.

"I've no patience with these young chaps!" he burst out, as soon as speech was possible. "Undermining the faith of their forefathers; putting our good old English Bible into 'Ebrew and Greek, just to parade their own learning, and confuse the minds of simple folk. 'Higher criticism,' they call it! Jolly low-down impudence, say I!"

Mrs. Smith watchfully bided her time. Then: "And popish too," she added, "to talk so much about the mother of our Lord."

"I don't think he mentioned *her*, my dear," said Mr. Churchwarden Smith. "Pass the mustard, Johnny."

Yes, as he thought it over during his lonely luncheon, David felt more and more convinced that his morning sermon had been a failure.

He did not know of a little curly-headed boy, whose young widowed mother was at her wit's end as to how to control his wilfulness; but who ran straight to his garret-room after service, and, kneeling beside his frosty window, looked up to the wintry sky and said: "Please God, make me a Manuel to my mother, like Jesus was to His, for Christ's sake. Amen."

David did not know of this; nor that, ever after, that cottage home was to be transformed, owing to the living power of his message.

So, down in the depths of discouragement, he dubbed his morning sermon a failure.

Notwithstanding, he prepared the evening subject with equal care, a spice of enjoyment added, owing to the fact that he would possibly—probably—almost to a certainty—have in the evening congregation a mind able to understand and appreciate each point; a mind of a caliber equal to his own; a soul he was bent on winning.

As he closed his Bible, put it into his pocket, and relaxed over the thought that his sermon was complete, he smiled into the glowing wood fire, saying to himself, in glad anticipation: "My Lady of Mystery will undoubtedly be there. Now I wonder if *she* believes that there were three Wise Men!"

CHAPTER II

THE LADY OF MYSTERY

DAVID thrust his hands deep into the pockets of his short coat, well cut, but inclined to be somewhat threadbare. He crossed his knees, and lay back comfortably in the Rector's big chair. An hour and a half remained before he need start out.

It was inexpressibly restful to have his subject, clear cut and complete, safely stowed away in the back of his mind, and to be able to sit quietly in this warmth and comfort, and let his thoughts dwell lightly upon other things, while Christmas snow fell softly, in large flakes, without; and gathering twilight slowly hushed the day to rest.

"Yes, undoubtedly my Lady of Mystery will be there," thought David Rivers, "unless this fall of snow keeps her away."

He let his memory dwell in detail upon the first time he had seen her.

It happened on his second Sunday at Brambledene.

The deadening effect of the mental apathy of the congregation had already somewhat damped his enthusiasm.

It was so many years since he had preached in English, that, on the first Sunday, he had allowed himself the luxury of writing out his whole sermon. This plan, for various reasons, did not prove successful,

Mrs. Churchwarden Jones and Mrs. Churchwarden Smith—good simple souls both, if you found them in their dairies making butter, or superintending the sturdy maids in the farm kitchens—seemed to consider on Sundays that they magnified their husbands' office by the amount of rustle and jingle they contrived to make with their own portly persons during the church services. They kept it up, duet fashion, on either side of the aisle. If Mrs. Jones rustled, Mrs. Smith promptly tinkled. If Mrs. Smith rustled, Mrs. Jones straightway jingled. The first time this happened in the sermon, David looked round, hesitated, lost his place, and suffered agonies of mortification before he found it again.

Moreover he soon realized that, with his eyes on the manuscript, he had absolutely no chance of holding the attention of his audience.

In the evening he tried notes, but this seemed to him neither one thing nor the other. So on all subsequent Sundays he memorized his sermons as he prepared them, and hardly realized himself how constantly, in their delivery, there flowed from his sub consciousness a depth of thought, clothed in eloquent and appropriate language, which had not as yet been ground in the mill of his conscious mind.

On that second Sunday evening, David had entered the reading-desk depressed and discouraged. In the morning he had fallen out with the choir. It was a mixed choir. Large numbers of young Smiths and Joneses sat on either side of the chancel and vied with one another as to which family could out sing the other. The rivalry was resulting in a specially loud and joyful noise in the closing verses of the Benedictus.

David, jarred in every nerve, and forgetting for the moment that he was not dealing with his African aborigines, wheeled round in the desk, held up his hand, and said: "Hush!" with the result that he had to declaim the details of John the Baptist's mission, as a tenor solo; and that the organist noisily turned over his music-books during the whole time of the sermon, apparently in a prolonged search for a suitable recessional voluntary.

Wishing himself back in his African forests, David began the service, in a chastened voice, on that second Sunday evening.

During the singing of the first of the evening Psalms, the baize-covered door at the further end of the church, was pushed gently open; a tall figure entered, alone; closed the door noiselessly behind her, and stood for a moment, in hesitating uncertainty, beneath the gallery.

Then the old clerk and verger, Jabez Bones, bustled out of his seat, and ushering her up the centre, showed her into a cushioned pew on the pulpit side, rather more than half-way up the church.

The congregation awoke to palpable interest, at her advent. The choir infused a tone of excitement into the chant, which, up to that moment, had been woefully flat. Each pew she passed, in the wake of old Jabez, thereafter contained a nudge or a whisper.

David's first impression of her, was of an embodiment of silence and softness,—so silently she passed up the church and into the empty pew, moving to the further corner, right against the stout whitewashed pillar. No rustle, no tinkle, marked her progress; only a silent fragrance of violets. And of softness— soft furs, soft velvet, soft hair; and soft grey eyes, beneath the brim of a dark green velvet hat.

But his second impression was other than the first. She was looking at him with an expression of amused scrutiny. Her eyes were keen and penetrating; her lips were set in lines of critical independence of judgment; the beautifully moulded chin was firm and white as marble against the soft brown fur.

She regarded him steadily for some minutes. Then she looked away, and David became aware, by means of that subconscious intuition, which should be as a sixth sense to all ministers and preachers, that nothing in the service reached her in the very least. Her mind was far away. Whatever her object had been in entering the little whitewashed church of Brambledene on that Sunday night, it certainly was not worship.

But, when he began to preach, he arrested her attention. His opening remark evidently appealed to her. She glanced up at him, quickly, a gleam of amusement and interest in her clear eyes. And afterwards, though she did not lift them again, and partly turned away, leaning against the pillar, so that he could see only the clear-cut whiteness of her perfect profile, he knew that she was listening.

From that hour, David's evening sermons were prepared with the more or less conscious idea of reaching the soul of that calm immovable Lady of Mystery.

She did not attract him as a woman. Her beauty meant nothing to him. He had long ago faced the fact that his call to Central Africa must mean celibacy. No man worthy of the name would, for his own comfort or delight, allow a woman to share such dangers and privations as those through which he had to pass. And, if five years of that climate had undermined his own magnificent constitution and sent him home a wreck of his former self, surely, had he taken out a wife, it would simply have meant a lonely grave, left behind in the African jungle.

So David had faced it out that a missionary's life, in a place where wife and children could not live, must mean celibacy; nor had he the smallest intention of ever swerving from that decision. His devotion to his work filled his heart. His people were his children.

Therefore no ordinary element of romance entered into his thoughts concerning the beautiful woman who, on each Sunday evening, leaned against the stone pillar, and showed by a slight flicker of the eyelids or curve of the proud lips, that she heard and appreciated each point in his sermon.

How far she agreed, he had no means of knowing. Who she was, and whence she came, he did not attempt to find out. He preferred that she should remain the Lady of Mystery. After her first appearance, when old Jabez bustled into the vestry at the close of the service, he abounded in nods and winks, inarticulate exclamations, and chuckings of his thumb over his shoulder backward toward the church. At length, getting no response from David, he burst forth: "Sakes alive, sir! I'm thinking she ain't bin seen in a place o' wash-up, since she was— —"

David, half in and half out of his cassock, turned on the old clerk in sudden indignation.

"Bones," he said, sternly, "no member of the congregation should ever be discussed in the vestry. Not another word, please. Now give me the entry book."

The old man muttered something inaudible about the Rector and young *h*upstarts, and our poor David had made another enemy in Brambledene.

He never chanced to see his Lady of Mystery arrive; but, after that first evening, she never failed to be in her place when he came out of the vestry; nor did he ever see her depart, always resisting the temptation to leave the church hurriedly when service was over.

So she remained the Lady of Mystery, and now—his last Sunday evening had come; and, as he thought of her, he longed to see a look of faith and joy dawn in her cold sad eyes, as ardently as another man might have longed to see a look of love for himself awaken in them.

But David wanted nothing for himself, and a great deal for his Lord, He wanted this beautiful personality, this forceful character, this strong, self-reliant soul; he wanted this obvious wealth, this unmistakable possessor of place and power, for his Master's service, for the Kingdom of his King. No thought of himself came in at all. How should it? He wanted to win her for her own sake; and he wanted to win her for his Lord, He wanted this more persistently and ardently than he had ever desired anything in his life before. He was almost perplexed at the insistence of the thought, and the way in which it never left him. And now—the last chance had come.

He rose, and went to the window. Snowflakes were falling gently, few and far between; but the landscape was completely covered by a pure white pall.

"Undoubtedly," said David, "my Lady of Mystery will be there, unless this fall of snow keeps her away."

He paced up and down the study, repeating stray sentences from his sermon, as they came into his mind.

Sarah brought in the lamp, and drew the maroon rep curtains, shutting out the snow and gathering darkness; Sarah, stout, comfortable, and motherly, who—accustomed to the rosy-cheeked plumpness of her easy-going master—looked with undisguised dismay at David's thin worn face, and limbs on which his clothes still hung loosely, giving him an appearance of not belonging to his surroundings, which tried the kind heart and practical mind of the Rector's good housekeeper.

"He do give me the creeps, poor young gentleman," she confided to a friend, who had dropped in for tea and a chat. "To see him all shrunk up, so to speak, in Master's big chair; and just where there would be so much of Master, there's naught of him, which makes the chair seem fair empty. And then he looks up and speaks, and his voice is like music, and his eyes shine like stars, and he seems more alive than Master, or anybody else one knows; yet not alive in his poor thin body; but alive because of something burning and shining *h*inside of 'im; something stronger than a body, and more alive than life—oh, *I* don't know!" concluded Sarah, suddenly alarmed by her own eloquence.

Creepy, I call it," said the friend.

"Creepy it is," agreed Sarah.

Nevertheless she watched carefully over David's creature comforts, and he owed it to Sarah's insistence, that he weighed nearly a stone heavier when he left Brambledene than on his arrival there.

She now brought in tea, temptingly arranged on a tray, poured out his first cup, and stood a minute to watch him drink it, and to exhort him to wrap up well before going out in this snow.

"My last Sunday, Sarah," said David, looking at her with those same deep-set shining eyes. "I shan't bother you much longer. I have a service to-morrow—Christmas Day; and must stay over Boxing Day for two weddings. Then I'm off to town; and in a couple of weeks I sail for Central Africa. I wonder how you would like Africa, Sarah. Are you afraid of snakes?"

"Don't mention 'em, Mr. Rivers, sir," replied Sarah, in a stage whisper; "nasty evil things! If Eve had been as fearful of 'em as I am, there'd never 'ave been no Fall. You wouldn't catch me staying to talk theology with a serpent. No, not me, sir! It's take to m'heels and run, would have been my way, if I'd 'a lived in Genesis three."

David smiled. "A good way, Sarah," he said, "and scriptural. But you forget the attraction of the tree, with its luscious fruit. Poor Eve! The longing of the moment, always seems the great essential. We are apt to forget the long eternity of regret."

Sarah sidled respectfully towards the door.

"Eat your hot-buttered toast, before it grows cold, sir," she counselled; "and give over thinking about snakes. Dear heart:, it's Christmas Eve!"

"So it is," said David. "And my sermon is about a star. Right you are, Sarah! I'll 'give over thinking about snakes,' and look higher. There can be no following of the star with our eyes turned earthward. . . . All right! Don't you worry. I'll eat every bit."

CHAPTER III

DAVID STIRS THE STILL WATERS

AS David tramped to church the moon was rising. The fir-trees stood, dark and stately, beneath their nodding plumes of feathery snow. The little village church, with its white roof, and brightly lighted windows, looked like a Christmas card.

Above its ivy-covered tower, luminous as a lamp in the deep purple sky, shone out one brilliant star.

David smiled as he raised his eyes. He was thinking of Sarah and the snakes. "If I had lived in Genesis three," he quoted. "What a delightful way of putting it; as if Genesis were a terrace, and three the number. Good old Sarah! Would she have been more successful in coping with the tempter? Undoubtedly Eve had the artistic temperament, which is always a snare; also she had a woman's instinctive desire to set others right, and to explain. Adam would have seen through the tempter's wilful distortion of the wording of God's command, and would not have been beguiled into an argument with so crafty and insincere an opponent. Poor Eve, in her desire to prove him wrong, to air her own superior knowledge, and to justify her Maker, hurried at once into the trap, and was speedily undone. Here, at the very outset of our history, we have in a nutshell the whole difference between the mentality of the sexes. Where Eve stood arguing and explaining—laying herself open to a retort which shook her own belief, and undermined her obedience—Adam would have said: "Liar!" and turned on his heel. Yet if Eve lived nowadays she would be quite sure she could set right all mistakes in our legislature, if only Adam could be induced to let her have a finger in every pie. Having lived in Genesis iii. Adam would know better than to try it!"

As David reached the old lich-gate, two brilliant lights shone down the road from the opposite direction, and the next moment a motor glided swiftly to the gate, and stopped.

A footman sprang down from beside the chauffeur, opened the door, touched a button, and the interior of the car flashed into light.

Seated within, half buried in furs, David saw the calm sweet face of his Lady of Mystery. He stood on one side, in the shadow of the gate, and waited.

The footman drew out a white fur rug, and threw it over his left arm; then held the door wide.

She stepped out, tall and silent. David saw the calm whiteness of her features in the moonlight. She took no more notice of her men, than if they had been machines, but passed straight up the churchyard path, between the yew-tree sentinels, and disappeared into the porch.

The footman bundled in the rug, switched off the lights, banged the door, took his place beside the chauffeur, and the large roomy motor glided silently away. Nothing remained save a delicate fragrance of violets under the lich-gate, beneath which she had passed.

The whole thing had taken twenty seconds. It seemed to David like the swift happenings of a dream. Nothing was left to prove its reality, but the elusive scent of violets, and the marks of the huge tyres in the snow.

But as David made his way round to the vestry door, he knew his Lady of Mystery was already in her corner beside the stout whitewashed pillar; and he also knew that he had been right in the surmise which placed her in an environment of luxury and wealth.

Christmas Eve had produced a larger congregation than usual. The service was as cheerful and noisy as the choir and organist could make it. David's quiet voice seemed only to be heard at rare intervals, like the singing of a thrush in the momentary lull of a storm.

The Lady of Mystery looked alternately bored and amused. Her expression was more calmly critical than ever. She had discarded her large velvet hat for a soft toque of silver-grey fur, placed lightly upon her wealth of golden hair. This tended to reveal the classic beauty of her features, yet made her look older, showing up a hardness of expression which had been softened by the green velvet brim. David, who had thought her twenty-five, now began to wonder whether she were not older than himself. Her expression might have credited her with full thirty years' experience of the world.

David mounted the pulpit steps to the inspiriting strains of "While shepherds watched their flocks by night, all seated on the ground." Already the inhabitants of Brambledene had had it at their front doors, sung, in season and out of season, by the school-children in every sort of key and tempo. Now the latter returned joyfully to the charge, sure of arriving at the final verse, without any sudden or violent exhortations to go away. They beat the choir's already rapid rendering; ignored the organist, and rushed on without pause, comma, or breathing space.

In the midst of this erratic description of the peaceful scene on Bethlehem's hills on that Christmas night so long ago, David's white earnest face appeared in the pulpit, looking down anxiously upon his congregation.

The words of his opening collect brought a sense of peace, though the silence of his long intentional pause after "Let us pray," had at first accentuated the remembrance of the hubbub which had preceded it. David felt that the weird chanting of his African savages, echoing among the trees of their primeval forests, compared favourably, from the point of view both of reverence and of music, with the singing in this English village church. His very soul was jarred. His nerves were all on edge.

As he stood silent, while the congregation settled into their seats, looking down he met the grey eyes of his Lady of Mystery. They said: "I am waiting. I have come for this."

Instantly the sense of inspiration filled him.

With glad assurance he gave out his text, "The gospel according to St. Matthew, the second chapter, the tenth and eleventh verses: 'When they saw the star, they rejoiced with exceeding great joy. . . . And when they had opened their treasures, they presented unto Him gifts; gold, and frankincense, and myrrh.'"

As soon as the text of a sermon was given out, Mr. Churchwarden Jones in his corner, and Mr. Churchwarden Smith in his, verified it in their Bibles, made sure it was really there, and had been read correctly. Then they closed their

Bibles and placed them on the ledges in front of them; took off their glasses, put them noisily into spectacle-cases, stowed these in inner pockets, leant well back, and proceeded to go very unmistakably and emphatically to sleep.

David had got into the way of reading his text twice over, slowly, while this performance took place.

Now, when he looked up from his Bible, the two churchwardens were in position. Their gold watch-chains, looped upon their ample waistcoats, produced much the same effect as the wreathing with which well-meaning decorators had accentuated the stoutness of the whitewashed pillars.

The attention of the congregation was already wandering. David made a desperate effort to hold it.

"My friends," he said, "although it is Christmas Eve, I speak to you to-night on the Epiphany subject, because, when the great Feast of Epiphany comes, I shall no longer have the privilege of addressing you. I expect to be on the ocean, on my way to carry the Christmas message of 'Peace on earth, good will toward men,' to the savage tribes of Central Africa."

No one looked responsive. No one seemed to care in the least where David Rivers would be on the great Feast of Epiphany. He tried another tack.

"Our text deals with the experience of those Wise Men of the East, who, guided by the star, journeyed over the desert in quest of the new-born King. Now, if I were to ask this congregation to tell me how many Wise Men there were, I wonder which of you would answer 'three.'"

No one looked in the least interested. What a silly question! What a senseless cause for wonder! Of course they would *all* answer "three." The youngest infant in the Sunday School knew that there were three Wise Men.

"But why should you say 'three'?" continued David. "We are not told in the Bible how many Wise Men there were. Look and see."

The Smith and Jones families made no move. They knew perfectly well that *their* Bibles said "three." If this young man's Bible omitted to mention the orthodox number, it was only another of many omissions in his new-fangled Bible and unsound preaching. It would be one thing more to report to the Rector on his return.

But his Lady of Mystery leaned forward, took up a Bible which chanced to be beside her, turned rapidly to Matthew ii., bent over it for a moment, then smiled, and laid it down, David knew she had made sure of finding "three," and had not found it. He took courage. She was interested.

He launched into his subject. In vivid words, more full of poetry and beauty than he knew, he rapidly painted the scene; the long journey through the eastern desert, with eyes upon the star; the anxious days, when it could not be seen, and the route might so easily be missed; the glad nights when it shone again, luminous, serene, still moving on before. The arrival at Jerusalem, the onward quest to Bethlehem, the finding of the King.

Then, the actual story fully dealt with, David turned to application.

"My friends," he said, "this earthly life of ours is the desert. Your pilgrimage lies across its ofttimes dreary wastes. But if your journey is to be to any purpose, if life is to be a success and not a failure, its main object must be the finding of the King. His guiding Spirit moves before you as the star. His word is also the heavenly lamp which lights your way. But I want, tonight, to give you a third meaning for the Epiphany star. The star stands for your highest Ideal. Pause a moment, and think. . . . Have you in your life to-night a heaven-sent Ideal, to which you are always true; which you follow faithfully, and which, as you follow it, leads to the King?"

David paused. Mrs. Jones rustled, and Mrs. Smith tinkled, but David heard them not. The Lady of Mystery had lifted her eyes to his, and those beautiful sad eyes said: "I *had.*"

"They lost sight of the star," said David. "Their hearts were sad, thinking they had lost it forever. But they found it again at Jerusalem—place of God's holy temple and worship. Here is your Jerusalem. Lift your eyes to-night, higher than the mere church roof, and find again your lost star; see where shines your Ideal—your faith, your hope, your love, your belief in things eternal. 'And when they saw the star they rejoiced.'"

David paused.

Long lashes veiled the grey eyes. Her hands were folded in her lap, and her eyes were not lifted from them.

"When these desert-travellers found the King," continued David, "they opened their treasures and presented unto Him gifts,—gold, and frankincense, and myrrh. I know this is usually taken in relation to Himself, and as being, in a threefold way, typical of His mission: Gold for the King; frankincense for the great High Priest; myrrh for the suffering, dying Saviour, who was to give His life for the redemption of the world.

"But I want to take it to-night in another sense. Let these three kinds of gifts emphasize the three kinds of things you have in your life to-day, which you may offer to the King, if your guiding star has led you to His feet. They opened *their* treasures. I want you to open *your* treasures, to-night. What are your treasures? Why yourself, and all you possess.

"First let us consider the gold."

The Lady of Mystery lifted her golden head and looked him full in the face. There was challenge in her eyes.

"I do not necessarily mean your money," said David, "though how much more you might all do with that, for the King and for His service, than you are already doing. Ah, if people could realize how greatly gold is needed for His work, they would soon open their treasures and pour it forth! I have told you of my vast parish, out in the unexplored forests, swamps, and jungles of Central Africa. Do you know what I want for my people, there? Think of all you have here—of all you have had, ever since you can remember. Then listen: I want a church; I want schools; I want books; I want a translation of the Bible, and a printing-press to print it with." David's eyes glowed, and he threw grammar to the winds! "I want a comrade to help me, and a steam-launch with which to navigate great lakes and rivers. I want all these things, and I want them for my Master, and for His work. I can give my own life, but it is all I have to give. I have been taking your Rector's place here for six weeks in order to earn twelve guineas, which will enable me to take out a good medicine-chest with which to doctor my people, and to complete my necessary outfit."

Mr. Churchwarden Jones was awake by now, and fidgeted uncomfortably. This young man should not have mentioned his stipend from the pulpit. It was decidedly unsuitable.

"Your Rector," continued David, "knowing why I need it, is generously doubling that payment. May God bless him for it when he takes up again his ministry among you."

They were all listening now. David's eyes glowed like hot coals in his thin face. His voice rang through the church.

"Ah, friends," he said, "those who have all they need for their comfortable spiritual life, cannot realize the awful, desperate want, in those wild places of the earth. We enjoy quoting what we call a 'gospel text': 'Whosoever shall call upon the name of the Lord shall be saved.' But too often we pause there, in self-appropriating complacency, forgetting that the whole point of the passage lies in what follows: 'How then shall they call on Him in Whom they have not believed? And how shall they believe in Him of Whom they have not heard? And how shall they hear, without a preacher? And how shall they preach except they be sent?' You must answer all these questions, when you open your treasures at the feet of the King.

"But forgive me for intruding my own interests. This is not a missionary sermon."—Here Mrs. Smith nodded energetically. That was exactly what she had already whispered to Mr. Smith.—"Also 'gold' stands for much besides money. Think of all the golden things in life. The joys, the brightness, the glory of success; all beauty, all gaiety, all golden mirth and laughter. Let all these golden things be so consecrated that, opening you treasures, you can at any moment bring them as offerings to your King.

"But the second gift was frankincense." David paused, giving each listener— and at last there were many—time to wonder what in his or her life stood for frankincense.

"Frankincense," said David, "is, first of all, your worship. And by worship, I do not necessarily mean public worship in church, important though that be. I mean the constant worship of an adoring heart. 'O worship the Lord in the beauty of holiness.' Unless your daily life from Monday to Saturday is a life of worship, there will not be much reality in your public worship on Sunday. And then, frankincense stands for all that appertains to the spirit part of you—your ideals, your noblest loves, your finest aspirations. Open your treasures, friends, and bring these to your King."

"And, lastly, myrrh." David paused, and a look so calm, so holy, so sublime, passed into his face, that to one who watched him then, and who chanced to know the meaning of that look, his face was as the face of an angel.

"The myrrh," he said, "stands for death. Some of us may be called upon definitely to face death, for the King's sake. But *all* who have lived unto Him in life, can glorify Him in death. 'Precious in the sight of the Lord is the death of

His saints.' We can all at last bring to Him this gift—a gift which, in the bringing, will indeed bring us into His very presence. But, meanwhile, your present offering of myrrh is the death of self; the daily crucifying of the self-life. 'For the love of Christ constraineth us; because we thus judge, that if one died for all, then were all dead; and that He died for all, that they which live should not henceforth live unto themselves, but unto Him, Who died for them, and rose again.' Your response to that constraining love, your acceptance of that atoning death, your acquiescence in that crucifixion of self, constitute your offering of myrrh.

"But myrrh, in the Bible, stands for other things besides death. We must not pause to do so now, but some time, at your leisure, look out each mention of myrrh. You will find it stands for love—love of the sweetest, tenderest kind; love so complete, that it must bring with it self-abnegation, and a mingling of pain with its bliss.

"And you will find it stands for sorrow; not bitterness of woe; but sorrow accepted as the Father's will, and therefore touched with reverent joy. Ah, bring your sorrows as gifts to your King. 'Surely He hath borne our griefs, and carried our sorrows.' Bring even these, and lay them at His feet."

David closed his Bible, placing it on the cushion, folded his hands upon it, and leaned down from the high pulpit.

"My friends," he said—and those who looked up responsive never forgot the light in his eyes—"I am leaving this dear home land of ours on the day when we shall be keeping the Feast of the Star. My star leads me to a place from which I do not ever expect to return. My offering of myrrh to my King, is a grave in an African forest, and I offer it gladly.

"But, may I now say to you, whose faces—after to-morrow—I never expect to see again: Do not lose sight of your star, as you travel across fife's desert. Look up, look on; ever, in earnest faith, move forward. Then I can leave with each one in this congregation, as a farewell promise "—he looked at all present; but his eyes met the grey eyes, now swimming in tears, of his Lady of Mystery; met, and held them, with searching solemn gaze, as he uttered his final words:

"Thine eyes shall see the King in His beauty; they shall behold the Land that is very far off."

CHAPTER IV

DIANA RIVERS, OF RIVERSCOURT

PERHAPS the greatest tribute to David's sermon, was the quiet way in which the good people of Brambledene rose to their feet at its close.

Lead, Kindly Light was sung with unusual feeling and reverence.

The collection, for Church Expenses, was the largest ever taken in Brambledene Church, within the memory of man. In one of the plates, there was gold. David knew quite well who had put in that sovereign.

He sat at the vestry table and fingered it thoughtfully. He had disrobed while the church-wardens counted the money and commented on the unusual amount of the collection, and the remarkable fact of a sovereign in the plate. They left the money in little piles on the red cloth, for David to carry home and lock up in the Rector's safe.

He had now to enter his text, and the amount of the collection, in the vestry book.

He had glanced down the church as he left the chancel. His Lady of Mystery was still on her knees in the comer near the pillar, her head bowed in her hands. He had seen the top of her grey fur hat, with soft waves of golden hair on either side of it.

He took up the pen and entered his text.

Then he laid the pen down, and glanced at back records of evening collections for Church Expenses. He did not hurry. He could hear very faintly in the distance the throbbing of a motor, waiting at the lich-gate. He knew exactly how it looked, waiting in the snow; two great acetylene lamps in front; delicate electric bulbs lighting the interior, one in each comer of the roof. He knew just how *she* would look, as the footman tucked the white fur rug around her. She would lean back, rather bored and impatient, and take no more notice of the man than if he were a machine. David hated that kind of behaviour toward those who serve. He held that every service, even the smallest, should receive a kindly acknowledgment.

He turned the pages of the vestry book. Six shillings and elevenpence. Two and fourpence halfpenny. Three and six. Four shillings and ninepence three farthings. Seven and tenpence. And now he was about to enter: "two pounds, eight shillings, and sevenpence halfpenny." Even without the gold *she* had put in, it was a large increase on former offerings. Truly these good people opened their treasures when at last their hearts were touched.

David was alone in the vestry. He could hear old Jabez Bones bustling about in the church, putting out the lamps, occasionally knocking down books, and picking them up again; doing in appearance three times as much as he accomplished in reality.

David took up the pen. He did not hurry. The rhythmic panting of the engine still reached him, faintly, across the snowy mounds He did not intend to arrive at the lich-gate until that dream-motor had glided noiselessly out of sight.

As he bent over the book to make the entry, the vestry door was pushed softly open. He heard no sound; but a subtle fragrance of violets suddenly surrounded him.

David looked up.

Framed in the Gothic arch of the narrow doorway, her large grey eyes fixed upon him in unwonted gentleness, stood his Lady of Mystery.

David was so completely taken by surprise that he forgot to rise to his feet. He dropped his pen, but still sat on the high vestry stool, and gazed at her in speechless wonderment.

"I have come," said his Lady of Mystery, and her low-pitched voice was full of music, "I have come to bring you my gifts—gold, frankincense, and myrrh."

"Not to me," said David, "You must not bring them to me. You must bring them to the King."

"I must bring them to you," she said, "because I know no other way. I have sought the Christ, and found HIM not, I had lost my way in the dreary darkness of the desert. To-night you have cleared my sky. Once more I see the shining of the Star. You have shown me that I have these three gifts to offer. But I must bring them to you, David Rivers, because you are the most Christlike man I have ever known, and you stand to me for your King."

"I cannot stand for my King," said David, unconscious of the light in his own eyes, or the divine radiance reflected on his face. "I am but His messenger; the voice in the wilderness crying: 'Prepare ye the way of the Lord.'"

The Lady of Mystery moved a step nearer, and laid one hand on the vestry table. She bent toward him. Two wax candles, in brass candlesticks, stood upon the table, on either side of the vestry book, providing the only illumination. In the light of these they looked into one another's faces.

"You have certainly prepared His way in my heart to-night," she said, "and I believe you are going to make straight for me the tangle of my life. Only, first of all, you must know who I am. Has anybody told you? Do you know?"

"Nobody has told me," said David, "and I do not know."

"What have you called me, to yourself, all these weeks?"

"My Lady of Mystery," answered David simply; wondering how she knew he had called her anything.

She smiled, and there seemed to be twenty wax candles in the vestry, rather than two.

"Quite pretty," she said, "but too much like a story-book, to be practically useful." She drew a small purple bag from her muff; took out a card, and laid it on the table in front of him, "You must know who I am," she said, "and where I live; because, you see, I am going to ask you to dinner."

She smiled again; and David bent over the card. She marked his involuntary movement of surprise.

"Yes," she said, "I am Diana Rivers, of Rivers-court. Had you heard of me before? I suppose we are, in some sort, cousins."

But David sat with his eyes bent upon the card before him. Alas, what was happening? His Lady of Mystery had vanished. This tall girl, in furs and velvet, with her brilliant smile. sweet low voice, and assured manner, was the greatest heiress in the county; Master of the Hounds; patron of four livings; notorious for her advanced views and fearless independence; a power and a terror in the whole neighbourhood. His Lady of Mystery who, under his guidance, was to become a meek and lowly follower of the Star! Poor David!

He looked so thin and forlorn, for the moment, that Diana felt an amused desire to put him into an armchair, and ply him with champagne.

"Of course I have heard of you, Miss Rivers," he said, slowly. "Mr. Goldsworthy told me all about you, during my first evening at the Rectory. He asked me whether we were related."

"Dear old thing!" remarked Diana, lightly. "He is my godfather, you know; and I think his anxiety over my spiritual condition is the one thing which keeps him of a size to pass through the pulpit door!"

"Don't," said David.

She looked at him, with laughter in her eyes.

"All right, Cousin David. I did not mean to be flippant. And we *are* cousins, you know."

"I think not," he answered, gravely. "I am of very humble origin; and I never heard of my people claiming kinship with courts of any kind."

"Oh, don't be silly!" retorted Diana, drumming on the vestry table with her firm, gloved fingers; but her tone was so gentle, that it almost held a caress. "Don't be silly, Cousin David. The humblest people live in courts in London; and all rivers run into the sea! Nothing but the genuine Rivers' pluck could have faced these good folk Sunday after Sunday; and only the fire of the real old Rivers' stock could have made them sit up and listen to-night. You look just like grandpapa, confounding the Opposition from his seat on the Government benches, when you attack Mrs. Smith for turning over the pages of her Bible in that distracting and senseless way. I can fancy myself back in the Ladies' Gallery, longing to cheer. We *must* claim kinship, Cousin David."

"I think not." he repeated, firmly. He looked very small, and thin, and miserable, huddled up on the vestry stool. His threadbare clerical jacket seemed several sizes too large for him, "Diana Rivers, of Riverscourt!" Oh, where was his dear Lady of Mystery?

If Diana wanted to shake him, she kept the desire well in hand. Her voice grew even deeper; more full of music, more softly gentle.

"Well, cousin or no cousin," she said, "I want your advice, and I can't do without your help Where do you take your Christmas dinner. David Rivers?"

"Why, at the Rectory," he answered, looking up. "I have no friends here." Then a gleam of amusement passed over his face: "Sarah says, a it is Christmas, she is 'going to a fowl,'" he said

"I see. And you are planning to eat your fowl in solitary grandeur at the Rectory? Well, *I* will 'go to a turkey' and a plum-pudding, and possibly, mince-pies; and you shall dine with me on Christmas night. The idea of a lonely meal on your last—I mean, your *one* Christmas Day in England!"

"You are very kind," said David; "but is not Riverscourt twelve miles from here?"

"My chauffeur does it in twenty minutes," replied Diana. "It would be as much as his place is worth to take twenty-one. I will send the motor for you at seven, and we will dine at half-past. They can run you back whenever you like. Does your household retire early? Or perhaps you are allowed a latch-key."

David smiled. "My household consists of Sarah, Mr. Goldsworthy's faithful housekeeper; and as I usually sit up reading until midnight, she retires early, and trusts me to put out the lamps and to lock up."

"Ah, I know Sarah," said Miss Rivers, "A worthy soul. She and I are excellent friends. We hold the same views on women's rights, and we love discussing them. Mere man—even godpapa—dwindles to nothing when arraigned at the bar of Sarah's intrepid judgment. Very well, then. The motor at seven."

But David still hesitated. "You are very kind," he said. "But—you see, we don't have dinner-parties in Central Africa. And since I came home, I have mostly been in hospital. I am afraid I haven't"—he looked down at his short jacket. "I don't even possess a long coat," he said, simply.

"Oh, don't be tiresome, Cousin David!" cried Miss Rivers. "If I wanted conventional evening dress, I know a dozen men whom I could invite to dinner. I want *you*, not your clothes. If one is greatly interested in a book does one bother to consider the binding? Bring your mind along, and come prepared to be helpful; for, God knows"—her eyes grew deep and earnest—"God knows I want helping, more than any of your African savages. Come as you are, Cousin David. Come as the Voice in the Wilderness. It is all I ask. Besides, there will only be myself and Chappie; and Chappie doesn't count."

She drew off a soft grey glove; then held out to him firm white fingers. He took them in his, They clasped hands silently; and, once more, by the light of the two wax candles, looked searchingly into each other's eyes. Each read there a quiet compact of friendship and of trust.

"I will come," said David. She paused with her hand on the door, looking back at him over her shoulder. Her tall head nearly touched the top of the archway.

"If you do," she said, "we must consider the question of your church, your schools, your printing-press, and your steamer. So, *au revoir*, to-morrow."

She threw him **a** little reassuring smile, and passed out.

The fragrance of violets, the sound of her low voice, the card upon the table, remained.

David took up the pen and made the entry in the vestry book: *two pounds, eight shillings, and sevenpence halfpenny.* Then he gathered up all the little piles of silver and copper, and put them into his coat pockets; but Diana's sovereign he slipped by itself into one waistcoat pocket, and her card into the other.

Then suddenly he realized—poor David—that she had stood beside him during the whole interview, while *he* had sat on the vestry stool.

He sprang to his feet. "Oh I say!" he cried. "Oh—I say!"

But there was nothing to say; and no one to whom to say it.

Poor David!

He sat down again, put his elbows on the table, and dropped his head into his hands.

Diana Rivers, of Riverscourt! Patron of four livings! Acknowledged leader of the gayest set in the county; known far and wide for her independence of character and advanced views!

Bones came shuffling up the chancel, rattling the church keys. There was also a sovereign of Diana's in *his* waistcoat pocket, and he showed no irritation as he locked up the vestry book, and returned David's good-night.

"A 'appy Christmas, sir," he said, "an' many of 'em; if they 'ave 'em in them wild parts."

As David plodded home through the snow, his mind dwelt, with curious persistence, on one question; "Now who on earth is 'Chappie'?"

CHAPTER V

THE NOISELESS NAPIER

"I AM morally certain 'Chappie' is a poodle," thought David to himself, at breakfast. "It would be just like her to have a large black poodle, abnormally clever, perfectly clipped, tied up with green ribbons to match her hat, and treated in all respects as a human being; excepting that, of course, his opinion on the cut of her guests' clothes would not matter. 'Chappie does not count,' she said; but I'll be bound he counts a lot, in most respects. I hope Chappie will like me. How does one whistle to a poodle?"

David was standing on the hearthrug, practising various seductive ways of whistling to Chappie, when Sarah came in to clear the breakfast table.

Sarah had put a Christmas card on David's plate that morning, and had kept nervously out of the way, while he opened the envelope. The card had evidently been chosen with great care, and an eye to its suitability. A large bunch of forget-me-nots figured in the centre, tied with a lover's knot of blue ribbon. Above this, two embossed hands—Sarah's and David's of course—were clasped. Above these again, flew two turtledoves. "They carried a scroll between them, depending from either beak, bearing in gold lettering, "The Compliments of the Season." At the bottom of the card were two blank lines beginning with "To— —" and "From— —." Sarah had filled in, with much labour, and rather brown ink:

To *the Reverant David rivers*
From *Yours rispectfully Sarah.*

David, delighted, stood the card in the place of honour on the mantelpiece, in front of the clock. When Sarah came in, he stopped whistling to Chappie, went forward at once and shook hands with her, thanking her warmly for the Christmas card.

"The only one I received, Sarah; and I do think it most awfully pretty."

Sarah admitted that it *was* that; explained at great length where she got it, and why she chose it; and described a good many other cards she had nearly bought, but eventually rejected in favour of the forget-me-nots, thinking they would "look homelike in them outlandish places," and ensure David's kind remembrance of her.

David protested that, card or no card, he would never forget Sarah, and all her thoughtful care of him; and Sarah wiped her eyes with a comer of her apron, and only wished there was more of him to care for,

David felt this rather embarrassingly personal, and walked over to the window to throw crumbs to a robin. Then he turned, as Sarah, having folded the cloth, was preparing to leave the room.

"Sarah," he said, "I have had an invitation. I am dining out to-night."

Sarah's face fell. "Oh, Mr. Rivers, sir! And me going to a chicking, being as it was Christmas!"

"Well, Sarah, you see my friend thought it was dull that I should dine by myself on Christmas night. And if you had gone to a chicken, I should indeed be left alone."

"Get along, sir!" chuckled Sarah. "You know my meaning. And, if it's Smiths or Joneses, I misdoubt if you'll get so good a dinner– –"

"It isn't Smiths or Joneses, Sarah. It is Miss Rivers, of Riverscourt. And she has promised me a turkey, and a plum-pudding, and possibly—only I must not count too much on those—possibly, mince-pies!"

Sarah's face expanded. "Oh, if it's Miss Diana, sir, you can't do better. There's none like Miss Diana, to my thinking. And we can have the chicking on Boxing Day. And, with your leave, if I'm not wanted, I'm asked out to friends this evening, which I hadn't no intention of mentioning. And Mr. Rivers, sir; mark my words. You can't do better than Miss Diana. We've known her from a babe, master an' me. Folks talk, because she don't hold with getting married, and because she don't do much church-going; but, begging your pardon, sir, I don't hold with either, m'self. Marriage means slaving away, with few thanks and fewer ha'pence; and church-going mostly means, for womenfolk, a vieing with one another's bonnets. I don't go to feathers, m'self; always having been well-content with beads. And I pay my respects to Almighty God at home."

"'Not forsaking the assembling of ourselves together, as the manner of some is,'" quoted David. "You forget the injunction of the writer to the Hebrews, Sarah."

"That don't hold good for now, Mr. Rivers, sir," replied Sarah, with conviction; "any more than many other *h*epistolic remarks."

"They all hold good for now, Sarah," said David, gravely.

"Then what about 'let your women keep silence in the churches'? Hark to them rowdy Miss Joneses in the choir!"

"They *do* make a row," admitted David, off his guard.

"And 'if they will learn anything, let them ask their husbands at home'?" Sarah was evidently well up in her Bible.

"Well, why not?" queried David.

"Why not, Mr. Rivers, sir?" repeated Sarah, scornfully. "Why not? Why because stay-at-home husbands ain't likely to be able to teach go-to-church wives! And, even if they did, how about me an' Miss Diana, as has none?"

This seemed unanswerable, though it had nothing whatever to do with the point at issue. But David had no suggestions to offer concerning the limitations contingent on the spinsterhood of Sarah and of Miss Diana. It therefore gave Sarah the last word; which, to the female mind, means victory; and she bore away the breakfast cloth in triumph.

When she brought in tea that afternoon, she lingered a few minutes, giving the fire a little unnecessary attention, and furtively watching David, as he put salt on his hot-buttered toast.

Then she said tentatively: "Mr. Rivers, sir, there are one or two things about Miss Diana you might as well know, before you go over there."

"No, thank you, Sarah," said David, with decision. "Whatever Miss Rivers wishes me to know, she will tell me herself. Anything she does not herself tell me, I prefer not to hear from others."

Sarah surveyed him; and her look expressed amazement and disapproval.

"Well I never!" she exclaimed. "You *are* different from master! All I hear in the village I tell master while I wait on him at dinner. He says: 'You may as well tell me what you hear, my good Sarah; and then I can judge how to act.'"

David smiled. He had already discovered the good Rector's love of gossip.

"But you see, Sarah," he said, "being only a *locum tenens,* I do not, fortunately, have to act."

"Don't disparage yourself, sir," advised Sarah, still disappointed, almost aggrieved. "And even if folks here *have* called you so, you won't be that to Miss Diana."

"Oh, no," said David, cheerfully. "I do not propose to be a *locum tenens* to Miss Diana!"

.   .   .   .   .

The motor glided up to the Rectory gate at seven o'clock to the minute. David saw the flash of the acetylene lamps on his bedroom blind.

He ran down the stairs, filled with a delightful sense of holiday-making and adventure.

His one clerical suit was carefully brushed, and Sarah had "pressed it," a mysterious process from which it emerged with a youthful, unwrinkled air, to which it had for long been a stranger. His linen was immaculate. He had shaved with extreme care. He felt so festive, that his lack of conventional evening clothes troubled him no longer. He slipped Sarah's Christmas card into his pocket. He knew Diana would appreciate the pathos and humour of those clasped hands and forget-me-nots.

Then he went down the garden path, and entered the motor. The footman arranged the fur rug over his knees, showed him how to switch off the electric lights if he preferred darkness, shut the door, took his seat beside the motionless chauffeur, and instantly they glided away down the lane, and turned into the high road leading to Riversmead.

It seemed wonderful to David to be flying along in Diana's sumptuous motor. He had never before been in a powerful noiseless Napier car, and he found it somewhat of an experience. Involuntarily he thought of the time when he had been so deadly weak from African fever, and his people had had somehow to get him to the coast; the rough little cart on wheels they made to hold him and his mattress, and tried to draw him along the apology for a road. But the shaking and bumping had been so absolutely unbearable, that he had eventually had to be slung and carried as far as the river. Even so, there had been the perpetual dread of the agonizing jerk if one of his bearers stumbled over a stone, or stepped unexpectedly into a rut. And to all this he was so soon returning. And quite right, too. No man should glide through life on cushioned tyres. For a woman, it was quite otherwise. Her womanhood constituted a sufficient handicap, without any roughness or hardship being allowed to come her way. He liked to know that Diana would always—literally and metaphorically—glide through life in a noiseless Napier. This method of progression need be no hindrance to her following of the Star.

He looked at his watch. In ten minute they would reach Riverscourt.

He switched off the lights, and at once the flying trees and hedges became visible in the pale moonlight. He enjoyed watching them as they whirled past. The great car bounded silently along the road, sounding a warning note upon the horn, if the distant light of any cart or carriage came in sight ahead of them; but passing it, and speeding on in the snowy darkness, before David had had time to look out and see what manner of vehicle it was.

They rushed through little villages, the cottage windows bright with seasonable festivity. In one of them David caught a glimpse of a Christmas-tree, decked with shining candles, and surrounded by the curly heads of happy little children. It was many years since he had seen a Christmas-tree. It brought wistful thoughts of home and boyhood's days. The first Christmas-tree he could remember had yielded to his enraptured hands a wooden popgun, which expelled a cork with great force and a terrifying sound, sufficiently loud to make all grown-up people jump, if it was done exactly behind their heads, when they were unaware of its near vicinity. This effect upon grown-ups, produced by his own popgun, had given him a sense of power which was limitless; until the sudden forcible confiscation of the popgun had set thereto an unexpected limit. He then mentioned it as a flute, and asked for it back; pointing out that its popgun propensities were a mere accident; its real nature was to be a flute. He received it back as a flute, upon condition that it should not immediately accidentally develop again into a popgun. He spent the remainder of that day blowing blissfully into the eight holes punched in the strip of red wood gummed to the side of the popgun. The resultant sounds were melancholy and fitful to a degree; and it is doubtful which was the greater trial to the nerves of the grownups, the sudden explosion of the popgun or the long drawn out piping of the flute. Anyway when his treasure suddenly and unaccountably disappeared, they assisted his tearful search in a half-hearted sort of way, and when eventually his unaided efforts discovered it, carefully concealed in one of their own wardrobes, his infantine faith in the sincerity of adult human nature had received its first rude shock.

David lay back in the motor and wondered whether life would ever hold for him a scene so enchanting as that first Christmas-tree, or a gift so priceless as that popgun-flute.

The motor sped through the old-world town of Riversmead, scarcely slacking speed, for the streets were clear; all its inhabitants were indoors, merry-making; and the one policeman they passed, saluted. Diana's car was well known and respected.

Then in at great iron gates, standing wide, and up an avenue of stately beeches, coming to sudden pause before the portico of a large stone house, gay with lighted windows.

CHAPTER VI

DAVID MAKES FRIENDS WITH "CHAPPIE"

THE door into the great hall opened as David stepped out of the motor. A footman took his overcoat, and he found himself following an elderly butler across the spacious hall toward a door, which he flung open, announcing in confidential tones: "The Reverend David Rivers"; then stood aside, that David might enter.

David had already been looking right and left for Chappie; and, even as he walked into the drawing-room, he had a seductive whistle ready in case the poodle came to meet him, before he could reach Diana's friendly hand.

But neither Diana nor the poodle were in the drawing-room.

Instead, on a large sofa, at right angles with the fireplace, in the midst of heaped-up cushions, sat a very plump elderly lady, of haughty mien, clad in claret-coloured velvet, a nodding ornament in her white hair, and much jewellery on her fat neck. She raised a lorgnon, on a long tortoiseshell handle, and looked through it at David as he advanced toward her.

There was such awe-inspiring majesty in the action, that David felt certain she must be, at the very least, a duchess.

He seemed to be hours in reaching the sofa It was like one of those long walks taken in dreams, covering miles, yet only advancing yards; and as he walked his clerical jacket grew shorter, and his boots more patently *not* patent leather.

When, at last, he reached the hearth-rug—nothing happened. The plump lady had, apparently, no disengaged hand; one held the lorgnon; the other a large feather fan.

"D'y do?" she said, in a rather husky voice. "I conclude you are Diana's missionary."

This was an almost impossible remark to answer. David was *not* Diana's missionary; yet he was, undoubtedly, the missionary Diana had asked to dinner. In his embarrassment he held his warm hands to the blaze of the log-fire, and said: "What a beautiful Christmas Day!"

The plump lady ignored the remark. She declined to recognize anything in common between her Christmas Day and David's.

"Where is your sphere of work?" she demanded hoarsely.

"Central Africa," replied David, in a meek voice, devoutly wishing himself back there.

At that moment the door burst open, by reason of a bump against it, and a black poodle trotted in, identical with the dog of David's imagining, excepting that its tufts were tied up with red ribbon.

David whistled joyfully. "Hullo, Chappie!" he said. "Come here, old fellow."

The poodle paused, surprised, and looked at him; one fore-paw uplifted.

The plump lady made an inarticulate sound, and dropped her lorgnon.

But David felt sure of his ground. "Come on Chappie," he said. "Let's be friends."

The poodle trotted up and shook hands. David bent down and patted his beautiful coat.

Then Diana herself swept into the room, "**A** thousand pardons, Cousin David!" she cried. "I should have been down to receive you. But Knox broke all records and did the distance in eighteen minutes!" In a moment her hand was in his; her eyes were dancing with pleasure; her smile enveloped him in an atmosphere of welcoming friendliness.

All David's shyness left him. He forgot his terror of the majestic person on the sofa. "Oh, that's all right!" he said. "I have been making friends with Chappie."

For a moment even Diana looked nonplussed. Then she laughed gaily. "I ought to have been down to introduce you properly," she said. "Let me do so now. Cousin David, this is Mrs. Marmaduke Vane. Chappie, dear, may I present to you my cousin, David Rivers?"

David never knew why the floor did not open and swallow him up! He looked helplessly at Diana, and hopelessly at the plump lady on the sofa, whose wrathful glance withered him.

Diana flew to the rescue. "Now, Chappie dear," she said, "the motor is at the door, and Marie has your fur cloak in the hall. Remember me to the Brackenburys, and don't feel obliged to come away early if you are enjoying the games after dinner. The brougham will call for you at eleven; but James can put up, and come round when you send for him. If I have gone up when you return, we shall meet at breakfast." She helped the plump lady to her feet, and took her to the door. "Good-bye, dear; and have a good time." She closed the door, and came back to David, standing petrified on the hearthrug.

"Mrs. Vane is my chaperon," she explained. "That is why I call her 'Chappie.' But—tell me, Cousin David; do you always call elderly ladies by their rather private pet-names, in the first moments of making their acquaintance?"

"Heaven help me! "said poor David, ruefully. "I thought 'Chappie' was the poodle."

Diana's peals of laughter must have reached the irate lady in the hall. She sank on to the sofa, and buried her golden head in the cushions.

"Oh, Cousin David!" she said. "I always knew you were unlike anybody else. Did you see the concentrated fury in Chappie's eye? And shall we improve matters by explaining that you thought she was the poodle? Oh, talk of something else, or I shall suffocate!"

"But you said: 'There will only be myself and Chappie; and Chappie doesn't count,'" explained David. "If that was 'Chappie,' she counts a lot. She looked me up and down, until I felt positively cheap; and she asked me whether I was your missionary. I made sure she was a duchess, at the very least."

"That only shows how very little experience you have had of duchesses. Cousin David. If Chappie had really been a duchess, she would have made you feel at home in a moment, and I should have found you seated beside her on the sofa talking as happily as if you had known her for years. Chappie has a presence, I admit; and a ducal air; which is partly why I keep her on as chaperon.

But she says: 'D'y do,' and looks down her nose at you in that critical manner, because her father was only a doctor in a small provincial town."

"My father was a doctor in a little country village," said David, quickly, "yet I hope I don't look down my nose at people."

"Ah," said Diana, "but then you are a man, and no foolish friends have told you that you look like a duchess, thus turning your poor head. Chappie is a kind old thing at heart, and must have attractive qualities of sorts, seeing she has been married no less than three times. She was my governess, years ago, before her first marriage. And when Uncle Falcon died, I had her back as chaperon; partly because she is very poor, and couples with that poverty an inordinate love of creature comforts, which is quite pathetic; partly because she makes an imposing figure-head, yet I can do with her exactly as I like. How would you define a chaperon, Cousin David?"

"We don't have them in Central Africa, Miss Rivers."

"Well, a chaperon is a person who should be seen and not heard. And she should be seen by the right people; not by those she is chaperoning, but by the tiresome people who think they ought to be chaperoned. My good Chappie satisfactorily fulfils these conditions. She is, to all intents, chaperoning you and me this evening; yet, in reality, she is dining with friends of hers in Riversmead; thus sparing us the unnecessary restraint of her presence, and the undesirable infliction of her quite mindless conversation."

David found himself wondering whether he ought not to have allowed Sarah to tell him "one or two things about Miss Diana" before he adventured over to Riverscourt.

At that moment the staid butler opened wide the door, with a murmured sentence about dinner.

Diana rose, with a gentle grace and dignity which reminded David of his Lady of Mystery's first progress up Brambledene church; and, laying her hand within his arm, guided him to the dining-room.

A small round table stood in the centre of the great oak-panelled room. It gleamed with glass and silver, wax candles and snowy linen. The decoration was Parma violets and lilies of the valley.

David sat at Diana's right hand, and when she leaned toward him and they talked in low voices, the old man at the distant sideboard could not overhear their conversation.

The poodle had followed them to the dining-room, and lay down contentedly in front of the log-fire.

Diana was wearing perfectly plain white satin. A Medici collar, embroidered with pearls, rose at the back of her shapely head. She wore violets at her bosom, and a dainty wreath of violets in her hair. Her gown in front was cut square and low, and embroidered with pearls. On the whiteness of her skin, below the beautiful firm neck, sparkled a brilliant diamond star. David hated to see it there; he could hardly have explained why. It rose and fell lightly, with her breathing. When she laughed, it scintillated in the light of the wax candles. It fascinated David—the sparkling star, on the soft flesh. He looked at it, and looked away;

but again it drew his unwilling eyes.

He tried to master his aversion. Why should not Miss Rivers wear a diamond star? Why should he, David, presume to dislike to see a star so worn?

Before they reached the second course, Diana said to the butler: "Send Marie to me."

In a few moments her French maid, in simple black attire, with softly braided hair, stood at her elbow. Diana, still talking gaily to David, lifted both arms, unclasped the thin gold chain from about her neck, and handed the pendant to her maid.

"*Serrez-moi ça*", she said, carelessly.

Then she turned her clear eyes on David. "You prefer it in the sky," she said. "I quite agree with you. A woman's flesh savours too much of the world and the devil, to be a resting-place for stars. It can have no possible connexion with ideals."

She spoke so bitterly, that David's tender
heart rose up in arms.

"True, I prefer it in the sky," he said, "and I prefer it not of diamonds. But I do not like to hear you speak so of—of your body. It seems to me too perfectly beautiful to be thus relegated to a lower sphere; not because it is not flesh; but because, though flesh, it clothes a radiant soul. The mortal body is but the garment of the immortal soul. The soul, in mounting, lifts the body with it."

"I do not agree with you," said Diana. "I loathe bodies; my own no less than other people's. And how little we know of our souls. I am afraid I shall shock you, Cousin David, but a favourite theory of mine is: that only a certain number of people have any souls at all. I have always maintained that the heathen have no souls."

David's deep eyes gleamed.

"The young natives of Uganda," he said, "sooner than give up their new-found faith, sooner than deny the Lord Who had bought them, walked calmly to the stake, and were slowly roasted by fire; their limbs, while they yet lived, being hacked off, one by one, and thrown into the flames. Their holy courage never failed; their last articulate words were utterances of faith and praise. Surely *bodies* would hardly go through so much, unless *souls—strong* immortal souls—dwelt within them."

"True," said Diana, softly. "Cousin David, I apologize. And I wonder how many of us would stand such a soul-test as slow fire I can't quite imagine Chappie, seated on a gridiron, singing hymns! Can you?"

"We must not judge another," said David, rather stiffly. "Conditions of martyrdom, produced the noble army of martyrs. Why should not Mrs. Vane, if placed in those conditions, rise to the occasion?"

"I am certain she would," said Diana. "She would rise quite rapidly—if the occasion were a gridiron."

Much against his will, David burst out laughing.

Diana leaned her chin in her hands; her luminous grey eyes observed him gravely. Little dimples of enjoyment dented either cheek; but her tone was entirely demure.

"I hope you are not a prig, Cousin David," she said, gravely.

"I have never been considered one," replied David, humbly. "But, if you say so— —"

"No, no!" cried Diana. "You are not a prig; and I know I am flippant beyond words. Have I you found out that I am flippant. Cousin David?

"Yes," he said, gently. "But I have found out something besides that."

Her eyes challenged him.

"And that is— —?"

"That you take refuge in flippancy, Miss Rivers, when you want to hide a deeper anxiety and earnestness of soul than you can quite understand, or altogether cope with."

"Really? Then you must explain it to me, and cope with it for me. I hope our Christmas dinner has come up to the dinner of Sarah's intentions. Have another pear; or some more nuts? I did not order crackers, because we are both grown up, and we should look so foolish in paper caps; and yet, if we had had them, we could not have resisted putting them on. Don't you know, at children's parties, the way in which grown-ups seize upon the most *outré* of the coloured headgear, don them, in a moment of gay abandonment, and—forget them! I can remember now, the delight, after one of the Christmas parties in my childhood, of seeing Chappie go gravely in to say good night to grandpapa, completely unconscious of a Glengarry bonnet, tilted waggishly on one side; or, on another occasion, of a tall peaked fool's cap, perched on her frizzled 'transformation.' Oh, to be a little child again, each Christmas Day! Yet here am I—twenty-eight! How old are you, Cousin David? . . . Twenty-nine? Well, I am glad you are not *quite* thirty. Being in another decade would have been like being in a cassock. . . . Why a cassock? How dense you are, my reverend cousin! My mildest jokes require explaining. Why, because it would have removed you so far away, and I want you quite near this evening, not perched in a distant pulpit! You cannot really help me, unless you fully sympathize and understand. And I am in such sore straits, Cousin David, that I look upon myself as a drowning man—why do we always say 'drowning *man*,' as if there never were any drowning women?—about to sink for the third time; and you as the rope, which constitutes my only hope of safety. Let us go to the drawing-room."

CHAPTER VII

THE TOUCH OF POWER

AS they passed into the drawing-room, David's eye fell on a grand piano, in black ebony case, fell of the door-way.

"Oh!" said David, and stopped short.

"Does that tempt you?" asked Diana. "Yes, I might have known you were full of Your sufferings, over the performances of the Brambledene choir, were more patent than you realized."

David's fingers were working eagerly.

"I so rarely get the chance of a piano," he said. "Like chaperons, we don't have them in Central Africa. I went without all manner of things to be able to afford one in my rooms at college; but, since then—Is it a Bechstein, or what?"

"I really do not know," laughed Diana. "It is an article of furniture I do not use. Once a quarter it lifts up its voice, poor dear, when a sleek person with a key of his own, arrives unexpectedly, asking for a duster, and announcing that he has come to tune it. He usually turns up when I have a luncheon party. Occasionally when Chappie is feeling low, and dwelling on the departed Marmaduke, she feels moved to play 'Home, Sweet Home'; but when Chappie plays 'Home, Sweet Home' you instantly discover that 'there's no place like'—being out; and be it ever so cheerless, you catch up a hat, and flee! You may carry off the piano to Africa, if you will, Cousin David. And, meanwhile, see how you like it now, while I try to collect my ideas, and consider how best to lay my difficulties before you."

She moved across the long room to the fireplace, drew forward a low chair, turning it so as to face the distant piano.

David, tingling with anticipation, opened the instrument with reverent care.

"It *is* a Bechstein," he said; then took his seat; pausing a moment, his hands upon his knees, his dark head bent over the keys,

Diana, watching him, laughed in her heart.

"What an infant it is, in some ways, she thought. "I do believe he is saying: 'For what we are about to receive'!" But in another minute her laughter ceased. She was receiving more than she had expected. David had laid his hands upon the keys; and, straightway, the room was filled with music.

It did not seem to come from the piano. It did not appear to have any special connexion with David. It came chiefly from an unseen purple sky overhead; not the murky darkness of an English winter, but the clear over-arching heavens of the Eastern desert—expansive, vas fathomless.

Beneath it, rode a cavalcade of travellers–anxious, perplexed, uncertain. She could hear the soft thud of the camels' feet upon the sane and see the slow swaying, back and forth, of the mysterious riders.

Suddenly outshone a star—clear, luminous, divine; so brilliant, so unexpected, that the listener by the fireplace said, "Oh!"—then laid her hand over her trembling lips.

But David had forgotten her. His eyes were shining; his thin face aglow.

Now all was peace and certainty. They travelled on. They reached Jerusalem. The minor key of doubt and disappointment crept in again. Then, once more, shone the star. They arrived at Bethlehem. In chords of royal harmony they found the King. *0 worship the Lord in the beauty of holiness!*

Diana's face sank into her clasped hands. The firelight played upon her golden hair.

She knew, now, just how far she had wandered from the one true Light; just how poor had been her response to the eternal love which brought the Lord of glory to the manger of Bethlehem; to the village home at Nazareth; to the cross of Calvary. The love of Christ had not constrained her. She had lived for self. Her heart had grown hard and unresponsive.

And now, in tenderest, reverent melody, the precious gifts were being offered—gold, frankincense, and myrrh. But what had *she* to offer? Her gold could hardly be accepted while she withheld *herself.* Yet how could love awaken in a heart so dead so filled with worldly scorn and unbelief?

The music had changed. It no longer came from unseen skies, or ranged back into past scenes and ancient history. It centred in David and the piano.

He was playing a theme so simple and so restful, that it stole into Diana's heart, bringing untold hope and comfort. At length, she lifted her head.

"What are you playing now, Cousin David?" she asked, gently.

David hushed the air into a whisper, as he answered: "A very simple setting of my own, to those wonderful words, 'At even, e'er the sun was set.' You know them? The old tune never contented me. It was so apt to drag, and did not lend itself to the crescendo of hope and thankfulness required by the glad certainty that the need of each waiting heart would be fully met, nor to the diminuendo of perfect peace, enfolding each one as they went away. So I composed this simple melody, and I sing it, by myself, out in the African forests most nights, when my day's work is over. But it is a treat to be able to play it here, with full harmonies."

"Sing it to me," said Diana, gently.

And at once David began to sing, to his own setting, the tender words of the old evening hymn. And this was what he sang:

"AT EVEN ERE THE SUN WAS SET"
Holy Star

1

At even ere the sun was set,
  The sick, O Lord, around Thee lay;
Oh, in what divers pains they met!
  Oh, with what joy they went away!

2

Once more 'tis eventide, and we
  Oppressed with various ills draw near;
What if Thy Form we cannot see?
  We know and feel that Thou art here.

3

O Saviour Christ, our woes dispel;
  For some are sick, and some are sad;
And some have never loved Thee well,
  And some have lost the love they had;

4

And some have found the world is vain.
  Yet from the world they break not free;
And some have friends who give them pain
  Yet have not sought a friend in Thee.

5

And none, O Lord, have perfect rest,
    For none are wholly free from sin;
And they who fain would serve Thee best,
    Are conscious most of sin within.

6

O Saviour Christ, Thou too art Man;
    Thou hast been troubled, tempted, tried;
Thy kind but searching glance can scan
    The very wounds that shame would hide.

7

Thy touch has still its ancient power;
    No word from Thee can fruitless fall;
Hear, in this solemn evening hour,
    And, in Thy mercy, heal us all;
        O heal us all!

The pure tenor voice rose and fell, giving full value to each line. As he reached the words: "And some have never loved Thee well, And some have lost the love they had," Diana's tears fell, silently. It was so true—so true. She had never loved Him well; and she had lost what little faith, what little hope, she had.

Presently David's voice arose in glad tones of certainty:

Thy touch has still its ancient power;
    No word from Thee can fruitless fall;
Hear, in this solemn evening hour,
    And, in Thy mercy, heal us all;
        Oh heal us all!

The last notes of the quiet Amen died away.

David closed the piano softly; rose, and walked over to the fireplace. He did not look at Diana; he did not speak to her. He knew, instinctively, that a soul in travail was beside him. He left her to his Lord.

After a while she whispered: "If only one were worthy. If only one's faith were strong enough to realize, and to believe."

"Our worthiness has nothing to do with it," said David, without looking round. "And we need not worry about our faith, so long as—like the tiny mustard seed—it is, however small, a living, growing thing. The whole point lies in the fact of the power of His touch; the changeless truth of His unfailing word; the fathomless ocean of His love and mercy. Look away from self; fix your eyes on Him; and healing comes."

A long silence followed David's words. He stood with his back to her, watching the great logs as the flames played round them, and they sank slowly, one by one, into the hot ashes.

At last he heard Diana's voice.

"Cousin David," she said, "will you give me your blessing?"

David Rivers turned. He was young; he was humble; he was very simple in his faith; but he realized the value and responsibility of his priestly office. He knew it had been given him as "a service of gift."

He lifted his hands, and as Diana sank to her knees, he laid them reverently upon the golden corona of her hair.

One moment of silence. Then David's voice, vibrant with emotion, yet deep, tender, and unfaltering, pronounced the great Triune blessing, granted to desert wanderers of old.

"The Lord bless thee and keep thee;

The Lord make His face shine upon thee, and be gracious unto thee:

The Lord lift up His countenance upon thee and give thee peace."

And the touch of power which Diana felt upon her heart and life, from that moment onward was not the touch of David Rivers.

CHAPTER VIII

THE TEST OF THE TRUE HERALD

AS DAVID sped back through the starry darkness, he was filled with an exultation such as he had never before experienced.

He had always held that every immortal soul was of equal value in the sight of God; and that the bringing into the kingdom of an untutored African savage was of as much importance, in the Divine estimation, as the conversion of the proudest potentate ruling upon any European throne.

But, somehow, he realized now the greatness of the victory which grace had won, in this surrender of Diana to the constraining touch of his Lord and hers.

It was one thing to see light dawn, where all had hitherto been darkness; but quite another to see the dispersion of clouds of cynical unbelief, and the surrender of a strong personality to the faith which requires the simple loving obedience of a little child: for, "whosoever shall not receive the kingdom of God as a little child, he shall not enter therein."

David leaned back in the motor, totally unconscious of his surroundings, as he realized how great a conquest for his King was this winning of Diana. Her immense wealth, her influence, her position in the county, her undoubted personal charm, would all now be consecrated, and become power on the side of right.

He foresaw a beautiful future before her. The very fact that he himself was so soon leaving England, and would have no personal share in that future, made his joy all the purer because of its absolute selflessness. Like the Baptist of old, standing on the banks of Jordan, he had pointed to the passing Christ, saying: "Behold!" She had beheld; she had followed; she had found Him and the messenger, who had brought about this meeting, might depart. He was needed no longer The Voice had done its work. All true heralds of the King rejoice when the souls they have strive to win turn and say: "Now we believe, not because of thy saying, for we have heard Him ourselves, and know that this is indeed the Christ, the Saviour of the world." This test was no David's; and being a true herald, he did not fail before it.

When Diana had risen from her knees, she had turned to him and said, gently: "Cousin David, do yon mind if I order the motor now? I could not speak or think to-night of other things; and I just feel I want to be alone."

During the few moments which intervened before the car was announced, they sat in silence, one on either side of the fireplace. There was a radiance of joy on both young faces, which any on entering unexpectedly, would doubtless have put down to a very different cause. Diana was not thinking at all of David; and David was thinking less of Diana than of the Lord Whose presence with them, in that evening hour, had made of a time of healing and of power.

As he rose to go, she put her band in his.

"Cousin David," she said "more than ever now, I need your counsel and your help. If I send over, just before one o'clock, can you come to luncheon to-morrow, and afterwards we might have the talk which I cannot manage to-night?"

David agreed. The weddings at which he had to officiate were at eleven o'clock. "I will be ready," he said, "and I will come. I am afraid my advice is not worth much; but, such as it is, it is altogether at your service."

"Good night. Cousin David," she said, "and God bless you I Doesn't it say somewhere in the Bible: 'They that turn many to righteousness shall shine as the stars for ever and ever'?"

David now remembered this farewell remark of Diana's, as he stood for a moment at the Rectory gate, looking upward to the clear frosty sky. But the idea did not suit his mood.

"Ah, no, my Lord," he said. "Thou art the bright and morning Star. Why should I want, for myself any glory or shining? I am content for ever to be but a follower of the Star."

CHAPTER IX

UNCLE FALCON'S WILL

LUNCHEON would have been an awkward affair, owing to David's nervous awe of Mrs. Marmaduke Vane and his extreme trepidation in her presence, had it not been for Diana's tact and vivacity.

She took the bull by the horns, explaining David's mistake, and how it was entirely her own fault for being so ambiguous and inconsequent in her speech— "as you have told me from my infancy, dear Chappie"; and she laughed so infectiously over the misunderstanding and over the picture she drew of poor David's dismay an horror, that Mrs. Marmaduke Vane laughed also, and forgave David.

"And to add to poor Cousin David's confusion, he had made sure, at first sight, that you were at least a duchess," added Diana tactfully; "and they don't have them in Central Africa; so Cousin David felt very shy. Didn't you, Cousin David?

David admitted that he did; and Mrs. Vane began to like "Diana's missionary."

"I have often noticed," pursued Miss River "that the very people who are the most braze in the pulpit, who lean over the side and read your thoughts; who make you lift your unwilling eyes to theirs, responsive; who direct the flow of the eloquence full upon any unfortunate person who is venturing at all obviously to disagree—are the very people who are most apt to be shy in private life. You should see my Cousin David fling challenge and proof positive at a narrow-minded lady, with an indignant rustle, and a red feather in her bonnet. I believe her husband is a tenant-farmer of mine. I intend to call, in order to discuss Cousin David's sermons with her, I shall insist upon her showing me the passage in *her* Bible where it says that there were three Wise Men."

Then Diana drew David on to tell of his African congregations, of the weird experiences in those wild regions; of the perils of the jungle, and the deep mystery of the forest. And he made it all sound so fascinating and delightful, that Mrs. Marmaduke Vane became quite expansive, announcing, as she helped herself liberally to *pâté de foie gras*, that she did not wonder people enjoyed being missionaries.

"You should volunteer, Chappie dear," said Diana. "I dare say the society sends out ladies. Only—fancy, if you came back as thin as Cousin David!"

In the drawing-room, she sent him to the piano; and Mrs. Vane allowed her coffee to grow cold while she listened to David's music, and did not ask Diana to send for more until David left the music stool.

Then Diana reminded her chaperon of an engagement she had at Eversleigh. "The motor is ordered at half-past two, dear; and be sure you stay to tea. Never mind if they don't ask you. Just remain until tea appears. They can but say: '*Must* you stay? *Can't* you go?' And they won't do that, because they are inordinately proud of your presence in their abode."

Mrs. Vane rose reluctantly, expressing regret that she had unwittingly made this engagement, and murmuring something about an easy postponement by telegram.

But Diana was firm. Such a disappointment must not be inflicted upon any family on Boxing Day. It could not be contemplated for a moment.

Mrs. Marmaduke Vane took David's hand in both her plump ones, and patted it, kindly.

"Good bye, my dear Mr. Rivers," she said with *empressement*. "And I hope you will have a quite delightful time in Central Africa. And mind" she added, archly, "if Diana decides to come out and sec you there, *I* shall accompany her."

Honest dismay leapt into David's eyes.

"It is no place for women," he said, helplessly Then looked at Diana. "I assure you. Miss Rivers, it is no place for women."

"Never fear, Cousin David," laughed Dian "You have fired Mrs. Vane with a desire to rough it; but I do not share her ardour, and she could not start without me. Could you, Chappie dear? Good-bye. Have a good time."

She turned to the fire, with an air of dismissal, and pushed a log into place with her toe.

David opened the door, waited patiently while Mrs. Vane hoarsely whispered final farewell pleasantries; then closed it behind her portly back.

When he returned to the hearth-rug, Diana was still standing gazing thoughtfully into the fire, one arm on the mantelpiece.

"Oh, the irony of it!" she said, without looking up. "She hopes you will have a quite delightful time; and, as a matter of fact, you are going o to die! Cousin David, do you *really* expect never to return?"

"In all probability," said David, "I shall never see England again. They tell me I cannot possibly live through another five years out there. They think two, or at most three, will see me through. Who can tell? I shall be grateful for three."

"Do you consider it right, deliberately to sacrifice a young life, and a useful life, by returning to a place which you know must cost that life? Why not seek another sphere?"

"Because," said David, quietly, "my call is there. Some one must go; and who better than one who has absolutely no home-ties; none to miss or mourn him but the people for whom he gives his life? It is all I have to give. I give it gladly."

"Let us sit down," said Diana, "just as we sat last night, in those quiet moments before the motor came round. Only now, I can talk—and, oh. Cousin David, I have so much to say! But first I want you to tell me, if you will, all about yourself. Begin at the beginning. Never mind how long it takes. We have the whole afternoon before us, unless you have anything to take you away early."

She motioned him to an easy chair, and herself sat on the couch, leaning forward in her favourite attitude, her elbow on her knee, her chin resting in the palm of her hand. Her grey eyes searched his face. The firelight played on her soft hair.

"Begin at the beginning. Cousin David," she said.

"There is not much to tell of my beginnings," said David, simply. "My parents married late in fife. I was their only child—the son of their old age. My home was always a little heaven upon earth. They were not well off; we only had what my father earned by his practice, and village people are apt to be slack about paying a doctor's bills. But they made great efforts to give me the best possible education; and, a generous friend coming to their assistance, I was able to go to Oxford." His eyes glowed. "I wish you could know all that that means," he said; "being able to go to Oxford."

"I can imagine what it would mean—to you," said Diana.

"While I was at Oxford, I decided to be ordained; and, almost immediately after that decision, the call came. I held a London curacy for one year, but, as soon as I was priested, by special leave from my Bishop, and arrangement with my Vicar, I went out to Africa. During the year I was working in London I lost both my father and my mother."

"Ah, poor boy!" murmured Diana. "Then you had no one."

David hesitated. "There was Amy," he said.

Diana's eyelids flickered. "Oh, there was 'Amy.' That might mean a good deal. Did 'Amy' want to go out to Central Africa?"

"No," said David; "nor would I have dreamed of taking her there. Amy and I had lived in the same village all our lives. We had been babies together. Our mothers had wheeled us out in a double pram. We were just brother and sister until I went to college; and then we though we were going to be—more. But, when the call came, I knew it must mean celibacy. No man could take a woman to such places. I knew, if I accepted, I must give up Amy. I dreaded telling her. But, when at last I plucked up courage and told her. Amy did not mind very much, be cause a gentleman-farmer in the neighbourhood was wanting to marry her. Amy was very pretty They were married just before I sailed. Amy wanted me to marry them. But I could not do that."

Diana looked at the thin sensitive face.

"No," she said; "you could not do that."

"I thought it best not to correspond during the five years," continued David, "considering what we had been to one another. But when I was invalided home, I looked forward, in the eager sort of way you do when you are very weak, to seeing Amy again. I had no one else. As soon as I could manage the journey, I went down—home; and—and called at Amy's house. I asked for Mrs. Robert Carsdale—Amy's married name. A very masculine noisy lady, whom I had never seen before, walked into the room where I stood awaiting Amy. She had just come in from hunting, and flicked her boot with her hunting-crop as she asked me what I wanted. I said: 'I have called to see Mrs. Robert Carsdale.' She said: 'Well? I am Mrs. Robert Carsdale,' and stared at me, in astonishment.

"So I asked for Amy. She told me where to—to find Amy, and opened the hall door. Amy had been dead three years. Robert Carsdale had married again. I found Amy's grave in our little churchyard, quite near my own parents'. Also the grave of her baby boy. It was all that was left of Amy; and, do you know, she had named her little son 'David.'"

"Oh, you poor boy!" said Diana. "You poor, poor boy! But, do you know, I think Amy in heaven was better for you, than Amy on earth. I don't hold with marriage. Had you cared very much?"

"Yes, I had cared a good deal," replied David, in a low voice, "but as a boy cares, I think. Not as I should imagine a man would care. A man who really cared *could* not have left her to another man. could he?"

"I don't hold with matrimony," said Diana again; and she said it with forceful emphasis.

"Nor do I," said David; "and my people out in Africa are all the family I shall ever know. I faced that out when I accepted the call. No man has a right to allow a woman to face nameless horrors and hardships, or to make a home in a climate where little children cannot live."

"Ah, I do so agree with you!" cried Diana. "I once attended a missionary meeting where a returned missionary from India told us how she and her husband had had to send their little daughter home to England when she was seven years old, and had not seen her again until she was sixteen. 'When we returned to England,' she told the meeting, 'I should not have known my daughter had I passed her in the street!' And every one thought it so pathetic, and so devoted. But it seemed to me false pathos, and unpardonable neglect of primary duties. Who could take that mother's place to that little child of seven years old? And, from the age of seven to sixteen, how a girl needs her own mother. What call could come before that first call—her own little child's need of her? And what do you think that missionary-lady's work had been? Managing a school for heathen children! All the time she was giving an account of these children of other people and her work among them, I felt like calling out: 'How about your own?' Cousin David, I didn't put a halfpenny in the plate; and I have hated missionaries ever since."

"That is not quite just," said David. "But I do most certainly agree with you, that first claims should come first. And, therefore, a man who feels called to labour where wife and children could not live, must forgo these tender ties and consider himself pledged to celibacy."

"It is the better part," said Diana.

David made no answer. It had not struck him in that light before. He had always thought he was forgoing an unknown but an undoubted joy.

A silence fell between them. He was pondering her last remark; she was considering him, and trying to fathom how much sincerity of conviction, strength of will, and tenacity of purpose lay behind that gentle manner and straightforward simplicity of character.

Diana was a fearless cross-country rider. She never funked a fence, nor walked a disappointed horse along, in search of a gap or a gate. But before taking a high jump she liked to know what was on the other side. So, while David pondered Diana's last remark, Diana studied David.

At length she said: "Do you remember my first appearance at Brambledene church, on a Sunday evening, about five weeks ago?"

Yes; David remembered.

"I arrived late," said Diana. "I walked up the church to blasts of psalmody from that noisy choir."

David smiled. "You were never late again," he said.

"Mercy, no!" laughed Diana. "You gave one the impression of being the sort of person who might hold up the entire service, while one unfortunate late-comer hurried abashed into her pew. Are many parsons so acutely conscious of the exact deportment of each member of their congregations?"

"I don't know," answered David. "I suppose the keen look-out one has to keep for unexpected and sometimes dangerous happenings at all gatherings of our poor wild people, has trained one to it. I admit I would sooner see the glitter of an African spear poised in my direction from behind a tree-trunk, than see Mrs. Smith nudge her husband, in obvious disagreement with the most important point in my sermon."

"Well," continued Diana, "I came. And what do you think brought me?"

David had no suggestion to make as to what had brought Diana.

"Why, after you had come down for an interview with my godfather and spent a night at the Rectory, I motored over to see him, just before he went for his cure. He told me all about you; and, among other things, that you were going back, knowing that the climate out there could only mean for you a very few years of life; and I came to church because I wanted to see a man whose religion meant more to him than even life itself—I, who rated life and health as highest of all good; most valuable of all possessions.

"I came to *see*—wondering, doubting, incredulous. I stayed to *listen*—troubled, conscience-stricken, perplexed. First, I believed in *you* Cousin David. Then I saw the Christ-life in you Then I longed to have what you had—to find Him myself. Yesterday, He found me. To-day, I can humbly, trustfully say: 'I know Whom I have believed, and am persuaded that He is able to keep that which I have committed unto Him against that day.' I am far from being what I ought to be; my life just now is one tangle of perplexities; but the darkness is over, and the true light now shineth. I hope, from this time onward, to be a follower of the Star."

"I thank God," said David Rivers.

"And now." continued Diana, after a few moments of happy silence, "I am going to burden you. Cousin David, with a recital of my difficulties; and I am going to ask your advice. Let me tell you my past history, as shortly as possible.

"This dear old place is my childhood's home. My earliest recollection is of living here with my mother and my grandfather. My father, Captain Rivers, who was heir to the whole property, died when I was three years old. I barely remember him. The property was entailed on male heirs, and failing my father, it came to a younger brother of my grandfather, a great-uncle of mine, a certain Falcon Rivers, who had fallen out with most of his relations, gone to live in America, and made a large fortune out there. My grandfather and my mother never spoke of Uncle Falcon, and I remember, as a child, having the instinctive feeling that even to think of Uncle Falcon was an insidious form of sin. It therefore had its attractions. I quite often thought of Uncle Falcon!

"Toward the close of his life, my grandfather became involved in money difficulties. Much of the estate was mortgaged. I was too young and heedless to understand details, but it all resulted in this: that when my grandfather died, he was unable to leave much provision for my mother or for me. We had to turn out of Riverscourt; Uncle Falcon was returning to take possession. So we went to live in town, on the merest pittance, and in what, after the luxuries to which I had always been accustomed, appeared to me abject poverty. I was then nineteen. My mother, who had been older than my father, was over fifty.

"Then followed two very hard years. Uncle Falcon wrote to my mother; but she refused to see him, or to have any communication with him. She would not show me his letter. We were absolutely cut off from the old home, and all our former surroundings. Once or twice we heard, in roundabout ways, how much Uncle Falcon's wealth was doing for the old place. Mortgages were all paid off; tumbled-down cottages were being rebuilt; the farms were put into proper order, and let to good tenants. American money has a way of being useful, even in proud old England.

"Any mention of all this filled my mother with an extreme bitterness, to which I had not then the key, and which I completely failed to understand.

"One morning, at breakfast, she received an envelope, merely containing a thin slip of paper. Her beautiful face—my mother was a very lovely woman— went, as they say in story-books, whiter than the tablecloth. She tore the paper across, and across again, and flung the fragments into the fire. They missed the flames, and fluttered down into the fender. I picked them up, and, right before her, pieced them together. It was a cheque from Uncle Falcon for a thousand pounds. 'Oh, Mamma dear!' I said. I was so tired of running after omnibuses, and pretending we liked potted meat lunches.

"She snatched the fragments out of my fingers, and dropped them into the heart of the fire.

"'Anyway, it was kind of Uncle Falcon,' I said.

"'Do not mention his name,' cried my mother, with white lips; and I experienced once more the fascination of the belief, which had been mine in childhood, that Uncle Falcon and the Prince of Darkness were somehow akin.

"To cut a long story short, at the end of those two hard years, my mother died. A close friend of ours was matron in the Hospital of the Holy Star—ah, yes, how curious! I had forgotten the name—a beautiful little hospital in the Euston Road, supported by private contributions. She accepted me for training. I found the work interesting, and soon got on. You may have difficulty in believing it, Cousin David, but I make a quite excellent nurse. I studied every branch, passed various exams., looked quite professional in my uniform, and should have been a ward Sister before long—when the letter came, which again changed my whole life.

"It was from Uncle Falcon! He had kept himself informed of my movements through our old family lawyer, Mr. Inglestry, who, during those years had never lost sight of poor mamma, nor of me. I can remember Uncle Falcon's letter, word for word.

"'My Dear Niece,' he wrote, 'I am told you are by now a duly qualified hospital nurse. My body is in excellent health, but my brain—which I suppose I have worked pretty strenuously—has partially given way; with the result that my otherwise healthy body is more or less helpless on the right side. My doctor tells me I must have a trained nurse; not in constant attendance—Heaven protect the poor woman, if *that* were necessary!—but somewhere handy in the house, in case of need.

"'Now why should I be tended in my declining years by a stranger, when my own kith and kin is competent to do it? And why should I bring a stray young woman to this beautiful place, when the girl whose rightful home it is, might feel inclined to return to it?

"'I hear from old What's-his-name that you bear no resemblance whatever to your father, but are the image of what your mother was, at your age. That being the case, if you like to come home, my child, I will make your life as pleasant as I can, for her sake.

"'Your affectionate unknown uncle,

"'FALCON RIVERS.'

"Well-I went.

"I arrived in uniform not sure what my standing was to be in the house but thankful to be back there on any terms and irresistibly attracted by the spell of Uncle Falcon.

"Our own old butler opened the door to me. I nearly fell upon his neck The housekeeper, who had known me from infancy took me up to my room. They wept and laughed and seemed to look upon my uniform as one of Miss Diana's pranks-half funny, half naughty. Truth to tell, I did feel dressed up, when I found myself inside the old hall again.

"In twenty-four hours Cousin David, I was installed as the daughter of the house.

"Of Uncle Falcon's remarkable personality, there is not time to tell you now. We took to each other at once, and, before long, he felt it right to put away at my request, the one possible cause of misunderstanding there might have been between us, by telling me the true reason of his alienation from home, and his breach with my grandfather and my parents.

"Uncle Falcon was ten years younger than my grandfather. My mother, then a very lovely woman, in the perfection of her beauty, was ten years older than my father, a young subaltern just entering the army. My mother was engaged to Uncle Falcon, who loved her with an intensity of devotion, such as only a nature strong, fiery, rugged as his, could bestow.

"During a visit to Riverscourt, shortly before the time appointed for her marriage to Uncle

Falcon, then a comparatively poor man with no prospects—my mother met my father. My father fell in love with her, and my mother jilted Uncle Falcon in order to marry the young heir to the house and lands of Riverscourt. Poor mamma! How well I could understand it, remembering her love of luxury, and of all those things which go with an old country place and large estates. Uncle Falcon never spoke to her again, after receiving the letter in which she put an end to their engagement; but he had a furious scene with my grandfather, who had connived at the treachery toward his younger brother; and then horsewhipped the young subaltern in his father's presence.

"Shortly afterwards, he sailed for America, and never returned.

"Then—oh, irony of fate! After three years of married life the young heir died without a son, and Uncle Falcon stood to inherit Riverscourt, as the last in the entail.

"Meanwhile everything he touched had turned to gold, and he only waited my grandfather's decease to return as master to the old home, with the large fortune which would soon restore it to its pristine beauty and grandeur.

"How well I could now understand my grandfather's silent fury, and my mother's remorseful bitterness! By her own infidelity she had made herself the *niece* of the man whose wife she might have been, and whose wealth, position, and power would all have been laid at her feet. Also, I am inclined to think she had not been long in realizing and regretting the treasure she had lost in the love of the older man. I always knew mamma had few ideals, and no illusions. Many of my own pronounced views on the vital things in life are the product of her disillusionising philosophy. Poor mamma! Oh, Cousin David, I see it hurts you each time I say '*poor* mamma'! Yet you cannot know what it means, when one's kindest thoughts of one's mother must needs be prefixed by the adjective 'poor.' Yes, I know it is a sad state of things when pity must be called in to soften filial judgment. But then life is full of these sad things, isn't it? Anyway I have found it so. Had my mother left me one single illusion regarding men and marriage, I might not now find myself in the difficult position in which I am placed to-day.

"However, for one thing I have always been thankful—one hour when I can remember my mother with admiration and respect; that morning at breakfast, in our humble suburban villa, when she tore up and flung to the flames Uncle Falcon's cheque for a thousand pounds.

"A close intimacy, and a deep, though undemonstrative, affection, soon arose between Uncle Falcon and myself. His lifelong fidelity to his love for my mother seemed to transfer itself to me, and to be at last content in having found an object. My every wish was met and gratified. He insisted upon allowing me a thousand a year, merely as pocket-money, while still defraying all large expenses for me, himself. Hunters, dogs, everything I could wish, were secured and put at my disposal. His last gift to me was the motor car which brought you here to-day.

"His sense of humour was delightful; his shrewd keen judgment of men and things instructive and entertaining. But—he had one peculiarity. So sure was he of his own discernment, and so accustomed to bend others to his iron will, that if one held a different view from his and ventured to say so, he could never rest until he had won in the argument and brought one round to his way of thinking. He was never irritable over the point; he kept his temper, and controlled his tongue. But he never rested until he had convinced and defeated a mental opponent.

"He and I agreed upon most subjects, but there was one on which we differed; and Uncle Falcon could never bring himself to let it be. In spite of his own hard experience and consequent bachelorhood—perhaps because of it—he was an ardent believer in marriage. He held that a woman was not meant to stand alone; that she missed her proper vocation in life if she refused matrimony; and that she attained her full perfection only when the marriage tie had brought her to depend, for her completion and for her happiness, upon her rightful master—man.

"On the other hand, I, as you may have discovered. Cousin David, regard the whole idea of marriage with abhorrence. I hold that, as things now stand in this civilization of ours, a woman's one absolute right is her right to herself. She is her own inalienable possession. Why should she give herself up to a man; becoming his chattel, to do with as he pleases? Why should she lose all right over her own person, her own property, her own liberty of action and regulation of circumstance? Why should she change her very name for his? If the two could stand on a platform of absolute independence and equality, the thing might be bearable—for some. It would still be intolerable to me! But, as the law and social usage now stand, marriage is—to the woman—practically slavery; and, therefore, an unspeakable degradation!"

Diana's eyes flashed; her colour rose; her firm chin seemed more than ever to be moulded in marble.

David, sole representative of the tyrant man, quailed beneath the lash of her indictment. He knew Diana was wrong. He felt he ought to say that marriage was scriptural; and that woman was intended, from the first, to be in subjection to man. But he had not the courage of his convictions; nor could he brook the thought of any man attempting to subjugate this glorious specimen of womanhood, invading her privacy, or in any way presuming to dispute her absolute right over herself. So he shrank into his large armchair, and took refuge in silence.

"When I proclaimed my views to Uncle Falcon," continued Diana, "he would hear me to the end, and then say: 'My dear girl, after the manner of most women orators, you mount the platform of your own ignorance, and lay down the law from the depths—or, perhaps I should say, shallows—of your own absolute inexperience. Get married, child, and you will tell a different story.'

"Then Uncle Falcon set himself to compass this result, but without success. However profound might be my inexperience, I knew how to keep men at arm's length, thank goodness! But, as the happy years went by, we periodically reverted to our one point of difference. At the close of each discussion, Uncle Falcon used to say: 'I shall win, Diana! Some day you will have to admit that I have won.' His eyes used to gleam beneath his shaggy brows, and I would turn the subject; because I could not give in, yet I felt it was becoming almost a mania with Uncle Falcon.

"It was the only thing in which I failed to please him. His pride in my riding, and in anything else I could do, was touching beyond words. He remodelled the kennels, and financed the hunt in our neighbourhood, on condition that I was Master.

"One day his speech suddenly became thick and difficult. He sent for Mr. Inglestry, our old family friend and adviser, and was closeted with him for over an hour.

"When Mr. Inglestry came out of the library, his face was grave ; his manner, worried.

"'Go to your uncle, Miss Rivers,' he said. 'He has been exciting himself a good deal over a matter about which I felt bound to expostulate, and I think he needs attention.'

"I went into the library.

"Uncle Falcon's eyes were brighter than ever, though his lips twitched. 'I shall win, Diana, he said. 'Some day you will have to admit that I have won. You will have to say: "Uncle Falcon, you have won."'

"I knelt down in front of him. 'No other man will ever win me, dear. So I can say it at once. Uncle Falcon, you have won.'

"'Foolish girl!' he said; then looked at me with inexpressible affection. 'I w-want you to be happy,' he said. 'I w-want you to be as h-happy as I would have made Geraldine.'

"Geraldine was my mother.

"On the following day Uncle Falcon sent for another lawyer, a young man just opening a practice in Riversmead. He arrived with his clerk, but only spent a very few minutes in the library, and as we have never heard from him since, no transaction of importance can have taken place. Mr. Inglestry had the will and the codicil.

"A few nights later I was summoned to my uncle's room. He neither spoke nor moved again; but his eyes were still bright beneath the bushy eyebrows. He knew me to the end. Those living eyes, in the already dead body, seemed to say: 'Diana, I shall win.'

"At dawn, the brave, dauntless soul left the body, which had long clogged it, and launched out into the Unknown. My first conscious prayer was: that he might not there meet either my father or my mother, but some noble kindred spirit, worthy of him. Cousin David, you would have liked Uncle Falcon,"

"I am sure I should have," said David Rivers.

"Go into the library," commanded Diana, "the door opposite the dining-room, and study the portrait of him hanging over the mantelpiece, painted by a famous artist, two years ago."

David went.

Diana rang, and sent for a glass of water; went to the window, and looked out; crossed to a mirror, and nervously smoothed her abundant hair. Hitherto she had been cantering smoothly over open country. Now she was approaching the leap. She must keep her nerve—or she would find herself riding for a fall.

"Did you notice his eyes?" she asked, as David sat down again.

"Yes," he answered; "wonderful eyes; bright, as golden amber. You must not be offended-you would not be, if you could know how beautiful they were-but the only eyes I ever saw at all like them, belonged to a *Macacus Cynomolgus*, a little African monkey—who was a great pet of mine."

"I quite understand," said Diana. "I know the eyes of that species of monkey. Now, tell me. Did Uncle Falcon's amber eyes say anything to you?"

"Yes," said David. "It must have been simply owing to all you have told me. But, the longer I looked at them—the more clearly they said: 'I shall win.'"

"Well, now listen," said Diana, "if my history does not weary you. When Mr. Inglestry produced Uncle Falcon's will, he had left everything to me: Riverscourt, the whole estate, the four livings of which he held the patronage, and—his immense fortune. Cousin David, I am so rich that I have not yet learned how to spend my money. I want you to help me. I have indeed the gift of gold to offer to the King, I wish you to have, at once, all you require for the church, the schools, the printing-press, and the boat, of which you spoke. And then, I wish you to have a thousand a year—two, if you need them —for the current expenses of your work, and to enable you to have a colleague. Will you accept this, Cousin David, from a grateful heart, guided by you, led by the Star, and able to-day to offer it to the King?"

At first David made no reply. He sat quite silent, his head thrown back, his hands clasping his knee; and Diana knew, as she watched the working of the thin white face, that he was striving to master an emotion such as a man hates to show before a woman.

Then he sat up, loosing his knee, and answered very simply:

"I accept—for the King and for His work. Miss Rivers; and I accept on behalf of my poor eager waiting people out there. Ah, if you could know how much it means— —!"

His voice broke.

Diana felt the happy tears welling up into her own eyes.

"And we will call the church," said David, presently, "the Church of the Holy Star."

"Very well," said Diana. "Then that is settled. You have helped me with my first gift. Cousin David. Now you must advise and help me about the second. And, indeed, the possibility of offering the first depends almost entirely upon the advice you give me about the second. You know you said the frankincense meant our ideals—the high and holy things in our lives? Well, my ideals are in sore peril. I want you to advise me as to how to keep them. Listen! There was a codicil to Uncle Falcon's will—a private codicil known only to Mr. Inglestry and myself, and only to be made known a year after his death, to those whom, if I failed to fulfil its conditions, it might then concern. Riverscourt, and all this wealth, are mine, only on condition that I am married within twelve months of Uncle Falcon's death. He has been dead, eleven."

Diana paused.

"Good God!" said David Rivers; and it was not a careless exclamation. It was a cry of protest from his very soul. "On condition that you are married!" he said. "And to whom?"

"No stipulation was made as to that," replied Diana. "But Uncle Falcon had three men in his mind, all of whom he liked, and each of whom considers himself in love with me: a famous doctor in London, a distinguished cleric in our cathedral town, and a distant cousin, Rupert Rivers, to whom the whole property is to go, if I fail to fulfil the condition."

David sat forward, with his elbows on his knees, and rumpled his hair with his hands. Horror and dismay were in his honest eyes.

"It is unbelievable" he said. "That he should really care for you, and wish you happiness, and yet lay this burden upon you after his death. His mind must have been affected when he made that codicil."

"So Mr. Inglestry says; but not sufficiently affected to enable us to dispute it. The idea of bending me to matrimony, and of forcing me to admit that it was the better part, had become a monomania with Uncle Falcon."

David sat with his head in his hands, his look bent upon the floor. Now that he knew of this cruel condition imposed upon the beautiful girl sitting opposite to him, he could not bring himself to lift his eyes to hers. She should be looked at only with admiration and wonder; and now a depth of pity would be in his eyes. Therefore he kept them lowered.

"So," said Diana, "you see how I am placed. If I refuse to fulfil the condition, on the anniversary of Uncle Falcon's death we must tell Rupert Rivers of the codicil; I shall have to hand over everything to him; leave my dear home, and go back to the life of running after omnibuses, and pretending to enjoy potted meat lunches! On the other hand, if—in order to keep my home, my income, all the luxuries I love, my position in the county, and the influence which I now for the first time begin to value for the true reason—I marry one of these men, or one of half a dozen others who would require only the slightest encouragement to propose to me at once, I fail to keep true to my own ideals; I practically barter myself and my liberty, in order to keep the place which is rightfully my own; I sink to the level of the women I have long despised, who marry for money."

"You must not do that," said David. "Nay, more; you *could* not do that. But is not your Cousin Rupert a man whom you might learn to love, a man you could marry for the real reasons?"

Diana laughed, bitterly.

"Cousin David," she said, "shortly before grandpapa died, I was engaged to Rupert Rivers for a fortnight. At the end of that time I loathed my own body. Young as I was, and scornfully opposed by my mother, I took matters into my own hands, and broke off the engagement."

David looked perplexed.

"It should not have had that effect upon you," he said, slowly. "I don't know much about it, but it seems to me that a man's love and worship should tend to make a woman reverence her own body, and regard her beauty in a new light because of his delight in it. I remember— —" a sudden flush suffused David's pale cheeks, but he brought forth his reminiscence bravely, for Diana's sake: "I remember kissing Amy's hand the evening before I first went to college, and she wrote and told me that for days afterwards that hand had seemed unlike the other, and whenever she looked at it she remembered that I had kissed it."

Diana's laughter was in her eyes. She did not admit it to her voice. She felt very much older, at that moment, than David Rivers.

"Oh, you dear boy!" she said. "What can you, with your Amy and your Africans, know of such men as Rupert, or the doctor, or even-even the church dignitary? *You* would love a woman's soul, and cherish her body because contained it. *They* make one feel that nothing else matters much, so long as one is beautiful And after having been looked at by them for a little while, one feels inclined to smash one's mirror."

David lifted quiet eyes to hers. They seemed deep wells of childlike purity; yet there was fire in their calm depths.

"When you *are* so beautiful," he said, simply, "you can't blame **a** man for thinking so when he looks at you."

Diana laughed, blushing. She was surfeited with compliments; yet this of David's, so unpremeditated, so impersonal, pleased her more than any compliment had ever pleased her.

But, in an instant, she was grave again. Momentous issues lay before her. Uncle Falcon had been dead eleven months.

"Then would you advise me to marry, and thus retain the property?" She suggested.

"God forbid!" cried David, "That you should be compelled to leave here, seems intolerable; but it would be infinitely more intolerable that you should make a loveless marriage. Give up all, if needs must, but—keep your ideals."

Diana glanced at him, from beneath half-lifted lids.

"That will mean, Cousin David, that you cannot have the money for your church, your school, your printing-press, and your steam-launch; nor the yearly income for current expenses."

Now, curiously enough, David had not thought of this. His mind had been completely taken up with the idea of Diana running after omnibuses and lunching cheaply on potted meat.

The great disappointment now struck him with full force; but he did not waver for an instant.

"How could I build the Church of the Holy Star on the proceeds of your lost ideals?" he said. "If my church is to be built, the money will be found in some other way."

"There *is* another way," said Diana, suddenly.

David looked up, surprised at the forceful decision of her tone.

"What other way is there?" he asked.

Diana rose; walked over to the window and stood looking across the spacious park, at the pale gold of the wintry sunset.

She was in full view, at last, of her high fence and did not yet know what lay beyond it. She headed straight for it; but she rode on the curb.

She walked back to the fireplace, and stood confronting him; her superb young figure drawn up to its full height.

Her voice was very quiet; her manner, very deliberate, as she answered his question.

"I want *you* to marry me, Cousin David," she said, "on the morning of the day on which you start for Central Africa."

CHAPTER X

DIANA'S HIGH FENCE

DAVID RIVERS sprang to his feet, and faced Diana.

"I cannot do that," he said.

Diana had expected this. She waited a moment, silently; while the atmosphere palpitated with David's intense surprise.

Then: "Why not, Cousin David?" she asked quietly.

And, as he still stood before her, speechless, "Sit down," she commanded, "and tell me. Why not?"

But David stood his ground, and Diana realized, for the first time, that he was slightly taller than herself.

"Why not?" he said. "Why not? Why, because, even if I wished—I mean, even if you wished—even if we both wished for each other—in that way—Central Africa is no place for a woman. I would never take a woman there!"

Diana's face flushed. Her white teeth bit sharply into her lower lip. Her hands clenched themselves suddenly at her sides. The fury of her eyes flashed full into the blank dismay of his.

Then, with a mighty effort, she mastered her imperious temper.

"My dear Cousin David," she said—and she spoke slowly, seating herself upon the sofa, and carefully arranging the silken cushions to her liking: "You totally mistake my meaning. I gave you credit for more perspicacity. I have not the smallest intention of going to Central Africa, or of ever inflicting my presence, or my companionship, upon you. Surely you and I have made it pretty clear to one another that we are each avowed celibates. But, just because of this—just because we both have everything to gain, and nothing to lose by such an arrangement—just because we so completely understand one another—I can say to you—as frankly as I would say: 'Cousin David, will you oblige me by witnessing my signature to this document?'—'Cousin David, will you oblige me by marrying me on the morning of the day upon which you return to Central Africa?' Do you not see that by doing so, you take no burden upon yourself, yet you free me at once from the desperate plight in which I am placed by Uncle Falcon's codicil? You enable me to give the gold and the frankincense, and you yourself have told me over and over, that you never expect to return to England."

David's young face paled and hardened.

"I see," he said. So *I* am to provide the myrrh! I could not promise to die, for certain, you know. I might pull through, and live, after all; which would be awkward for you."

This was the most human remark she had, as yet, heard from David; but the bitterness of his tone brought the tears to Diana's eyes. She had not realized how much her proposal would hurt him.

"Dear Cousin David," she said, with extreme gentleness, "God grant indeed that you may live, and spend many years in doing your great work. But you told me you had nothing to bring you back to England, and that you felt you were leaving it now, never to return. It was not *my* suggestion. And don't you see, that if you help me thus, you will also be helping your poor African people; because it will mean that you can have your church, and your schools, and all the other things you need, and a yearly income for current expenses?"

"So these were all bribes," cried David, and his eyes flamed down into hers—"bribes to make me do this thing! And you called them gifts for the King!"

Diana flushed. The injustice of this was hard to bear. But the indignant pain in his voice helped her to reply with quiet self-control.

"Cousin David, I am sorry you think that of me. It is quite unjust. Had there been no codicil to my uncle's will, every penny I hope to offer for your work would have been gladly, freely, offered. Since I knew that my gold could be useful in helping you to bring light into that darkness, the thought has been one of pure joy. Oh, Cousin David, say 'No' to my request, if you like, but don't wrong me by misjudging the true desire of my heart to bring my gifts, all unworthy though they be. Remember you stand for the Christ to me. Cousin David; and He was never unjust to a woman."

David's face softened; but instantly hardened again, as a fresh thought struck him.

"Was this plan—this idea—in your mind," he demanded, "on that Sunday night when you first came to Brambledene church?" Then, as Diana did not answer, "Oh, good heavens! he cried, vehemently, "say it wasn't! My Lady of Mystery! Say you came to worship, and that all this was an after-thought!"

Diana's clear eyes met his. They did not flinch, though her lips trembled.

"I cannot lie to you, Cousin David," she said, bravely. "I had heard you were never coming back—it seemed a possible way out—it seemed my last hope. I—I came—to see if you were a man I could trust."

David groaned; looked wildly round the room, as if for a way of escape; then sank into a chair, and buried his face in his hands.

"I cannot do it, Miss Rivers," he said. "It would be making a mockery of God's most holy ordinance of matrimony—to wed you in the morning, knowing I should leave you for ever in the afternoon. How could I promise, in the presence of God, to love, comfort, honour, and keep you? The whole thing would be a sacrilege."

He lifted a haggard face, looking at her with despairing eyes.

Diana smiled softly into them. A moment before she had expected to see him leave the room and the house, for ever. That he should sit down and discuss the matter, even to prove the impossibility of acceding to her request, seemed, in some sort, a hopeful sign. She held his look while she answered.

"Dear Cousin David, why should it be a mockery? Let us consider it reasonably. Surely, in the best and highest of senses, it might be really *rather* true. I know you don't love me; but—you do *like* me a little, don't you?"

"I like you very much indeed," said David, woefully; and then, all of a sudden, they both laughed. The rueful admission had sounded so funny.

"Why of course I like you," said David, with conviction; "better than any one else I know. But— —"

He paused; looked at her, helplessly, and hesitated.

"I quite understand," said Diana, quickly. "*Like* is not *love;* but in many cases 'like' is much better than 'love,' to my thinking. I know a very Christian old person, whom I once heard say: 'We are commanded in the Bible to love the brethren. I always *love* the brethren, though I cannot always *like* them.' Now I had much rather you liked me, and didn't love me. Cousin David, than that you loved me, and didn't like me! Wouldn't you?

"And remember how St. John began one of his epistles: 'The Elder unto the well beloved Gaius, whom I love in the truth.' I am sure, if you had occasion to write to me, and began: 'David, unto the well beloved Diana, whom I love in the truth,' no one could consider it an ordinary love-letter, and yet it would answer the purpose. Wouldn't it, Cousin David?"

David laughed again, in spite of his desire to maintain an attitude of tragic protest. And, as he laughed, his face grew less haggard, and his eyes regained their normal expression of steadfast calm.

Diana hurried on.

"So much for love. Now what comes next? Comfort? Ah, the comfort you would bring into my life! Comfort of body; comfort of mind; the daily, hourly, constant comfort wrought by the solving of this dark problem. And then—'honour.' Why, you can honour a woman as much by your thought of her at a distance, as by any word or action in her presence. Not that I fed worthy of honour from such a man as you, Cousin David. Yet I know you would honour all women, and all women worth anything would try to deserve it. What comes next? Keep? Oh what could be a truer form of keeping, than to keep me from a lowering marriage, on the one hand; or from poverty, and all the ups and downs of strenuous London life, on the other; to keep me in the entourage of my childhood's lovely home? It seems to me, Cousin David, that you would be doing more 'keeping' for me than falls to the lot of most men to do for the girls they marry And, best of all, you would be keeping me true to the purest, highest ideals."

David's elbows had found his knees again He rumpled his hair, despairingly.

"Miss Rivers," he said, "I admit the truth of all you say. I would gladly do anything to beer—useful to you under these difficult circumstances; anything *right*. But could it be right to go through the solemn marriage service, without having the slightest intention of fulfilling any of the causes for which matrimony was ordained? And could it be right for a man to take upon himself solemn obligations with regard to a woman; and a few hours later leave her, never to return?"

"It seems to me," said Diana "that the cause for our marriage would be a more important and vital one than most of those mentioned in the Prayer-book. And, as to the question of leaving me—why, before the Boer War, several friends of mine married their soldiers on the eve of their departure for the front, simply because if they were going out to die, they wished the privilege of being their widows."

David's eyes softened.

"That was love." he said.

"Not in every case. I know a girl who married an old Sir Somebody on the morning of the day his regiment sailed, making sure he would be killed in his first engagement; he offered such a vast, expansive mark for the Boer sharpshooters. She wished to be Lady So-and-So, with a delicate halo of tragic glory, and no encumbrance. But back he came unscathed, and stout as ever—he did not even get enteric! They have lived a cat-and-dog life ever since."

"Abominable!" said David. "I hate hearing such stories."

"Well, are not our motives better? And are they not better than scores of the loveless marriages which are taking place every day?"

"Other people's wrong does not constitute our right," said David, doggedly.

"I know that," she answered, with unruffled patience; "but I cannot see any wrong in what we propose to do. We may be absolutely faithful to one another, though continents divide us. I should most probably continue faithful if you were on another planet. We can be a mutual help and comfort the one to the other, by our prayers and constant thought, and by our letters; for surely, Cousin David, we should write to one another—occasionally? Is not our friendship worth something?"

"It is worth everything," said David, "except wrongdoing. Look here!" he exclaimed suddenly, rising to his feet. "I must go right away, by myself, and think this thing over, for twenty-four hours. At the end of that time I shall have arrived at a clear decision in my own mind. Then, if you do not object, and can allow me another day, I will run up to town, and lay the whole matter—of course without mentioning your name —before the man whose judgment I trust more than that of any man I know. If he agrees with me, my own opinion will be confirmed; and if he differs— —"

"You will still adhere to your own opinion," said Diana, with a wistful little smile.

She rang the bell.

"I am beginning to know you pretty well, Cousin David.—The dogcart, Rodgers.—Who is this Solon?"

"A London physician, who has given me endless care, refusing all fees, because of my work, and because my father was a doctor. Also he gives a more hopeful report than any."

"Really? Does he think you will stand the climate after all?"

David smiled. "He gives me a possible three years, under favourable circumstances. The other people give me two, perhaps only one."

"I think you must tell me his name. He may be my undesirable suitor!"

"Hardly," said David. "He has a charming wife of his own, and two little children. But of course I will tell you who he is."

David named a name which brought a flush of pleasure to Diana's face.

"Why, I know him well. He is honorary consulting physician to our Hospital of the Star and is constantly called in when we have specially interesting or baffling cases. You couldn't go to a better man. Tell him everything if you like—my name, and all. He is absolutely to be trusted. But—Cousin David– –" They heard the horse's hoofs on the drive, and she rose and faced him. "Ah, do remember, how much this means to me! Don't make an abstract case of it, when you consider it alone. Don't dissolve it from its intensely personal connexion with you and me. We are so unlike ordinary people. We are both alone in the world. Your work is so much to you. We could make your—your *three* years so gloriously fruitful. You would leave such a strongly established church behind you, and I would go on supporting it. My home is so much to me; and I am just beginning to understand the influence I possess. Think if, as these four livings become vacant, I can put in really earnest men. Think of the improvements I could make in the condition of the villages. At present I have been able to do so little, because Mr. Inglestry is holding back as much as possible of this year's income, to which I have any way the right, in order to buy me a small annuity when I lose all. For, let me tell you frankly, Cousin David, if you cannot do as I ask, that is what it will mean. I have no intention whatever of selling my body into slavery, or my soul to hopeless degradation, by marrying Rupert Rivers, or any of the others. I lose all, if you say 'no'; and I lose it on the Feast of the Star. At the same time, ah, God knows, I do not want to do wrong! Nor do I want to urge you to do violence to your own conscience. You know that?"

David took her hand, holding it very firmly in his.

"I know that," he said; "and I think you can trust me. Miss Rivers, not to forget how much it means to us both. If it meant more, there could be no doubt. If it meant less, there would be no question. It is because it means exactly what it does mean, that the situation is so difficult. I believe light will soon come; and when it comes, it will come clearly. I think it will come to me to-night. If so, I need not keep you waiting forty-eight hours. I will go up to town early to-morrow morning, and see Sir Deryck, if possible, in time to catch the 2.35 for Riversmead. Could you be here, alone, at that hour to-morrow?"

"I will send to meet the 2.35," said Diana; "and I will be here alone. Good-bye, Cousin David."

"Good-bye. Miss Rivers."

Diana went into the hall, watched him climb into the dogcart and be driven rapidly away without looking back.

Then she entered the library, closed and locked the door, and stood on the hearth-rug looking up at the portrait of Falcon Rivers. The amber eyes seemed to twinkle kindly into hers; but they still said: "I shall win, Diana."

"Oh, Uncle Falcon," she whispered, "was this the way to secure my happiness? Ah, if you could know the loneliness, the pain, the humiliation the shame! To have had to ask this of any man—even of such a saint as David Rivers. And how cruelly I hurt him, by seeming to build the whole plan upon the certainty of his death."

Suddenly she broke down under the prolonged strain of the afternoon's conversation. Kneeling at her uncle's empty chair—where she had so often knelt, looking up into his kind eyes—she buried her face on her arms and wept, and wept, until she could weep no longer.

"If only he had cared a little," she whispered between her paroxysms of sobbing; "not enough to make him troublesome, but enough to make him pleased to marry me, on any terms. Why was he so indignant and aghast? It seemed to me quite simple. Well, twenty-four hours of suspense are less trying than forty-eight. But—what will he decide? Oh, what will he decide! . . . Sorry, but you can't come in, Chappie; I am not visible to any one just now." This in response to a persistent trying of the handle and knocking at the door . . . . "Yes, he went some time ago." . . . "Yes, in the dogcart.". . . "I wish you would not call him *my* missionary. I am not a heathen nation!". . . . "No, he did not propose to me. How silly you are!". . . . "Oh, I am glad the tea was good. Yes, we will find out where those tea cakes can be had." . . . "No; he has not once called me' Diana.'". . . . "Why, 'Miss Rivers' of course! Chappie, if you don't go away this very moment I shall take down Uncle Falcon's shot-gun and discharge both barrels through the panel of the door at the exact height at which I know your face must be, on the other side!" . . . "Of course I can tell by your voice, even had I not heard the plump, that you are now on your knees. I shall blow out the lower panel." . . . "No, I am not communing with spirits, but *you* soon will be, if you don't go away!". . . "Chappie! In ten seconds, I ring the bell; and when Rodgers answers it, I shall order him to take you by the arm, and lead you upstairs!"

As Mrs. Vane rustled indignantly away, and quiet reigned once more, Diana buried her head again in the seat of the chair. She laughed and wept, alternately; then cried bitterly: "Ah, it is so lonely—so lonely! Nobody really cares!"

Then, suddenly she remembered that she could pray—pray, with a new right of access, to One Who cared. Whose love was changeless; Whose wisdom was infinite. If *He* went on before, the way would become clear.

Her morning letters lay on the library table.

From a pile of Christmas cards she drew out one which held a motto for the swiftly coming year. She breathed it, as a prayer, and her troubled heart grew still.

> Dear Christ, move on before!
> Ah, let me follow where Thy feet have trod;
> Thus shall I find, 'mid life's perplexities,
> The Golden Pathway of the Will of God.

After that, all was peace. In comparative rest of soul, Diana waited David's answer.

CHAPTER XI

THE VOICE IN THE NIGHT

THE fire burned low in the study grate.

The black marble clock on the mantelpiece had struck midnight, more slowly and sonorously than it ever sounded the hour by day. Each stroke had seemed a knell—a requiem to bright hopes and golden prospects; and now it slowly and distinctly ticked out the first hour of a new day.

Sarah, and her assistants, had long been sleeping soundly, untroubled by any difficult questions of casuistry.

The one solitary watcher beneath the roof of Brambledene Rectory sat huddled up in the Rector's large armchair, his elbows on his knees, his head in his hands.

His little worn Prayer-book had fallen to the floor, unnoticed. He had been reading the marriage service. The Prayer-book lay on its back, at his feet, open at the Burial of the Dead, as if in silent suggestion that that solemn office had an important bearing on the case.

The fire burned low; yet David did not bestir himself to give it any attention. The hot embers sank together, in the grate, with that sound of finality which implies no further attempt to keep alight—a sitting-down under adverse circumstances, so characteristic of human nature, and so often caused by the absorbed neglect of others.

David had as yet arrived at no definite decision regarding the important question of marriage with Diana.

He had reviewed the matter from every possible standpoint. Diana had begged him not to let the question become an impersonal one—not to consider it as an abstract issue.

There had been little need for that request. Diana's brilliant personality dominated his whole mental vision, just as the sun, bursting through clouds, illumines a grey scene, touching and gilding the heretofore dull landscape, with unexpected glory.

It puzzled David to find that he could not consider his own plans, his most vital interests, as apart from her. The whole future seemed to hinge upon whether she were to be happy or disconsolate; surrounded by the delights of her lovely home, or cast out into the world, alone and comfortless.

A readjustment had suddenly taken place in his proportionate view of things. Hitherto, Africa had come first; all else, his own life included, being a mere background.

Now—DIANA stepped forth, in golden capitals; and all things else receded, appearing of small importance; all save his sensitive conscientiousness; his unwavering determination to adhere to the right and to shun the wrong.

It perplexed David that this should be so. It was an experience so new that it had not as yet found for itself a name, or formulated an explanation.

As he sat, wrapt in thought, in the armchair in which he had prepared so many of his evening sermons, she became once more his Lady of Mystery. He reviewed those weeks, realizing, for the first time, that the thought of her had never left him; that the desire to win the unawakened soul of her had taken foremost place in his whole ministry at Brambledene. She seemed enfolded in silent shadows, from which her grey eyes looked out at him, sometimes cold, critical, appraising, incredulous; sometimes anxious, appealing, sorrowful; soft, with unshed tears; sad, with unspoken longing.

Then—she came to the vestry; and his Lady of Mystery vanished; giving place to Diana Rivers, imperious, vivid, radiating vitality and friendliness; and when he realized that it was little more than forty-eight hours since he had first known her name, he marvelled at the closeness of the intimacy into which she had drawn him. Yet, undoubtedly, the way in which she had dominated his mind from the very first, was now accounted for by the fact that, from the very first, she had planned to involve him in this scheme for the unravelling of her own tangled future.

David clenched his hands and battled fiercely with his instinctive anger against Diana in this matter. It tortured him to remember his wistful gladness at the appearance of an obviously unaccustomed worshipper in the holy place of worship; and later, his sacred joy in the thought that he was just the Voice sent to bring the message; and, having brought it, to pass on unrecognized. Yet, all the while, he had been the tool she intended using to gain her own ends; while the most sacred thing in his whole life, was the fact, which, chancing to become known to her, had led her to pounce upon him as a suitable instrument. As priest and as man, David felt equally outraged. Yet Diana's frank confession had been so noble in its truthfulness, at a moment when a less honourable nature would have been sorely tempted to prevaricate, that David had instantly matched it with a forgiveness equally noble, and now fought back the inclination to retrospective wrath.

But the present situation must be faced, She was asking him to do this thing.

Could he refuse? Could he leave England knowing he had had it in his power to do her so great a service, to make the whole difference in her future life, to rid her of odious obligations, to right an obvious wrong— and yet, he had refused? Could he sail for Africa, leaving Diana homeless;

confronted by hardships of all kinds; perhaps facing untold temptations? The beautiful heiress, in her own ancestral home, could keep Rupert Rivers at arm's length, if she chose. But if Rupert Rivers reigned at Riverscourt; if all she held so dear, and would miss so overwhelmingly, were his; if, under these circumstances, he set himself to win the hospital nurse— —?

David clenched his cold hands and ground his teeth; then paused amazed, to wonder at himself.

Why should it fill him with impotent fury, to contemplate the possibility of any man winning and subjugating Diana? Had she infected him with her own irrational and exaggerated views?

The more he thought over it, the more clearly he realized that this thing she asked of him would undoubtedly bring good—infinite good—to herself; to the many dependents on the Riverscourt estate; to the surrounding villages, where, as each living became vacant, she would seek to place earnest men, true preachers of the Word faithful tenders of the flock. It would bring untold good to his own poor waiting people, in that dark continent, eagerly longing for more light. To all whom his voice could sway, whom her money could benefit, whom their united efforts could reach, this step would mean immeasurable gain. Nobody walked the earth whom it could wrong. He recalled, with unexpected clearness of detail, a lengthy account of Rupert Rivers, given him in that very room by his garrulous host, during the only evening they spent together. At the time it had made no impression upon an intentionally inattentive mind; but now it came up from his subconsciousness, and provided him with important information. If Mr. Goldsworthy's facts were correct, Rupert Rivers already possessed more money than was good for him, and lived the life of a gay spendthrift, having chambers in town, a small shooting-box in Scotland; much of his time being spent abroad, flitting from scene to scene, and from pleasure to pleasure, with absolutely no sense of responsibility, and no regard for the welfare of others. His one redeeming point appeared to be: that he wanted to marry Diana. But that was not to be thought of.

Again David's hands clenched, painfully. Why was it such sudden fierce agony to contemplate Diana as the wife of Rupert Rivers? That bewildered question throbbed unanswered into the now chilly room.

Yes, undoubtedly, it would mean untold gain to many; loss to none. But no sooner did his mind arrive at the possibility of agreeing to Diana's suggestion, than up rose, and stalked before him, the spectre of mockery; the demon of unreality; the ghastly horror, to the mind of the earnest priest, of having to stand before God's altar, there to utter solemn words, under circumstances which would make of those words a hollow mockery, an impious unreality The position would be different, had he but a warrant for believing that any conditions could justify him, in the sight of God, in entering into the holy bond of marriage for reasons other than those for which matrimony was ordained.

For a moment a way out of the difficulty had suggested itself, in the registry-office; but he had not harboured the thought for many seconds. An act which could not face the light of God's holy church, most certainly could not stand in the light of the judgment day.

The Rector's black marble clock struck one.

David shivered. One hour had already passed of the day on which he had promised to give Diana his decision; yet, after hours of deliberation, he was no nearer arriving at any definite conclusion.

"My God," he prayed, "give me light Ah, give me a clear unmistakable revelation of Thy will!"

The hours from one to two, and from two to three, are apt to hold especial terrors for troubled souls—for lonely watchers, keeping vigil. This is the time of earth's completest silence, and the sense of the nearness of the spirit-world seems able to make itself more intimately felt.

The cheerful cock has not yet bestirred himself to crow; the dawn has made no rift in the heavy blackness of sky

The Prince of Darkness invades the world, unhindered. The Hosts of Light stand by, with folded wings; their glittering swords close sheathed. "This is you hour, and the hour of darkness." Murder, robbery, lust, and every form of sin, lift their heads, unafraid.

Christian souls, waking, shudder in nameless fear; then whisper:

Keep me, O keep me. King of Kings,
Beneath Thine Own almighty wings!

and sleep again, in peace.

Next comes the coldest hour—the hour before the dawn. This is the hour of passing souls. Death, drawing near, enters unchecked; and, ere the day breaks and busy life begins to stir again, the souls he has come to fetch, pass out with him; and weary watchers close the eyes which will never see another sun rising, and fold the hands whose day's work in the world is over.

All life, in this hour, is at its lowest ebb.

From one to two, David prayed: "Give me light! Oh, my God, give me light!"

Evil thoughts, Satanic suggestions, diabolic whisperings, swarmed around him but failed to force an entrance into the guarded garrison of his mind.

The clock struck two.

The study lamp grew dim, flickered spasmodically; and, finally, went out. David reached for matches, and lighted one candle on the table at his elbow.

He saw his Prayer-book on the floor, picked it up, and glanced at the open page. "Forasmuch as it hath pleased Almighty God of His great mercy to take unto Himself the soul of our dear brother here departed, we therefore commit his body to the ground– –"

David smiled. It seemed so simple a solution to all earthly difficulties—"we therefore commit his body to the ground." It promised peace at the last.

Who would read those words, over the forest grave in Central Africa? Would he be borne, feet foremost, down the aisle of the Church of the Holy Star—his church and Diana's—or would he be carried straight from his own hut to the open grave beneath the mighty trees? It would not matter at all to his wasted body, which it was; but, ah, how much it would matter to the people he left behind!

"Oh God, give me light—give me light!"

The clock struck three.

The study grate was black. The last red ember had burned itself out.

David shuddered. He was too completely lost to outward things to be conscious of the cold; but he shuddered in unison with the many passing souls.

Then a sense of peace stole over his spirit. He lifted his head from his hands, leaned back in the Rector's armchair, and fell into a light sleep. He was completely exhausted, in mind and body.

"Send me light, my Lord," he murmured for the last time; and fell asleep.

He did not hear the clock strike four; but, a few moments later, he was awakened by a voice in the silent room, saying, slowly and distinctly, in tones of sublime tenderness: "Son of man!"

David, instantly wide awake, started up, and sat listening. The solitary candle failed to illumine the distant corners of the study, but was reflected several times in the glass doors of the book-cases.

David pushed back his tumbled hair. "Speak again," he said, in tones of awe and wonder. Then, as his own voice broke the silence, he realized that the voice which had waked him had not stirred the waves of outward sound, but had vibrated on the atmosphere of his inner spirit-chamber, reaching, with intense distinctness, the hearing of his soul. He lay back, and closed his eyes.

"Son of man!" said the voice again.

This time David did not stir. He listened in calm intentness.

"Son of man," said the low tender tones again; "behold, I take away from thee the desire of thine eyes with a stroke."

Then David knew where he was. He sat up, eagerly; drew the candle close to him; took out his pocket-Bible; and, turning to the twenty-fourth chapter of Ezekiel, read the whole passage.

"Son of man, behold, I take away from thee the desire of thine eyes with a stroke: yet neither shalt thou mourn nor weep, neither shall thy tears run down. Forbear to cry, make no mourning for the dead, bind the tire of thine head upon thee, and put on thy shoes upon thy feet, and cover not thy lips, and eat not the bread of men.

"So I spake unto the people in the morning; and at even my wife died: and I did in the morning as I was commanded.

"And the people said unto me: Wilt thou not tell us what these things are to us, that thou doest so? Then I answered them. The word of the Lord came unto me saying: Speak unto the house of Isreal: Thus saith the Lord God: . . . Ezekiel is unto you a sign: according to all that he hath done, shall ye do; and when this cometh ye shall know that I am the Lord.

"Also, thou son of man, shall it not be in the day when I take from them their strength, the joy of their glory, the desire of their eyes, and that whereupon they set their minds. . . . In that day shall thy mouth be opened, . . . and thou shalt speak, . . . and thou shalt be a sign unto them; and they shall know that I am the Lord."

As David read this most touching of all Old Testament stories, his mind was absorbed at first in the tragedy of the simply told, yet vivid picture. The young prophet, standing faithfully at his post, preaching to a stiff-necked, hardhearted people, though knowing, all the while, how rapidly the shadow of a great sorrow was drawing near unto his own heart and home. The Desire of his eyes—how tenderly that described the young wife who lay dying at home. He who knoweth the hearts of men, knew she was just that to him. Each moment of that ebbing life was precious; yet the young preacher must remain and preach; he must yield to no anguish of anxiety; he must show no sign of woe. Throughout that long hard day, he stood the test. And then—in the grand unvarnished simplicity of Old Testament tragedy—he records quite simply: "And, at even, my wife died; and I did in the morning, as I was commanded." A veil is drawn over the night of anguish, but—"I did in the morning, as I was commanded."

David, as he read, felt his soul attune with the soul of that young prophet of long ago. He also had had a long night of conflict and of vigil. He also, would do in the morning as he was commanded.

Then, suddenly—suddenly—he saw light!

Here was a marriage tie, close, tender, perfect; broken, apparently for no reason which concerned the couple themselves, for nothing connected with the causes for which matrimony was ordained; broken simply for the sake of others; solely in order that the preacher might himself be the text of his own sermon; standing before the people, bereaved, yet not mourning; stricken suddenly, all unprepared—in order that he might be a living sign to all men who should see and question, of Jehovah's dealings with themselves.

David's mind, accustomed to reason by induction, especially on theological points, grasped this at once: that if the marriage tie could be *broken* by God's direction, for purposes of influence, and for the sake of bringing good to others, it might equally be *formed* for the same reasons—unselfish, pure, idealistic—without the man and the woman, who for these causes entered into the tie, finding themselves, in so doing, outside the Will or the Word of God.

From that moment David never doubted that he might agree to Diana's proposal.

To many minds would have come the suggestion that the twentieth century differed from ancient times; that the circumstances of the prophet Ezekiel were probably dissimilar, in all essentials, to his own. But David had all his life lived very simply by Bible rules. The revealed Will of God seemed to him to hold good through all the centuries, and to apply to all circumstances, in all times. His case and Diana's was unique ; and this one instance which, to him, seemed clearly applicable, at once contented him.

He laid his open Bible beside the candle on the table.

"I shall say 'Yes,'" he said, aloud. "How pleased she will be." He could see her face, radiant in its fair beauty.

"The Desire of thine eyes." What a perfect description of a man's absorbing love for a woman. Two months ago, he would not have understood it; but he remembered now how he used to look forward, all the week, to the first sight, on Sunday evening, of the sweet face and queenly head of his Lady of Mystery, in her corner beside the stone pillar. And on Christmas Eve, when he stood in the snow, under the shadow of the old lich-gate, while the footman flashed up the lights in the interior of the car, and her calm loveliness was revealed among the furs. Then these two days of intimacy had shown him so much of vivid charm in that gay, perfect face, as she laughed and talked, or hushed into gentle earnestness. She had talked for so long—he sitting watching her; he knew all her expressive movements; her ways of turning her head quickly, or of lowering her eyelids, and hiding those soft clear eyes. To-day—this very day—he would see her again; and every anxious cloud would lift, when she heard his decision. Her grateful look would beam upon him.

"The Desire of thine eyes." Yes; it was a truly Divine description of a man's– –

Suddenly David sprang to his feet.

"My God!" he cried; "I love Diana!"

The revelation was overwhelming in its Suddenness. Having resolved upon a life of celibacy, his mental attitude towards women had never contemplated the possibility of this. He had stepped fearlessly out into this friendship, at the call of her need, and of his duty. And now– –

He stood quite still in the chill silence of the dimly lighted study, and faced the fact.

"I—love—Diana! And, in two weeks I am to wed Diana. And a few hours afterwards, I am to leave Diana—for ever! 'Son of man behold I take away from thee the Desire of thine eyes with a stroke.' To sail for Central Africa; and never to look upon her face again—the face of my own wife. 'And at even my wife died.' but my wife will not die," said David, "Thank God, it is I who bring the offering of myrrh. Because of this that I can do for her, my wife will live, rich, happy, contented, useful. Her home, her wealth, her happy life, will be my gift to her. But—if Diana knew I loved her, she would never accept this service from me."

David had been pacing the room. He now stood still, leaning his hands on the table, where glimmered the one candle.

"Can I," he said, slowly, asking himself deliberately the question: "Can I carry this thing through, without letting Diana suspect how much more it means to me, than she intends; how much more than it means to her? Can I wed the Desire of mine eyes in the morning, look my last upon her in the afternoon, and leave her, without her knowing that I love her?"

He asked himself the question, slowly, deliberately, leaning heavily on the study table.

Then he stood erect, his head thrown back, his deep eyes shining, and answered the question with another.

"Is there anything a man cannot do for the woman he loves?" said David Rivers.

He went to the window, drew back the heavy rep curtains, unbarred the shutters, and looked out.

There was, as yet, no sign of dawn. but through the frosty pane, right before him, as a lamp in the purple sky, shone the bright morning star.

Cold though he was, stiff from his long night vigil David threw up the window-sash, that he might see the star shine clearly, undimmed by frosty fronds, traced on the window-pane.

He dropped on one knee, folding his arms upon the woodwork of the sill.

"My God," he said, looking upward, his eyes on the morning star; "I thank Thee for light; I thank Thee for love; I thank Thee for the guiding star! I thank Thee, that heavenly love and earthly love can meet, in one bright radiant Ideal. I thank Thee that, expecting nothing in return, I love Diana!"

CHAPTER XII

SUSPENSE

"YOU old flirt!" laughed Diana. "How many more hearts of men do you contemplate capturing, before you shuffle off this mortal coil? Chappie, you are a hardened old sinner! However, I suppose if one had committed matrimony three times already, one would feel able to continue doing so, with impunity, as many more times as circumstances allowed. Did poor old Dr. Dapperly actually propose?"

Mrs. Marmaduke Vane smiled complacently, as she put a heaped-up spoonful of whipped cream into her coffee.

"He made his meaning very clear, my dear Diana," she whispered, hoarsely; "and he held my arm more tightly than was necessary, as he assisted me to the motor. He remarked that the front steps were slippery; but they were not. A liberal supply of gravel had been placed upon them."

"Had he been having *much* champagne?" asked Diana. "Oh, no, I remember! It was tea, not dinner. One does not require to hold on to people's arms tightly when going down! steps with a liberal supply of gravel on them, after tea. Chappie dear, congratulations! I think it must be a case."

"He made his meaning very clear," repeated Mrs. Vane, helping herself to omelette and mushrooms.

"Isn't it rather hard on god-papa?" inquired Diana, her eyes dancing.

"I have a great respect for Mr. Goldsworthy," whispered Mrs. Vane, solemnly; "and I should grieve to wound or to disappoint him. But you see—there was Sarah."

"Ah, yes," said Diana; "of course; there was Sarah. And Sarah has god-papa well in hand."

"She is an impertinent woman," said Mrs. Vane; "and requires keeping in her place."

"Oh, what happened?" cried Diana. "Do tell me, Chappie dear!"

But Mrs. Vane shook her head, rattling her bangles as she attacked a cold pheasant; and declined to tell "what happened."

The morning sun shone brightly in through the oriel window of the pleasant breakfast-room, touching to gold Diana's shining hair, and causing the delicate tracery of frost to vanish quickly from the window-panes.

Breakfast-time, that supreme test of health—mental and physical—always found Diana radiant. She delighted in the beginning of each new day. Her vigorous vitality, reinforced by the night's rest, brought her to breakfast in such overflowing spirits, that Mrs. Vane—who suffered from lassitude, and never felt "herself" until after luncheon —would often have found it a trying meal, had she not had the consolations of a bountiful table, and a boundless appetite.

On this particular morning, however, a more observant person might have noted a restless anxiety underlying Diana's gaiety. She glanced often at the clock; looked through her pile of letters, but left them all unopened; gazed long and yearningly at the wide expanse of snowy park, and at the leafless arms of ancient spreading trees; drank several cups of strong coffee, and ate next to nothing.

This was the day which would decide her fate. Before evening she would know whether this lovely and beloved home would remain hers, or whether she must lose all, and go out to face a life of comparative poverty.

If David had taken the nine o'clock train he was now on his way to town, to consult Sir Deryck Brand.

What would be Sir Deryck's opinion? She knew him for a man of many ideals, holding particularly exalted views of marriage and of the relation of man to woman. On the other hand, his judgment was clear and well-balanced; he abhorred morbidness of any kind; his view of the question would not be ecclesiastical; and his very genuine friendship for herself would hold a strong brief in her behalf.

No two men could be more unlike one another than David Rivers and Deryck Brand. They were the two on earth of whom she held the highest opinion. She trusted both, and knew she might reply implicitly upon the faithful friendship of either. Yet her heart stood still, as she realized that her whole future hung upon the conclusion reached in the conversation to take place, that very morning, between these two men.

She could almost see the consulting-room in the doctor's house in Wimpole Street; the doctor's calm strong face, as he listened intently to David's statement of the case. There would be violets on the doctor's table; and his finger-tips would meet very exactly, as he leaned back in his revolving chair.

David would look very thin and slight. in the large armchair, upholstered in dark green leather, which had contained so many anxious bodies, during the process of unfolding and revealing troubled minds. David would tie himself up in knots, during the conversation. He would cross one thin leg over the other, clasping the uppermost knee with long nervous fingers. The whiteness of his forehead would accentuate the beautiful line of his thick black hair. Sir Deryck would see at once in his eyes that look of mystic, the enthusiast; and Sir Deryck's common sense would come down like a sledge-hammer! Ah, God grant it might come down like a sledge-hammer! Yet, if David had made up his mind, it would take more than a sledge-hammer to bend or to break it.

Mrs. Vane passed her cup for move coffee, as she concluded a detailed account of all she had had for tea at Eversleigh, the day before. "And really, my dear Diana," she whispered, "if we could find out where to obtain those, scones, it would give us just cause to look forward every day, to half-past four o'clock in the afternoon."

"We *will* find out," cried Diana, gaily "Who would miss hours of daily anticipation for lack of a little judicious pumping of the households of our friends? We have but to instruct my maid to call upon their cook. The thing is as good as done! You may embark upon you pleasurable anticipations, Chappie. . . .If I were as stout as you, dear, I should take on spoonful of cream, rather than two. . . . But, as we are anticipating, tell me: What is to become of me, after I have duly been bridesmaid at your wedding? I shall have to advertise for a stately but *plain* chaperon, who will not be snapped up by all the young sparks of the neighbourhood."

Mrs. Marmaduke Vane's many chains and necklets tinkled with the upheaval of her delighted laughter.

"Foo-foolish girl!" she whispered, spasmodically. "Why, of course, you must get married, too."

"Not I, sir," laughed Diana. "You will not find me importing a lord and master into my own domain. My liberty is too dear unto me. And who but a Rivers should reign at Rivers-court?"

"Marry your cousin, child," whispered Mrs. Vane, hoarsely. "One of your silly objections to marriage is changing your name. Well—marry your cousin, child, and remain Diana Rivers."

"Your advice is excellent, dear Chappie. But we must lose no time in laying your proposition before my cousin. He sails for Central Africa in ten days."

"Gracious heavens!" cried Mrs. Vane, surprised out of her usual thick whisper. "I do not mean the thin missionary! I mean Rupert!"

"Rupert, we have many times discussed and dismissed," said Diana. "The 'thin missionary,' as you very aptly call my cousin David, is quite a new proposition. The idea is excellent and appeals to me. Let us— –"

The butler stood at her elbow with a telegram on a salver.

She took it; opened it, and read it swiftly,

"No answer, Rodgers; but I will see Knox in the hall, in five minutes. Let us adjourn, my dear Chappie. I have a full morning before me; and, by your leave, I intend spending it in the seclusion of the library. We shall meet at luncheon."

Diana moved swiftly across the hall, and stood in the recess of a bay window overlooking the park.

She heard Mrs. Vane go panting and tinkling upstairs, and close the door of her boudoir. Then she drew David's message from the envelope, and read it again.

"If convenient kindly send motor for me early this morning. Not going to town. Consultation unnecessary. Have decided."

Diana screwed the paper and envelope into two little hard balls, between her strong white fingers.

"*Have decided.*" Those two words were rock impregnable, when said by David Rivers. No cannon of argument; no shrapnel of tears; no battery of promise or reproaches, would prevail against the stronghold of his will, if David River; had decided that he ought to refuse her request.

It seemed to her that the words, "Consultation unnecessary," implied an adverse decision; because, had he come round to her view of the matter, he would have wished it confirmed by Sir Deryck's calm judgment; whereas, if he had made up his mind to refuse, owing to conscientious reasons, no contrary opinion, expressed by another, would serve to turn him from his own idea of right.

Already Diana seemed to be looking her last on her childhood's lovely and beloved home.

She turned from the window as her chauffeur stepped into the hall.

"Knox," she said, "you will motor immediately to Brambledene to fetch Mr. Rivers from the Rectory. He wishes to see me on a matter of business. His time is valuable; so do not lose a moment."

The automaton in leather livery lifted his Land to his forehead in respectful salute; turned smartly on his heel, and disappeared through a swing-door. Five minutes later, Diana saw her Napier car flying down the avenue.

And soon—she would be chasing after omnibuses, in the Euston Road. And grimy men, with no touch to their caps, would give her five dirty coppers for her sixpence; and a grubby ticket, with a hole punched in it.

And David Rivers would be in Central Africa, educating savages. And it could have made no possible difference to him, to have stood beside her for a few minutes, in an empty church, and repeated a few words, entailing no after consequences; whereas to her– –

Diana's beautiful white teeth bit into her lower lip. She had always been accustomed to men who did her bidding, without any "Why" or "Wherefore" Yet she could not feel angry with David Rivers. He and his Lord were so one in her mind. Whatever they decided must be right.

As she crossed the hall, on her way to the staircase, she met the butler.

"Rodgers," she said, "Mr. Rivers wishes to see me on business this morning. He will be here in about three-quarters of an hour. When he arrives show him into the library, and see that we are not disturbed."

Diana mounted the stairs. Every line of carving on the dark oak balustrades was dear and was familiar.

The clear wintry sun shone through stained glass windows on the first landing, representing

Rivers knights, in silver armour, leaning on their shields. One of these, with a red cross upon his breast, his plumed helmet held in his arm, his close-cropped dark head rising firm and strong above his corselet, was not unlike David Rivers.

"Ah," said Diana, "if he had but cared a little! Not enough to make him troublesome; but just enough to make him glad to do this; thing for me."

CHAPTER XIII

DAVID'S DECISION

DIANA found it quite impossible to await in the library the return of the motor.

She moved restlessly to and fro in her own bedroom, from the windows of which she could see far down the avenue.

When at last her car came speeding through the trees, it seemed to her a swiftly approaching Nemesis, a relentless hurrying Fate, which she could neither delay nor avoid. It ran beneath the portico; paused for one moment; then glided away towards the garage. She had not seen David alight; but she knew he must now be in the house.

She waited a few moments, then passed slowly down the stairs.

Oh, lovely and belovèd home of childhood's days!

White and cold, yet striving bravely after complete self-control, Diana crossed the hall, and turned the handle of the library door.

As she entered, David was standing with his back to her, looking up intently at the portrait of Falcon Rivers.

He turned as he heard the door close, and came forward, a casual remark upon his lips, expressing the hope that it bad not been inconvenient to send the motor so early—then saw Diana's face.

Instantly he took her trembling hands in his saying gently: "It is all right. Miss Rivers. I can do as you wish. I am quite clear about it to-day. You must forgive me for not having been able to decide yesterday."

Diana drew away her hands and clasped them upon her breast.

Her eyes dilated.

"David? Oh, David! You will? You will! You will– –!"

Her voice broke. She gazed at him, helplessly—dumbly.

David's eyes, as he looked back into hers, were so calmly tender, that it somehow gave her the feeling of being a little child. His voice was very steadfast and unfaltering. He smiled reassuringly at Diana.

"I hope to have the honour and privilege, Miss Rivers," he said, "of marrying you on the morning of the day I sail for Central Africa."

Diana swayed for one second; then recovered, and walked over to the mantelpiece.

Not for nothing was she a descendant of those old knights in silver armour, in the window on the staircase. She leaned her arms upon the mantelpiece, and laid her head upon them. She stood thus quite still, and quite silent, fighting for self-control.

David, waiting silently behind her, lifted his eyes from that bowed head, with its mass of golden hair, and encountered the keen quizzical look of the portrait above her.

"*I shall win,*" said Uncle Falcon silently to David, over Diana's bowed head. But David, who knew he was about to defeat Uncle Falcon's purpose utterly, looked back in silent defiance.

The amber eyes twinkled beneath their shaggy brows. "*I shall win, young man,*" said Uncle Falcon.

Presently Diana lifted her head. Her lashes were wet, but the colour had returned to her cheeks. Her lips smiled, and her eyes grew softly bright.

"David," she said, "you must think me *such* a goose! But you can't possibly know what my home means to me; my home and—and everything. Do you know, when I read your telegram saying: 'Consultation unnecessary. Have decided,' I felt quite convinced you had decided that you could not do it; and, oh, David, I have left Riverscourt for ever, a hundred times during this terrible hour! Really it would have been kinder to have said: 'I will marry you,' in the telegram."

David smiled. "I am afraid that might have caused a good deal of comment at both post-offices," he said. "But I was a thoughtless ass not to have put in a clear indication as to which way the decision had gone."

"Hush! "cried Diana, with uplifted finger. "Don't call yourself names, my dear David, before the person who is going to promise to honour and obey you!" Diana's spirits were rising rapidly. "Now sit down and tell me all about it. What made you feel you could do it? Why didn't you need to consult Sir Deryck? Did you come to a decision last night, or this morning? You will keep to it, David?"

David sat down in an armchair opposite to Diana, who had flung herself into Uncle Falcon's.

The portrait, hanging high above their heads, twinkled down on both of them.

"*I shall win,*" said Uncle Falcon.

David did not "tie himself up in knots" to-day. He sat very still, looking at Diana with those calm steadfast eyes, which made her feel so young and inconsequential, and far removed from him.

He looked ill and worn, but happy and at rest; and, as he talked, his face wore an expression she had often noted when, in preaching, he became carried away by his subject; a radiance, as of inner glory shining out; a look as of being detached from the world, and independent of all actual surroundings.

"Undoubtedly I shall keep to it, Miss Rivers," he said, "unless, for any reason, you change your mind. And I saw light on the subject this morning."

"Oh, then you 'slept on it,' as our old nurses used to say?"

David smiled.

"I never had an old nurse," he said. "My mother was my nurse."

Diana did not notice that her question had been parried. "And what made you feel it right this morning? "she asked.

David hesitated.

"Light came—through—the Word," he said at last, slowly.

"Ha!" cried Diana. "I felt sure you would look for it there. And I sat up nearly all night—I mean until midnight—searching my Bible and Prayer-book. But the only applicable thing: I found was: 'I will not fail David.' It would have been more comforting to have found: 'David will not fail *me!*'"

David laughed

"We shall not fail each other, Miss Rivers."

"Why do you call me 'Miss Rivers'? It is quite absurd to do so, now we are engaged."

"I do not call ladies by their Christian names, when I have known them only a few days," said David.

"Not when you are going to marry them?"

"I have not been going to marry them, before," replied David.

"Oh, don't be tiresome. Cousin David! Are you determined to accentuate our unusual circumstances?"

David's clear eyes met hers, and held them.

"I think they require accentuating," he said, slowly.

Diana's eyes fell before his. She felt reproved. She realized that in the reaction of her immense relief, she was taking the whole thing too lightly.

"Cousin David," she said, humbly, "indeed I do realize the greatness of this that you are doing for me. It means so much; and yet it means so little. And just because it means so little, and never can mean more, it was difficult to you to feel it right to do it. Is not that so? Do you know, I think it would help me so much, if you would tell me exactly what seemed to you doubtful; and exactly what it was which dispelled that doubt."

"My chief difficulty," replied David, speaking very slowly, without looking at Diana—"my chief difficulty was: that I could not consider it right, in the sight of God, to enter into matrimony for reasons other than those for which matrimony was ordained; and to do so, knowing that each distinctly understood that there was never to be any question of fulfilling any of the ordinary conditions and obligations of that sacred tie."

David paused.

"In fact," he said, after a few moments of deliberation, "we proposed marrying each other for the sake of other people."

"Yes," cried Diana, eagerly; "your savages and my tenantry. We wrong no one; we benefit many. Therefore—it *must* be right."

"Not so," resumed David, gently. "We are never justified in doing wrong in order that good may result. No amount of after good can justify one wrong or crooked action. It seemed to me that, according to the revealed mind and will of God, the only admissible considerations in marriage were those affecting the man and the woman themselves; that to wed one another, entirely for the sake of benefiting other people, would make of that sacred act an impious unreality and could not be done by those seeking to live in accordance with the Divine Will."

Again David paused.

"Well?" breathed Diana, rather wide-eye and anxious. This undoubted impediment to her wishes sounded insuperable.

David heard the trepidation in her voice, and smiled at her, reassuringly.

"Well," he said, "I was guided to a passage in the Word—a wonderful Old Testament story—which proved that, at all events in one case, God Himself had put out of consideration the man and the woman, their personal happiness, their home together, and had dealt with that wedded life in a manner which was solely to benefit a community of people. This one case was enough for me. It furnished the answer to all my questions; set at rest all my doubts. True, the case was unique. But so is ours. Undoubtedly it took place many centuries ago; but were not the Divine Law and Will, in their entirety, revealed in what we call 'olden days'? Biblical manners and customs may vary according to clime, century, or conditions; but Bible ethics are the same from Genesis to Revelation; they never vary throughout the centuries, and are therefore changeless for all time. I stand or fall by the Word of my God, revealed in Eden; just as confidently as I stand or fall by the Word of my God, spoken from the rainbow throne of Revelation; or, as it shall one day be spoken, from the great white throne, which is yet to come. It is the same, yesterday, to-day, and for ever. I hold the Bible to be inspired from the first word to the last. Let one line go, and you may as well give up the whole. If men begin to pick and choose, the whole great book is swept into uncertainty. Either it is impregnable rock beneath our feet, or it is mere shifting sand of man's concoction and contrivance; in which case, where can essential certainties be found?"

David's eyes shone. His voice rang, clarion clear in its assurance. He had forgotten Diana; he had forgotten himself; he had forgotten the vital question under discussion.

Her anxious eyes recalled him.

"Ah, where were we? Yes; the Divine ethics are unchangeable. We can say of our God: 'He is the Father of Lights, with Whom is no variableness, neither shadow that is cast by turning.' Therefore there is no shadow in the clear light which came to me last night—from above, I honestly believe. I may be wrong, Miss Rivers; a man can but act according to his conscientious convictions. I am convinced, to-day, that your suggestion is God's will for us, in order that we may be made a greater blessing to many. I believe I was guided to that passage so that it might dispel a doubt, which otherwise would certainly have remained an insurmountable obstacle in the way of the fulfilment of your wishes."

"Who were the people?" asked Diana, eagerly,

"Where was the passage?"

David turned his head, and looked out of the window.

He had expected this, but, until Diana actually put the question, he had postponed a definite decision as to what he should answer.

He looked at the clear frosty sky. A slight wind was stirring the leafless branches of the beeches. He could see the powdery snow fall from them in glistening showers.

He did not wish Diana to read that passage in Ezekiel. It seemed to him, she could not fail to know at once, that *she* was the desire of his eyes, if she read it. This would dawn on he as it had dawned on him—a sudden beam of blinding illumination—and there would be an end to any service he might otherwise have rendered her.

"I would rather you did not read the passage," he said. "Much of it is not applicable. In fact, it required logical deduction, and reasoning by analogy, in order to arrive at the main point."

"And do you not consider me capable of logical deduction, or of reasoning by analogy, Cousin David?"

He flushed.

"How stupidly I express myself. Of course I did not mean that. But—there are things the story. Miss Rivers, I do not wish you to see."

Diana laughed.

"My good Cousin David, it is quite too late to begin shielding me! In fact I never have been the carefully guarded 'young person.' I have read heaps of naughty books, of which, I daresay, you have never even heard!"

David winced. "Once more, I must have expressed myself badly," he said. "I will not try again. But you must forgive me if I still decline to give you the passage."

"Very well. But I shall hunt until I find it," smiled Diana, in playful defiance. "Did you use a concordance last night. Cousin David? I did. I looked out 'David'—pages and pages of it! I wondered whether you were looking out 'Diana.'"

He smiled. "I should only have found 'Diana of the Ephesians,'" he said; "and, though she fell mysteriously from heaven, she was quite unlike my Lady of Mystery."

"Who arrived in a motor-car," laughed Diana. "Do you know, when you told me you had called me—that, I thought it quite the most funnily unsuitable name I had ever heard. I realized how the Hunt would roar if they knew."

"You see," said David, "the Greek meaning of 'mystery' is: 'What is known only to the initiated.'"

"And you were not yet initiated?" suggested Diana.

"No," replied David. "The Hunt was not initiated."

Diana looked at him keenly. Cousin David was proving less easy to understand than she had imagined.

"Let us talk business," she said. "I will send for Mr. Inglestry this afternoon. How immensely relieved he will be! He can manage all legal details for us—the special licence, and so forth. Of course we must be married in London; and I should like the wedding to be in St. Botolph's, that dear old church in Bishopsgate; because Saint Botolph is the patron saint of travellers, and that church is one where people go to pray for safe-keeping, before a voyage; or for absent friends who are travelling. I can return there to pray for you, whenever I am in town. So shall it be St. Botolph's, David?"

"If you wish it," he said.

"You see, we could not have the wedding here or at Brambledene. It would be such a nine days' wonder. We should never get through the crowds of people who would come to gaze at us. I don't intend to make any mystery of it. I shall send a notice of our engagement to the papers. But I shall say of the wedding: 'To take place shortly, owing to the early date already fixed for the departure of the Rev. David Rivers to Central Africa.' Then no one need know the exact day. Chappie and Mr. Inglestry can be our witnesses; and you might get Sir Deryck. What time does the boat start?"

"In the afternoon, from Southampton. The special train leaves Waterloo at noon."

"Capital!" cried Diana. "We can be married at half-past ten, and drive straight to the station afterwards. There is sure to be a luncheon-car on the train. We can have our wedding-breakfast *en route,* and I can see you off from Southampton. I have always wanted to see over one of those big liners. I may see you off, mayn't I, Cousin David?"

"I If you wish," he said, gently.

"I can send my own motor down to Southampton ton the day before, and it will be an easy run back home, from there. We can hire a car for the wedding. Wouldn't that be a good plan?"

"Quite a good plan," agreed David.

"God-papa shall marry us," said Diana; "and then I can make him leave out anything in the service I don't want to have read."

David sat up instantly.

"No," he said; "to that I cannot agree. Not one word must be omitted. If we are married according to the prescribed rules of our Church, we must not pick and choose as to what our Church shall say to us, as we humbly stand before her altar. I refuse to go through the service if a word is omitted."

Diana's eyes flashed rebellion.

"My dear Cousin David, have you read the wedding service?"

"I know it by heart," said David Rivers.

"Then you must surely know that it would simply make a farce of it, to read the whole, at such a wedding as ours."

"Nothing can make a farce of a Church service," said David firmly. "We may make a sham of our own part in it; but every word the Church will say to us, will be right and true."

"I *must* have certain passages omitted," flashed Diana.

"Very well," said David, quietly. "Then there can be no wedding."

"David, you are unreasonable and obstinate!"

David regarded her quietly, and made no answer.

Diana's angry flush was suddenly modified by dimples.

"Is this what people call finding one's master?" she inquired, "It is fortunate for our peace, dear Cousin, that we part on the wedding-day! I am accustomed to having my own way."

David's eyes, as he looked into hers, were sad, yet tender.

"The Church will require you, Miss Rivers, to promise to obey. Even your god-father will hardly go on with the ceremony, if you decline to repeat the word. I don't think I am a tyrant, or a particularly domineering person. But if, between the time we leave the church and the sailing of my boat, I should feel it necessary to ask you to do—or not to do—a thing. I shall expect you to obey."

"Brute!" cried Diana. "I doubt if I shall venture so far as the station. Just to the church door, we might arrive, without a wrangle!" Then she sprang up, all smiles and sunshine. "Come, my lord and master! An it please you, I hear the luncheon-gong. Also the approach of Chappie, who responds to the call of the gong with a prompt and unhesitating obedience, which is more than wifely! Quick, my dear David, you hand. . . . Come in Chappie! We want you to congratulate us! Your advice to me at breakfast appeared so excellent, that I have lost no time in following it. I have promised to marry my Cousin David, before he sails for Central Africa!"

CHAPTER XIV

THE EVE OF EPIPHANY

IT was the eve of the wedding-day.

Diana lay back in an easy-chair in the sitting-room of the suite she always occupied at the Hotel Metropole, when in town.

A cheerful fire blazed in the grate. Every electric light in the room—and there were many—was turned on. Even the little portable lamp on the writing-table, beneath its soft silken shade, illumined its own corner. Diana's present mood required a blaze of light everywhere. The gorgeous colouring, the rapid movement, the continual bustle and rush of life in a huge London hotel, exactly suited her just now; especially as the movement was noiseless, on the thick Persian carpets; and the rush went swiftly up and down, in silently rapid elevators.

Within five days of her wedding, Diana had reached a point, when she could no longer stand the old oak staircase; the fatherly deportment of Rodgers; and meals alone with Mrs. Marmaduke Vane. Also David, pleading many pressing engagements in town, came no more to Rivers-court.

So Diana had packed her chaperon and her maid into the motor, and flown up to London, to be near David.

There was, for Diana, a peculiar and indefinable happiness in the days that followed. It was so long since she had had anybody who, in some sort really belonged to her. David, when once they had met again, proved more amenable to reason than Diana had dared to hope. He allowed himself to be taken about in the motor to his various appointments each day. He let Diana superintend his simple outfit; he even let her supplement it, where she considered necessary. He was certainly very meek, for a tyrant; and very humbly gentle, for a despotic lord and master.

When he found Diana's heart was set upon it, he allowed her to pay for the elaborate medicine-chest he was taking out, and spent the money he had earned for this purpose, on the wedding-ring; and on a simple, yet beautiful, guard-ring. This, Diana wore already, upon the third finger of her left hand; a plain gold band with just one diamond, cut star shape, inset. Round the inside of the ring, David had had engraved the three words: Gold, frankincense, and myrrh.

Diana, who quickly formed habits, had already got into the way of twisting this ring, with the diamond turned inwards, when anything tried or annoyed her. Rather often, during those few days, the stone was hidden from Mrs. Vane's complacent sight; but when David was with her, it always shone upon her hand.

One afternoon, when they were out together, he mentioned, with pleasure, having secured a berth in the cabin he had had on the homeward voyage, on that same ship.

"It will seem quite home-like," said David.

"You have it to yourself?" inquired Diana.

"Oh, no!" replied David. "Two other fellows will share it with me. A state-room all to myself would be too palatial for a missionary."

"But supposing the two other fellows are not the kind of people you like to be cooped up with at close quarters, during a long voyage?"

"Oh, one chances that," replied David. "And it is always possible to make the best of the most adverse circumstances."

Diana became suddenly anxious to be rid of David. At their next place of call, she arranged to leave him for twenty minutes.

No sooner had David disappeared, than Diana ordered her chauffeur to speed to Cockspur Street.

She swept into the office of the steamship company, asking for a plan of the boat, the manager of the booking department, the secretary of the company, and the captain of the ship, if he happened to be handy, all in a breath, and in so regal a manner, that she soon found herself in an inner sanctum, and in the presence of a supreme official. While there, after much consultation over a plan of the ship, she sat down and wrote a cheque for so large a sum, that she was bowed out to her motor by the great man himself.

"And mind," said Diana, turning in the doorway, "no mention of my name is to appear. It is to be done 'with the compliments of the Company.'"

"Your instructions shall be implicitly obeyed, madam," said the supreme official, with a final bow.

"Nice man," remarked Diana to herself as the motor glided off into the whirl of traffic. "Now that is the kind of person it would be quite possible to marry, and live with, without ructions. No amount of training would ever induce David to bow and implicitly obey instructions."

The ready dimples peeped out, as Diana leaned back, enjoying the narrow shaves by which her chauffeur escaped collisions all along Piccadilly.

"Between the time we leave the church, and the sailing of my boat. . . . I shall expect you to *obey*," she whispered, in gleeful amusement. "Poor David! I wonder how he will behave between Waterloo and Southampton. And, oh, I wonder how *I* shall behave! I am inclined to think it might be wise to let Chappie come with us."

Diana's eyes danced. It never failed to provide her with infinite amusement, when her chaperon and David got on each other's nerves.

"No, I won't do that," she decided, as they flew up Park Lane; "it would be cowardly. And he can't bully me much, in two hours and a half. Poor David!"

So the days had passed, and the eve of the wedding had now arrived.

David had refused to dine and spend the evening, pleading a promise of long standing to his friend, the doctor. But they had had tea together, an hour before; Mrs. Marmaduke Vane absorbing most of the conversation, and nearly all the tea cake; and David had risen and made his adieux, before Diana could think of any pretext for dismissing her chaperon.

She would not now meet David again, until they stood together, on the following morning, at the chancel step of St. Botolph's Church.

All preparations were complete; yet Diana was now awaiting something unforeseen and unexpected.

David had not left the room ten minutes—Mrs, Vane was still discussing the perfectly appointed teas, the charming roseleaf china, and debating which frock-coated official in the office would be the correct person of whom to make inquiries concerning the particular brand of the marmalade—when the telephone-bell rang sharply; and Diana, going to the mantelpiece, took up the receiver.

Mr. Inglestry was speaking from his club. He must see her at once, on a matter of importance. Mr. Ford, of the firm of Ford & Davis, of Rivers-mead, was with him, having brought up a sealed package to hand over to Miss Rivers in his—Mr. Inglestry's—presence. Would they find her at home and disengaged, if they called in half an hour's time?

"Certainly," said Diana, "I will be here." Adding, as an after-thought, before ringing off: "Mr. Inglestry! Are you there?—No, wait a minute. Central!—Mr, Inglestry! What is it about?" just for the fun of hearing old Inglestry sigh at the other end of the telephone and patiently explain once more that the package was sealed.

There was no telephone at Riverscourt, and Diana found endless amusement in a place where she had one in her sitting-room and one in her bedroom. She loved ringing people up, when Mrs. Vane was present; holding mysterious one-sided conversations, for the express purpose of exciting her chaperon's curiosity to a positively maddening extent. One evening she rang up David, and gave him a bad five minutes. She could say things into the telephone to David, which she could not possibly have said with his grave clear eyes upon her. And David always took you quite seriously, even at the other end of the telephone; which made it all the more amusing; especially with Chappie whispering hoarsely from the sofa;

"My *dear* Diana! What *can* your Cousin David be saying!" when, as a matter of fact, poor Cousin David was merely gasping inarticulately, unable to make head or tail of Diana's remarks.

But now Diana waited; a query of perplexity on her brow. Mr. Ford was the young lawyer sent for in haste by Uncle Falcon, shortly before his death. What on earth was in the sealed package?

All legal matters had gone forward smoothly, so far, in the experienced hands of Mr. Inglestry. In his presence, David had quietly acquiesced in all Diana wished, and in all Mr. Inglestry arranged. Settlements had been signed; Diana's regal gifts to David's work had been duly put into form and ratified. Only—once or twice, as David's eyes met his, the older man had surprised in them a look of suffering and of tragedy, which perplexed and haunted him. What further development lay before this unexpected solution to all difficulties, arranged so suddenly, at the eleventh hour, by his fair client? The old family lawyer was too wise to ask many questions, yet too shrewd not to foresee possible complications in this strange and unusual marriage. Of one thing, however, he was certain: David Rivers was a man to be trusted.

CHAPTER XV

THE CODICIL

AS the gilt clock on the mantelpiece hurriedly struck six, corroborated in the distance by the slow booming of Big Ben, a page boy knocked at Diana's sitting-room door, announcing two gentlemen waiting below, to see Miss Rivers.

"Show them up," commanded Diana; and, rising, stood on the hearthrug to receive them.

Mr. Inglestry entered, suave and fatherly, as usual; followed by a dark young man, who, hat in hand, looked with nervous admiration at the tall girl in green velvet, standing straight and slim, with her back to the fire.

She shook hands with Mr. Inglestry, who presented Mr. Ford, of the firm of Ford & Davis, of Riversmead.

"Well?" said Diana.

She did not sit down herself, nor did she offer a chair to Mr. Ford, of the firm of Ford & Davis, of Riversmead. A gleam of sudden anger had come into her eyes at sight of the young man. She evidently intended to arrive at once at the reason for this unexpected interview.

So Mr. Ford presented a sealed envelope to Diana.

"Under private instructions, Miss Rivers," he said, with a somewhat pompous air of importance; "under private instructions, from your uncle, the late Mr. Falcon Rivers, of Riverscourt, I am to deliver this envelope unopened into your hands, in the presence of Mr. Inglestry, on the eve of your marriage; or should no marriage previously have taken place, on the eve of the anniversary of the death of your late uncle."

Diana took the envelope, and read the endorsement in her uncle's characteristic and unmistakable handwriting.

"So I see," she said. "And, furthermore, if you carry out these instructions, and deliver this envelope at the right time, and in every respect in the manner arranged, payment of fifty guineas is to be made to you, out of the estate, for so doing. Also, I see I am instructed to open this envelope in the presence of Mr. Inglestry alone. Well, you have exactly carried out your instructions, Mr. Ford, and no doubt Mr. Inglestry will see that you receive your fee. Good evening."

"Wait for me downstairs, Ford," said Mr. Inglestry, nervously. "You will find papers in the reading-room. Miss Rivers is naturally anxious to acquaint herself with the contents of this package."

Mr. Ford, of the firm of Ford & Davis, of Riversmead, bowed himself out of the room. He afterwards described Miss Rivers, of Riverscourt, as "a haughty woman; but handsome as they make' em!"

Alone with her old friend and adviser, Diana turned to him, impetuously.

"What is the meaning of this?" she inquired, wrath and indignation in her voice. "Why did my uncle instruct that greasy young man to intrude upon me with a sealed letter from himself, a year after his death?

"Open it, my dear; open it and see," counselled Mr. Inglestry, removing his glasses and polishing them with a silk pocket-handkerchief. "Sit down quietly and open it. And it is not prudent to allude to Mr. Ford as 'greasy,' when the door has barely closed upon him. I cannot conceive what Mr. Ford has done, to bring upon himself your evident displeasure."

"Done!" cried Diana. "Why I knew him the moment he entered the room! He had the impudence, the other day, to join the hunt on a hired hack, and to ride in among the hounds, while they were picking up the scent. Of all the undesirable bounders— —"

"My dear young lady," implored Mr. Inglestry, "do lower your voice. Mr. Ford is probably still upon the—the, ah—mat. He is merely the bearer of your uncle's missive. I do beg of you to turn your thoughts from offences in the hunting-field, and to give your attention to the matter in hand."

"Well, shoo him off the mat," said Diana, "and hustle him into the lift! I decline to receive letters from a person who comes into the room heralded by hair-oil. . . . All right! Don't look so distressed. Sit down in this comfy chair, and we will see what surprise Uncle Falcon has prepared for us. Really, when one comes to think of it, a letter from a person who has been dead a year is a rather wonderful thing to receive."

Diana seated herself on the sofa, after pushing forward an armchair for the old lawyer. Then, in the full blaze of the electric light, she opened the sealed envelope, and drew out a letter addressed to herself, in her uncle's own handwriting. A folded paper from within it, fell unheeded on her lap.

She read the letter aloud to Mr. Inglestry. As she read her grey eyes widened; her colour came and went; but her voice did not falter.

And this was Uncle Falcon's letter:

"MY DEAR NIECE,—If Ford does his duty—and most men do their duty for fifty guineas—you will be reading these words either on the eve of your wedding-day, or on the eve of the day on which you will be preparing to leave Rivers-court, and to give up all that which, since my death, has been your own.

"Feeling sure that I was right, my dear Diana, in our many arguments, and that I have won in the contest of our wills, I would bet a good deal— if betting is allowed in the other world—that you are reading this on the eve of your wedding-day—am I right, Inglestry, old chap?—having found a man who will soon teach you that wifehood and motherhood and dependence on the stronger sex are a woman's true vocation, and her best chance of real happiness in life.

"If so, look up, honestly, and say: 'Uncle Falcon, you have won'; and I hereby forgive Inglestry all his fuss and bluster, and you, the obstinacy of years—and may Heaven bless the wedding-day.

"But—ah, there's a 'but' in all things human! Perhaps the world where I shall be, when you are reading these lines, is the only place where buts cease to be, and where all things go straight on to fulfilment.

"But—your happiness, my own dear girl, is of too much real importance for me to risk it, on the possible chance of the right man not having turned up; or of you—true Rivers that you are—proving obstinate to the end.

"Therefore—enclosed herewith you will find a later codicil than that known to you and Inglestry, duly witnessed by Ford and his clerk, nullifying the other, and leaving you my entire property as stated in my will, subject to no conditions whatsoever.

"Thus, my dear Diana, if you are on the eve of preparing to leave Riverscourt, you may unpack your trunks, and stay there, with your uncle's love and blessing. It is all your own.

"Or—but knowing you as I do, I hardly think this likely—if you are on the eve of making a marriage which is not one of love, and which is causing you in prospect distress and unhappiness—why, break it off, child, and send the man packing. If he is marrying you for you money, he deserves the lesson; and if he loves you for your splendid self, why he is not much of a man if he has been engaged to such a girl as my niece Diana without having been able to win her, before the eve of the wedding-day!

"Anyway you now have a free hand, child; and if my whim of testing fate for you with the first codicil has put you in a tight place, old Inglestry will see you through, and you must forgive your departed uncle, who loves you more than you ever knew,

"FALCON RIVERS."

Diana dropped the letter, flung herself down on the sofa cushions, and burst into a passion of weeping.

Mr. Inglestry. helpless and dismayed, took off his glasses and polished them with his silk pocket-handkerchief; put them on again; leaned forward and patted Diana's shoulder; even ventured to stroke her shining hair, repeating, hurriedly: "It can all be arranged my dear. I beg of you not to upset yourself. It can all be arranged."

Then he picked up the codicil and examined it carefully. It was correct in every detail. It simply nullified the previous codicil, and confirmed the original will.

"It can all be arranged, my dear," he repeated, laying a fatherly hand on Diana's heaving shoulder. "Do not upset yourself over this unfortunate marriage complication. I will undertake– –"

"It is not that!" cried Diana, sitting up and pushing back her rumpled hair. "Oh, you unimaginative old thing! Can't you understand? All these months it has been so hard to have to think that Uncle Falcon's love for me had really been worth so little, that, in order to prove himself right on one silly point, he could treat me as he did in that cruel codicil. He could not have foreseen the simply miraculous way in which Providence and my Cousin David were coming to my rescue, at the eleventh hour. Otherwise it must have meant, either a hateful marriage, or the loss of home, and money, and everything I hold most dear. But by far the worst loss of all was to lose faith in the truest love I had ever known. In my whole life, no love had ever seemed to me so true, so faithful, so completely to be trusted, as Uncle Falcon's. To have lost my belief in it, was beginning to make of me a hard and a bitter woman. That codicil was costing me more than home and income And now it turns out to have been merely a test— a risky test, indeed! Think if either of us had told Rupert of it, before the time specified; or if I had been going to marry Rupert or any other worldly-minded man, who would have made endless trouble over being jilted! But—dear old thing! He didn't think of that. He was so sure his plan would lead to may making a happy marriage, not-withstanding my prejudices and my principles. He was wrong, of course. But the main point brought out by this second codicil is: that he really cared. I can forgive him all the rest, now I know that Uncle Falcon loved me too well really to risk spoiling my life."

Diana dried her eyes; then raised her head, snuffing the air with the keenness of one of her own splendid hounds.

"Oh, Mr. Inglestry," she said; "do go and see if that person is still on the mat! I have been talking at the top of my voice, and I believe I scent hair-oil!"

The old lawyer tiptoed to the door, opened it cautiously, and looked up and down the brightly lighted corridor. From the distance came the constant clang of the closing of the elevator gates, and the sharp ting of electric bells.

He shut the door, and returned to his seat.

Diana was reading the codicil.

"I wonder why he called in that Ford creature," she said, "Why did he not intrust this envelope to you?"

"My dear," suggested Mr. Inglestry, "knowing my affection for you, knowing how deeply I have your interests at heart, your uncle may have feared that, if I saw you in much perplexity, in great distress of mind over the matter, I might have let fall some hint—have given you some indication— —"

"Why, of course!" said Diana. "Think how you would have caught it to-day, if you hadn't. You would have been much more afraid of me. on earth, than of Uncle Falcon, in heaven!"

Mr. Inglestry lifted his hand in mute protest; then took off his glasses, and polished them. The remarks of Miss Rivers were so apt to be perplexing and unanswerable.

"Let us leave that question, my dear young lady" he said. "Your uncle adopted a remarkably shrewd course for attaining the end he desired. Meanwhile, it remains for us to deal with the present situation. I advise that we send immediately for your cousin David Rivers Of course this marriage of—of convenience, need not now take place."

Diana looked straight at the old lawyer for a few moments, in blank silence. She turned the ring upon her finger, so that the diamond was hidden. Then she said, slowly:

"You suggest that we send for David Rivers, and tell him that—this second codicil having turned up—we shall not, after all, require his services: that he may sail for Central Africa to-morrow, without going through the marriage ceremony with me?"

"Just so," said Mr. Inglestry, "just so." Something in Diana's eyes arresting further inspiration, he repeated rather nervously: "Just so."

"Well, I absolutely decline to do anything of the kind," flashed Diana. "Think of the intolerable humiliation to David! After overcoming his own doubts in the matter; after disposing of his first conscientious scruples; after making up his mind to go through with this for my sake, and being so faithful about it. After all the papers we have signed, and the arrangements we have made! To be sent for, and calmly told his services are no longer required! Besides—though I don't propose to be much to him, I know—I am all he has in the world. He will sail to-morrow feeling that at least there is one person on this earth who belongs to him, and to whom he belongs; one person to whom he can write freely, and who cares to know of his joys or sorrows; his successes or failures. Poor boy I Could I possibly, to avoid a little bother to myself, rob him of this? I—who owe him more than I can ever express? Besides, he could never—after such a slight on my part—accept the money I am giving to his work. In fact, I doubt if he would accept so much, even now, were it not that he believes

I owe my whole fortune to the fact of his marriage with me."

Diana turned the ring again; and the diamond shone like a star on her hand.

"No, Mr. Inglestry," she said, with decision. "The marriage will take place to-morrow, as arranged; and my Cousin David must never know of this new codicil."

The lawyer looked doubtful and dissatisfied.

"The fact of the codicil remains," he said. "Your whole property is now safely your own, subject to no conditions whatever. You have nothing to gain by this marriage with your cousin; you might—eventually—have serious cause to regret the loss of liberty it will entail. I do not consider that we are justified in allowing the ceremony to take place without informing him of the complete change of circumstances, and acquainting him with the existence of this second codicil."

"Very well," said Diana.

With a sudden movement, she rose to her feet, whirled round on the hearthrug, tore the codicil to fragments, and flung them into the flames.

"There!" she cried, towering over the astonished little lawyer in the large armchair. "Now, no second codicil exists! I can still keep my restored faith in the love of Uncle Falcon; but I shall owe my home, my fortune, and all I possess to my husband, David Rivers."

CHAPTER XVI

IN OLD ST. BOTOLPH'S

AT twenty minutes past ten, on the morning of the Feast of Epiphany, David Rivers stood in the empty church of St. Botolph's, Bishopsgate, awaiting his bride.

Perhaps no man ever came to his wedding looking less like a bridegroom than did David Rivers.

Diana had scorned the suggestion, first mooted by Mrs. Marmaduke Vane, of clerical broadcloth of more fashionable cut, to be worn by David for this one occasion.

"Rubbish, my dear Chappie!" had said Diana. "You are just the sort of person who would marry the clothes, without giving much thought to the man inside them. *I* don't propose to be in white satin; so why should David be in broadcloth? I shall not be crowned with orange-blossom, so why should David go to the expense of an unnecessary topper? He could hardly wear it out, among his savages in Central Africa. They might get hold of it; make of it a fetish; and, eventually, build for it a little shrine, and worship it. An article might then be written for a missionary magazine, entitled: 'The Apotheosis of the silk top-hat of the Rev. David Rivers!' I shall not wear a train, so why should David appear in a long coat. Have a new one for the occasion, David, because undoubtedly this little friend, though dear, is an *old* friend. But keep to your favourite cut. You would alarm me in tails or clerical skirts, even more than you do already."

So David on his wedding morning looked, quite simply, what he really was: the young enthusiast, to whom outward appearance meant little or nothing, just ready to start on his journey to Central Africa.

His friend, the doctor, with whom David had spent his last night in England, might, with his frock-coat, lavender tie, and buttonhole, easily have been mistaken for the bridegroom, as the two stood together in the chancel of St. Botolph's.

"I cannot be your best man, old boy," Sir Deryck had said, "because, years ago, I did, myself, the best thing a man can do. But I will come to your wedding, and see you through, if it is really to take place at half-past ten in the morning, and if I may be off immediately afterwards. You are marrying a splendid girl, old chap. I only wish she were going with you to Ugonduma. Yet, I admit, you are doing the right thing in refusing to let her face the dangers and hardships of such life and travel. Only—David, old man—if you want any married life at all, you must be back within the year. With this unexpected attraction drawing you to England and home, you will hardly keep to your former resolution, or remain for longer in that deadly climate."

David had smiled, bravely, and gripped the doctor's hand. "I must see how the work goes on," he said; and prayed to be forgiven the evasion.

Mr. Goldsworthy was robing in the vestry, and kept peeping out, in order to make his entry into the chancel just before Diana's arrival There could not, under the circumstances, be much processioning in connexion with this wedding; but, what there was should be dignified and might as well be effectively timed.

Mr. Goldsworthy had passed through some strenuous moments in the vestry with David over the question of omissions or non-omissions from the wedding service. He knew Diana's point of view; in fact he had received private instructions from his god-daughter to bully David into submission—"just as Sarah bullies you, you know, godpapa." He knew Sarah" methods of bullying, quite well; but felt doubtful about applying them to David. In fact, when the question came up, and the moment for bullying had arrived, he turned his attention to buttoning his cassock, and meekly agreed to David's firmly expressed ultimatum.

You cannot button a casssock—a somewhat tight cassock—(why do cassocks display so in-convenient a tendency to grow tighter each week?) and at the same time satisfactorily discuss a difficult ecclesiastical point (why do ecclesiastical points become more and more involved ever year?) with a very determined young man. This should be his excuse to Diana for failing to bully David into submission.

In his heart of hearts he knew the younger man was right. He himself had grown slack about these matters. It was years since he had repeated the creed of Saint Athanasius. It had a tendency to make him so breathless. When David had recited it on Christmas morning, the congregation had not known where to find it in the prayer-book; and Mr. Churchwarden Smith had written the absent Rector an indignant letter accusing David of popery. He was glad to remember that, in his reply, though feeling very unequal to letter-writing, he had fully justified his *locum tenens*.

The clock struck the half-hour, Mr. Goldsworthy peeped out again.

David and the doctor were walking quietly about in the chancel, examining the quaint oak carvings. At that moment they stood, with their backs to the body of the church, studying the lectern. David did not need to watch for the arrival of Diana. He knew Mrs. Marmaduke Vane was to enter first, with Mr. Inglestry. Diana had told him she should walk up the church alone.

As yet, beside the usual church officials, Sarah Dolman was the only person present. Sarah, having a married niece in town, who could put her up for the night, had insisted upon attending the wedding of her dear Miss Diana and that "blessèd young gentleman," of whom the worst that could be said, in Sarah's estimation, appeared to be: that it was a pity there was not more of him!

She was early at the church, "to get a good place"; and had shifted her seat several times, before David arrived. In fact she tried so many pews, that the careful woman always on duty as verger at St. Botolph's, began to look upon her with suspicion.

Sarah had feared she would not succeed in catching David's eye; but David had seen her directly he came into the chancel. He had also noticed, in Sarah's bonnet, the exact counterpart of Mrs. Churchwarden Smith's red feather. He knew at once how much this meant, because Sarah had told him that she only "went to beads."

Often in the lonely times to come, when David chanced to see a gaily plumaged bird in the great forests of Ugonduma, he thought of Sarah's bonnet, and the red feather worn in honour of his wedding.

He now went straight down the church and shook the good woman by the hand: Which was beyond m' proudest dreams," Sarah always explained in telling the story afterwards.

"Hullo, Sarah! How delightful of you to come; and how nice you look!" Then as he felt Sarah's white cotton glove still warmly clasping his own hand, he remembered the Christmas card. David possessed that priceless knack of always remembering the things people expected him to remember.

"Sarah," he said, glancing down at their clasped hands, "you should have brought me a buttonhole of forget-me-nots."

Sarah released his hand, and held up an impressive cotton finger.

"Ah, Mr. Rivers, sir," she said; "I knew you would say that. But who could 'a' thought that card of mine would ha' bin prophetic!"

"Prophetic?" repeated David, quite at a loss.

"The turtle-doves," whispered Sarah, with wink, infinitely romantic and suggestive.

Then David understood. He and Diana were the pair of turtle-doves, flying above the forget me-nots, united by a festoon of ribbon, held in either beak.

At first he shook with silent laughter. Good old Sarah, with her prophetic card! He and Diana were the turtle-doves! How it would amuse Diana!

Then a sharp pang smote him. Tragedy and comedy moved on either side of David, as he walked back to the chancel.

He and Diana were the turtle-doves.

Soon after the half-hour, a stir and bustle occurred at the bottom of the church. Mrs. Marmaduke Vane entered, on the arm of Mr. Inglestry. The dapper little lawyer was completely overshadowed by the large and portly person of Diana's chaperon. She tinkled and rustled up the church, all chains, and bangles, and nodding plumes. She seemed to be bowing right and left to the empty pews. Mr. Inglestry put her into the front seat on the left, just below the quaintly carved lectern; then went himself to the vestry for a word with Mr. Goldsworthy.

Sarah, from her pew on the opposite side, glared at Mrs. Marmaduke Vane. The glories of her own new bonnet and crimson feather had suffered eclipse. Yet—though the nodding purple plumes opposite seemed to beckon him—she marked, with satisfaction, that David did not even glance in their direction. She—Sarah—had had a handshake from the bridegroom. Mrs. Marmaduke Vane, in all her grandeur, had failed to catch his eye.

Truth to tell, no sooner did David become aware of the arrival of Diana's chaperon and of her lawyer, who were, he knew, accompanying her, than he ceased to have eyes for any one or anything save for the place where she herself would presently appear.

He took up his position alone, at the chancel step, slightly to the right; and, standing sideways to the altar, fixed his eyes upon the distant entrance at the bottom of the church.

Suddenly, from the organ-loft above it, where the golden pipes and carved wood casing stand so quaintly on either side of a stained-glass window there wafted down the softest, sweetest strains of tender harmony. A musician, with the touch and soul of a true artist, was playing a lovely setting of David's own, to "Lead, kindly Light." This was a surprise of Diana's. Diana loved arranging artistic surprises.

In his astonishment and delight at hearing so unexpected and so beautiful a rendering of hi own theme, David lifted his eyes for a moment to the organ-loft.

During that moment the door must have opened and closed without making any sound for, when he dropped his eyes once more to the entrance, there, at the bottom of the church, pausing—as if uncertain whether to advance or to retreat—was standing his Lad of Mystery.

David's heart stood still.

He had been watching for Diana—that bewildering compound of sweetness and torment, for whose sake he had undertaken to do this thing—and here was his own dear Lady of Mystery, the personification of softness and of silence, waiting irresolute at the bottom of this great

London church, just as she had waited in the little church at Brambledene, on that Sunday evening, seven weeks ago.

How far Diana consciously intended to appear thus to David, it would be difficult to say; but she purposely wore in every detail just what she had been wearing on the Sunday evening when he saw her first; and possibly the remembrance of that evening, now also strongly in her own mind accounted for her seeming once more to be enveloped in that atmosphere of soft, silent detachment from the outer world, which had led David to call her his Lady of Mystery.

In a swift flash of self-revelation, David realized, more clearly than before, that he had loved this girl he was now going to marry, ever since he first saw her, standing as she now stood—tall, graceful, irresolute; uncertain whether to advance or to retreat.

Down the full length of that dimly lighted church, David's look met the hesitating sweetness of those soft grey eyes; met, and held them.

Then—as if the deep earnestness of his gaze drew her to him, she moved slowly and softly up the church to take her place beside him.

The fragrance of violets came with her. She seemed wafted to him, in the dim light, by the melody of his own organ music: "Lead, kindly Light, amid the encircling gloom; lead Thou me on."

David's senses reeled. He turned to the altar, and closed his eyes.

When he opened them again, his Lady of Mystery stood at his side, and the opening words of the marriage service broke the silence of the empty church.

CHAPTER XVII

DIANA'S READJUSTMENT

DIANA had waited a minute or two in the moto in order to allow time for the entrance and seating of Mrs. Vane; also, Mr. Inglestry was to give the signal to the musician at the organ.

Even after she had left the motor, and walked down the stone paving, leading from Bishops gate to the main entrance of St. Botolph's, she paused, watching the sparrows and pigeons at the fountain, in the garden enclosure—now very bare and leafless—opposite the church. Here she waited until she heard the strains of organ music within. Then she pushed open the door and entered.

Once inside, a sudden feeling of awe and hesitancy overwhelmed Diana. There seemed an unusual brooding sense of sanctity about this old church. All light, which entered there, filtered devoutly through some sacred scene, and still bore upon its beams the apostle's halo, the Virgin's robe, or the radiance of transfiguration glory.

The shock of contrast, as Diana passed from the noise and whirl of Bishopsgate's busy traffic into this silent waiting atmosphere of stained glass, old oak carving, and the sheen of the distant altar, held her senses for a moment in abeyance.

Then she took in every detail: Mr. Goldsworthy peeping from the vestry, catching sight of her, and immediately proceeding within the communion rails, and kneeling at the table; Mrs. Vane and Mr. Inglestry on one side of the church; Sarah and Sir Deryck, in different pews, on the other. Lastly, she saw David, and the place at his side which awaited her; David, looking very slim and youthful, standing with his left hand plunged deep into the pocket of his short coat—a boyish attitude he often unconsciously adopted in moments of nervous strain. Slight and boyish he looked in figure; but the intellectual strength and spiritual power in the thin face had never been more apparent to Diana than at this moment, as he stood with his head slightly thrown back, awaiting her advance.

Then a complete mental readjustment came to Diana. How could she go through with this marriage, for which she herself had worked and schemed? It suddenly stood revealed as a thing so much more sacred, so far more holy, so infinitely deeper in its significance, than she had ever realized.

She knew, now, why David had felt it impossible, at first, for any reasons save the one paramount cause—the reverent seeking of the Church's sanction and blessing upon the union of two people who needed one another utterly.

Had she loved David—had David loved her—she could have moved swiftly to his side, without a shade of hesitancy.

As it was, her feet seemed to refuse to carry her one step forward.

Then Diana realized that had this ceremony beer about to take place in order that the benefits accruing to her under her uncle's will should remain hers, she must, at that moment, have fled back to the motor, bidding the chauffeur drive off—anywhere, anywhere—where she would never see St. Botolph's church again, or look upon the face of David Rivers.

But, by the happenings of the previous evening the conditions were changed—ah, thank God they were changed! David still thought he was; doing this for her; but she knew she was doing it for him. He believed he gave her all. She knew he actually gave her nothing, save this honest desire to give her all. And, in return she could give him much:—not herself—*that* he did not want—but much, oh, much!

All this passed through Diana's mind, in those few moments of paralysing indecision, while she stood, startled and unnerved, beneath the gallery.

Then, as her eyes grew more accustomed to the dim light, David's look reached her—reached her, and called her to his side.

And down from the organ-loft wafted the prayer for all uncertain souls: "Lead, kindly Light, amid the encircling gloom; lead Thou—lead Thou—lead Thou me on."

With this prayer on her lips, and her eyes held by the summons in David's, Diana moved up the church, and took her place at his side.

No word of the service penetrated her consciousness, until she heard her godfather's voice inquire, in confidential tones: "Who giveth this woman to be married to this man?"

No one replied. Apparently no one took the responsibility of giving her to David, to whom she did not really give herself. But in the silence of the slight pause following the question, Uncle Falcon's voice said, with startling clearness, it her ear: "*Diana—I have won.*"

This inarticulate sentence seemed to Diana the clearest thing in the whole of that service. She often wondered afterwards why all actual spoken words had held so little conscious meaning. She could recall the strong clasp of David's hand, and when his voice, steadfast yet quiet, said: "I will," she looked at him and smiled; simply because his voice seemed the only real and natural thing in the whole service.

When they walked up the chancel together, and knelt at the altar rail, she raised her eyes to the pictured presentment of the crucified Christ; but there was something too painful to be borne, in the agony of that suffering form as pictured there. "Myrrh! "cried her troubled heart;

"myrrh, was *His* final offering. Must gold and frankincense always culminate in myrrh?"

. . . . .

In the vestry. Sir Deryck Brand was the first to offer well-expressed congratulations. But, after the signing of the registers, as he took her hand in his in bidding her farewell, he said with quiet emphasis: "I have told your husband, Mrs. Rivers, that he must come home within the year."

Diana, at a loss what to answer, turned to David.

"Do you hear that, David?"

"Yes," said David, gently; "I hear."

As they passed out together, her hand resting lightly on David's arm, Diana looked up and saw above the organ-gallery, between the golden pipes, the beautiful stained-glass window, representing the Infant Christ brought by His mother to the temple, and taken into the arms of the aged Simeon.

"Oh, look, David," whispered Diana; "I like this window better than the others. It doe not give us our Wise Men from the East, but it gives us the newborn King. Do you see Him in the arms of Simeon?"

David lifted his eyes; and suddenly she saw the light of a great joy dawn in them.

"Yes," he said, "yes. And do you remember what Simeon said?"

They had reached the threshold of St. Botolph's Diana took her hand from his coat sleeve; and pausing a moment, looked into his face.

"What did he say, David?"

"Lord, *now* lettest Thou Thy servant depart in peace," replied David, quietly.

"And what have you just remembered, David which has filled your face with glory?"

"That this afternoon, I start for Central Africa," replied David Rivers, as he put his bride into the motor.

CHAPTER XVIII

DAVID'S NUNC DIMITTIS

THE doctor was responsible for Diana's shyness during the drive from St. Botolph's to Waterloo.

Ho had said: "I have told your husband, Mrs. Rivers." This was unlike Sir Deryck's usual tact. It seemed so impossible that that dreamlike service had transformed her from *Miss* Rivers, into *Mrs.* Rivers; and it was so very much calling "a spade a spade," to speak of David as "your husband."

The only thing which as yet stood out clearly to Diana in the whole service, was David's resolute "I will"; and the essential part of David's "I will," in his own mind, and therefore of course in hers, appeared to be: "I will go at once to Central Africa; and I will start for that distant spot in four hours' time!"

Diana took herself instantly to task for the pang she had experienced at sight of the sudden flash of intense relief in David's eyes, as he quoted the Nunc Dimittis.

That he should "depart" on the wedding-day, had been an indispensable factor in the making of her plan; and, that he should depart "in peace," untroubled by the fact that he was leaving her, was surely a cause for thanksgiving, rather than for regret.

Diana, who prided herself upon being far removed from all ordinary feminine weaknesses and failings, now rated herself scornfully for the utter unreasonableness of feeling hurt at David's very obvious relief over the prospect of a speedy departure, now he had faithfully fulfilled the letter of the undertaking between them. He had generously done as she had asked, at the cost of much preliminary heart-searching and perplexity; yet she, whose express stipulation had been that he should go, now grudged the ease with which he was going, and would have had him a little sad—a little sorry.

"Oh," cried Diana, giving herself a mental shake, "it is unreasonable; it is odious; it is like an ordinary woman! I don't want the poor boy to stay, so why should I want him to regret going? How perfectly natural that he should be relieved that this complicated time is over; and how glad *I* ought to be, that whatever else connected with me he has found difficult, at all events he finds; it easy to leave me! Any mild regrets would spoil the whole thing, and reduce us to the level of an ordinary couple. Sir Deryck's remark in the vestry was most untactful. No wonder it has had the immediate effect of making us both realize with relief that, excepting in outward seeming, we each leave the church as free as when we entered it."

Yet, undoubtedly David *was* now her husband; and as Diana sat silently beside him, she felt as: an experienced fighter might feel, who had handed over all his weapons to the enemy. What advantage would David take, of this new condition of things, during the four hours which remained to him? She felt defenceless.

Diana plunged both her hands into her muff. If David took one of them, there was no knowing what might happen next. She remembered the compelling power of his eyes, as they drew her up the church, to take her place at his side. How would she feel, what would she do, if he turned and looked so, at her—now?

But David appeared to be quite intent on the sights of London, eagerly looking his last upon each well-known spot.

"I am glad this is a hired motor," he said, "and not your own chauffeur. This fellow does not drive so rapidly. One gets a chance to look out of the window. Ah, here is the Bank of England. I have never felt much interest in that. But I like seeing the Royal Exchange, because of the Prince Consort's text on the marble slab, high up in the centre of its facade."

They were held up for a moment in the stream of cross-traffic.

"My father pointed it out to me when I was a very little chap," continued David. "I really must see it again, for the last time."

He leaned forward to look up through the window on her side of the motor. His arm rested for a moment against Diana's knee.

"Yes, there it is, in golden letters, on the marble slab! 'The earth is the Lord's, and the fullness thereof.' Wasn't it a grand idea? That those words should dominate this wonderful centre of the world's commerce, wealth, and enterprise. As if so great, so mighty, so influential a nation as our own, upon whose glorious flag the sun never sets, is yet humbly proud to look up and inscribe, in letters of gold, upon the very pinnacle of her supremacy: 'The earth is the Lord's!' All this wealth, all this power; these noble colonies, this world-encircling influence, may be mine; but—'The earth is the Lord's.'"

David's eyes glowed. "I am glad I have seen it once more. It is not so clear as when, holding tightly to my father's hand, I first looked up and saw it, twenty-two years ago. The letters are tarnished. If I were a rich man, I should like to have them re-gilt."

"You *are* a rich man," said Diana, smiling, "and it shall be done, David, if private enterprise is allowed the privilege,"

"Ah, thanks," said David. "That would really please me. You must write and say whether it proved possible. Sometimes when alone, it the utter silence of our great expanse of jungle and forest, I like to picture the rush and rumble the perpetual movement of this very heart of our grand old London, going on—on—on, all the time. It is my final farewell to it, to-day. Ah here is the Mansion House. On the day my old dad showed me the Royal Exchange, we also saw the Lord Mayor's show. I remember I was much impressed. I fully intended then to be Lord Mayor, one day! I always used to imagine myself as being every important personage I admired."

"You remind me," said Diana, "of a very great man of whom it has been said that he never enjoys a wedding, because he cannot be the bride; and that he hates attending funerals, because he cannot be the corpse."

David laughed. "A clever skit on an undoubted trait," he said; "but that trail makes for greatness. All who climb high: see themselves at the top of the tree, long before they get there." Then suddenly he remarked: "There won't be any éclat about *my* funeral. It will be a very simple affair; just a stowing away of the worn-out suit of clothes, under a great giant tree in our silent forests."

"Please don't be nasty," said Diana; and, though the words were abrupt, there was such a note of pain in her voice, that David turned and looked at her. There was also pain in her sweet grey eyes. David put out his hand, impulsively, and laid it on Diana's muff.

"You must not mind the thought," he said. "We know it has to come; and I want you to get used to it, just as I have done. To me it only seems like a future plan for a quite easy journey; only there's a lot to be done first. Oh, I say! The Thames. May I tell the man to go along the Embankment, and over Westminster Bridge? I should like a last sight of the Houses of Parliament, and Big Ben; and, best of all, of Westminster Abbey."

David leaned out of the window, and directed the chauffeur.

Diana slipped her hands out of her muff.

They passed the royal statue of England's great and beloved Queen. David leaned forward and saluted.

"The memory of the Just is blessed," he said. "I always like to realize how truly the Royal Psalm applies to our Queen Victoria. 'Thou gavest him a long life; even for ever and ever' She lives on for ever in the hearts of her people. This—is true immortality!"

Diana removed her gloves, and looked at the bright new wedding-ring, encircling the third finger of her left hand.

David glanced at it also, and looked away.

"Good-bye. old Metropole!" he said, as they sped past Northumberland Avenue. "We have had some jolly times there. Ah, here is the Abbey! I must set my watch by Big Ben."

"Would you like to stop, and go into the Abbey?" suggested Diana. "We have time."

"No, I think not," said David. "I made my final adieu to English cathedrals at Winchester, last Monday. And I had such a surprise and pleasure there. Nothing the Abbey could provide would equal it."

"What was that? "asked Diana, and her hand stole very near to David's.

David folded his arms across his breast, and turned to her with delight in his eyes.

"Why, the day before you came to town, I went down to Winchester to say good-bye to some very old friends. Before leaving that beautiful city I went into the cathedral, and there I found—what do you think? A side-chapel called the Chapel of the Epiphany, with a stained-glass window representing the Wise Men opening their treasures and offering their gifts to the Infant Saviour."

"Were there three Wise Men?" asked Diana. For some reason, her lips were trembling.

David smiled. "Yes, there were three. Mrs. Churchwarden Smith would have considered her opinion triumphantly vindicated. But, do you know, that little chapel was such a holy place. I knelt there and prayed that I might live to see the completion and consecration of our 'Church of the Holy Star.'"

Diana drew on her gloves, and slipped her hands back into her muff.

"Where did you kneel, David? I will make a pilgrimage to Canterbury, and kneel there too."

"It wasn't Canterbury," said David gently. "It was Winchester. I knelt at the altar rail; right in the middle."

"I will go there," said Diana. "And I will kneel where you knelt, David."

"Do." said David, simply. "That little chapel meant a lot to me."

They had turned out of York Road, and plunged into the dark subway leading up to the main station at Waterloo.

Diana lifted her muff to her lips, and looked at David over it, with starry eyes.

"Shall you remember sometimes, David, when you are so far away, that I am making pilgrimages, and doing these things which you have done?"

"Of course I shall," said David. "Why, here we are; with plenty of time to spare."

He saw Diana to their reserved compartment in the boat train; then went off to the cloakroom to find his luggage.

Before long they were gliding out of Waterloo Station, and David Rivers had looked his last on London; and had bidden a silent farewell to all for which London stands, to the heart of every true-born Englishman.

CHAPTER XIX
DAVID STUDIES THE SCENERY

THE railway journey passed with surprising ease and swiftness. David's unusually high spirits were perhaps responsible for this.

To Diana it seemed that their positions were suddenly and unaccountably reversed. David led, and she followed. David set the tone of the conversation; and, as he chose that it should be gay and bantering, Diana found it impossible to strike the personal and pathetic note, bordering on the intimate and romantic, which she, somehow, now felt suitable to the occasion.

So they had a marry wedding-breakfast in the dining-car; and laughed much over the fact that they had left Mrs. Marmaduke Vane, with two strings to her bow—Diana's godfather and Diana's lawyer.

"Both are old flames of Chappie's," explained Diana. "She will be between two fires. But I am inclined to think Sarah's presence will quench godpapa's ardour. In which case, Mr. Inglestry will carry Chappie off to luncheon, and will probably dance attendance upon her during the remainder of the day. After which, even if he does not actually propose, I shall have to hear the oft-told tale: 'He made his meaning very clear, my dear Diana.' How clever all these old boys must be, to be perpetually 'making their meaning clear' to Chappie, which, I admit, must be a fascinating occupation, and yet remaining triumphantly unwed! Chappie does not return home until to-morrow. David—I shall be quite alone at Riverscourt to-night."

"Oh, look at the undulating line of those distant hills! "cried David, polishing the window with his table-napkin. "And the gorse in bloom, on this glorious common. It seems a waste to look for a moment on one's plate, while passing, for the last time, through beautiful England. Even in winter this scenery is lovely, gentle, home-like. I don't want to miss the sight of one cosy farmhouse, leafless orchard, nestling village, or old church tower. All upon which I am now looking, will be memory's treasured picture-gallery to visit eagerly in the long months to come."

Apparently there were to be only landscapes in David's picture gallery. Portraits, however lovely, were not admitted. A very lovely face was opposite to him at the little table. A firm white chin rested thoughtfully in the rounded palm of the hand on which gleamed his golden wedding-ring. Soft grey eyes, half-veiled by drooping lids and long dark lashes, looked wistfully, earnestly, at the thin lines of his strong eager face. Diana was striving to imprint upon her memory a portrait of David, which should not fade. But David polished the window at intervals with his table-napkin, and assiduously studied Hampshire orchards, and frost-covered fields and gardens.

.   .   .   .   .

Back in their own compartment, within an hour of Southampton, Diana made a desperate attempt to arrive at a clear understanding about the rapidly approaching future—those two years possibly three, while they would be husband and wife, yet on different sides of the globe.

She was sitting beside David, who occupied the corner seat, facing the engine, on her left. Diana had been seated in the corner opposite to him; but had crossed over, in order to sit beside him; and now asked him, on pretext of being dazzled, to draw down the blinds on his side of the compartment.

David complied at once, shutting out the pale wintry sunlight; which, pale though it was, yet made a golden glory of Diana's hair.

Thus excluded from his refuge in the leafless orchards, David launched into a graphic description of the difficulties and adventure of African travel.

"You see," he was saying, "the jungle grasses grow to such a height that it becomes almost impossible to force one's way through them; and they make equally good cover for wild beasts, or mosquitoes"—when Diana laid her hand upon his coat sleeve.

Either the sleeve was thick, or David was dense—or both. The account of African swamps continued, with increased animation.

"As soon as the wet season is over, the natives fire the grass all around their villages; and then wild beasts get no cover for close approach; shooting becomes possible, and the women can get down to the river to fetch water, or into the forests to cut firewood. The burning kills millions of mosquitoes, makes it possible to go out in safety, and to shoot game. When the grass is high, mosquitoes are rampant, and game impossible to view. Before the burning was done round my place, last year, I found a hippopotamus in my flower garden, when I came down to breakfast one morning. He had danced a cake-walk among my oleanders, which was a trial, because oleanders bloom gloriously all the year round when once they get a hold."

Suddenly Diana turned upon him, took his right hand between both hers, and caught it to her, impulsively.

"David," she said, "do you consider it right in our last hour together, completely to ignore the person you have just married?"

David's startled face showed very white against the green window-blind.

"I—I was not ignoring you," he stammered, "I was telling you about——"

"Oh, I know!" cried Diana, uncontrollable pain in her voice, and the look of a wounded leopard in her eyes, "Bother your tall grasses, and your oleanders, and your hippopotamus!" Then more gently, but still holding his hand pressed against her velvet coat: "Oh, don't let's quarrel, David! I don't want to be horrid! But we can't ignore the fact that we were married this morning, and you are wasting the only time left to us, in which to discuss our future."

David gently drew away his hand, folded his arms across his breast, leaned back in his comer, and looked at Diana, with that expression of patient tenderness which always had the effect of making her feel absurdly young, and far removed from him.

"Have we not said all there is to say about it?" he asked, gently.

"No, silly, we have not!" cried Diana, furiously. "Oh, how glad I am that you are going to Central Africa!"

David's face whitened to a terrible pallor.

"There is nothing new in that," he said, speaking very low. "It has been understood all along."

"Oh, David, forgive me," cried Diana. "I did not mean to say anything unkind. But I am so miserable and unhappy; and if you say another word about Hampshire scenery or African travel, I shall either swear and break the windows, or fall upon your shoulder and weep. Either course would involve you in an unpleasant predicament. So, for your own sake, help me, David."

David's earnest eyes searched her face.

"How can I help you?" he asked, his deep voice vibrating with an intensity which assured Diana of having gained at last his full attention. "What has made you miserable?"

"Our wedding-service," replied Diana, with tears in her voice. "It meant so much more than I had ever dreamed it possibly could mean."

Then a look leapt into David's eyes such as Diana had never seen in mortal eyes, before.

"How?" he said; the one word holding so much of question, of amazement, of hope, of suspense, that its utterance seemed to arrest the train; to stop the beating of both their hearts; to stay the universe a breathing space; while he looked, with a world of agonized hope and yearning, into those sweet grey eyes, brimming over with tears.

Perhaps the tears blinded them to the meaning of the look in David's. Anyway, his sudden "How?" bursting as a bomb-shell into the silent railway-carriage, only brought an expression of startled surprise, to add to the trouble in Diana's sweet face.

David pulled himself together.

"How?" he asked again, more gently; while the train, the hearts, and the universe went on once more.

"Oh, I don't know," said Diana, with a little break in her voice. "I think I realized suddenly, how much it might mean between two people who really cared for one another—I mean really *loved*—for we do 'care'; don't we, Cousin David?"

"Yes, we do care," said David, gently.

"I want you to talk to me about it; because the service was so much more solemn than I had expected; I have never been at any but flippant weddings—what? . . . Oh, yes, weddings are often 'flippant,' Cousin David. But ours was not. And I am so afraid, after you are gone, it will come back and haunt me. I want you to tell me, quite plainly, how little it *really* meant; although it seemed to mean so appallingly much."

David laid his hand gently on hers, as it lay upon her muff, and the restless working of her fingers ceased.

"It meant no more," he said, quietly, "than we intended it should mean. It meant nothing which could cause you distress or trouble. AH was quite clear between us, beforehand; was it not? That service meant for you—your home, your fortune, your position in the county, your influence for good; deliverance from undesired suitors; and—I hope—a friend you can trust—though far away—until death takes him—farther."

He kept his hand lightly on hers, and Diana's mind grew restful. She laid her other hand over his. She was so afraid he would take it away.

"Oh, go on David." she said. "I feel better."

"You must not let it haunt you when I am: gone," continued David. "You urged me to do this thing, for a given reason; and, when once I felt convinced we were not wrong in doing it, I went through with it, as I had promised you I would. There was nothing in that to frighten or to distress you. We could not help it that the service was so wonderful. That was partly your fault," added David, with a gentle smile, "for providing organ music, and for choosing to impersonate my Lady of Mystery."

Diana considered this. Then: "Oh, I am so comforted, Cousin David," she said. "I was so horribly afraid it had—somehow—meant more than I wanted it to mean."

"How could it have meant more than you wanted it to mean?"

"I don't know. I begin to think Uncle Falcon was right, when he called me ignorant and inexperienced."

David laughed. "Oh, you mustn't begin to give in to Uncle Falcon," he said. "And today, of all days, when our campaign has succeeded and we have defeated him. You can go into the library this evening, look Uncle Falcon full in the eyes, and say: 'Uncle Falcon, *I* have won!'"

"Can I?" said Diana, doubtfully. "I am a little bit afraid of Uncle Falcon. I could, if you were there, Cousin David."

David tried to withdraw his hand; but the hand lying lightly upon it immediately tightened.

"Are you *sure* I shan't be haunted after you are gone?" asked Diana, with eyes that searched his face.

"Not by me," smiled David.

"Of course not. But by the service?"

"Are any special words troubling you? "he asked, gently.□

"Goodness, no!" cried Diana. "I realized nothing clearly excepting 'I will,' when you said it. I haven't a ghost of a notion what I promised."

"Then if you haven't ghost– –" began David.

"Oh, don't joke about it," implored Diana. "I am really in earnest. I was horribly afraid; and I did not know of what. I began to think I should be obliged to ask you to put off, and to go by a later boat."

"Why?"

"So as to have you here, to tell me it had not meant more than we intended it should mean,"

Diana took off her large hat, and threw it on to the seat opposite. Then she rested her head against the cushion, close to David's.

"Oh, this is so restful," she sighed; "and I am so comforted and happy I Do let's stop arguing."

"We are not arguing," said David.

"Oh, then let's stop *not* arguing!"

She lifted his hand and her muff together, holding them closer to her.

"Let's sit quite still, David, and realize that the whole thing is safely over, and we are none the worse for it; and have got all we wanted in the world."

David said nothing. He had stopped "not arguing."

The train sped onward.

A sense of complete calm and rest came over the two who sat silent in their compartment, moving so rapidly toward the moment of inevitable parting. Diana's head was so near to David's that a loose strand of her soft hair blew against his face. She let her muff drop, but still held his hand to her breast. She closed her eyes, sitting so still that David thought she had fallen asleep.

At length, without stirring, she said: "We shall write to each other. Cousin David?"

"If you wish."

"Of course I wish. Will you promise to tell me exactly how you are?"

"I never speak, think, or write, about my own health."

"Tiresome boy! Do you call this 'obeying' me?"

"I did not promise to obey you."

"Oh, no; I forgot. How wickedly one-sided the marriage service is! That is one reason why I always declared I never would marry. One law for the man, and another for the woman; and in a civilized country! We might as well be Hottentots! And what a slur on a woman to have to change her name—often for the worse, I knew a Miss Pound who married a Mr. Penny,"

David did not laugh. He had caught sight of the distant ships on Southampton Water,

"Everybody made endless puns on the wedding-day," continued Diana. "I should have been in such a rage before the reception was over, had I been the bride, that no one would have dared come near me. It got on her nerves, poor girl; and when some one asked her just as they were starting whether she was going to take care of the Penny and leave the Pounds to take care of themselves, she burst into tears, and drove away, amid showers of rice, weeping! I think Mr. Penny must have felt rather 'cheap'; don't you? Well, anyway, I have kept my own name."

"You have taken mine," said David, with his eyes on the masts and funnels.

"How funny it will seem to get letters addressed: *Mrs. David Rivers*. If my friends put D only, it might stand for 'Diana.' David—"she turned her head suddenly, without lifting it, and her soft eyes looked full into his dark ones—"David, what shall you call me, when you write? I am no longer *Miss Rivers,* and you can hardly begin your letters: *My dear Mrs. Rivers!* That would be too formal, even for you! At last you will *have* to call me 'Diana.'"

David smiled. "Not necessarily," he said. "In fact, I know how I shall begin my letters; and I shall not call you 'Diana.'"

"What then? "she asked; and her lips were very close to his.

David sat up, and touched the springs of the window-blind.

"I will tell you, as we say good-bye; not before. Look! We are running through Southampton. We shall be at the quay in two minutes."

CHAPTER XX
WITH THE COMPLIMENTS OF THE COMPANY

DIANA followed David up the gangway of the big liner, and looked around with intense interest at the floating hotel he was to inhabit during so many days; the vessel which was to bear him away to the land from which he never intended to return.

Diana experienced an exhilarating excitement as she and David stepped on board, amid a bustling crowd of other passengers and their friends; the former already beginning to eye one another with interest; the latter, to follow with wistful gaze those from whom they would so soon be parted.

Diana had left the train, at the dock station, with very different sensations from those with which she had entered it at Waterloo. She now felt so indescribably happy and at rest; so completely reassured as to the future. David had been so tender and understanding, so perfect in all he had said and done, when once she had succeeded in making him realize how much more their new relationship meant to her, than it did to him. He had so patiently allowed her to hold his hand, during the remainder of the journey. She could feel it still, where she had pressed it against her bosom. It seemed to her that she Would always feel it there, in any time of doubt or of difficulty. It must be because of David's essential goodness, that his touch possessed such soothing power. The moment he had laid his hand on hers, she had thought of the last verse of his favourite hymn.

Her car, sent down from town the day before to be in readiness to take her home, awaited her as near the gangway of the steamer as the regulations of the wharf would allow. It was comforting to know that there would not be the need for a train journey, after David's departure. It might have seemed lonely without him. Once safely tucked into her motor, she was at home, no matter how long the run to Riverscourt might chance to be.

David caught sight of the car; and she had to stand, an amused spectator, while he ran quickly down to say good-bye to her footman and to her chauffeur. She saw the wooden stiffness of the footman, and the iron impassivity of the chauffeur, subside into humanity, as David shook them each by the hand, with a kindly word of remembrance and farewell. Both automata, for the moment, became men. Diana could see the glow on their faces, as they looked after David. Had he tipped them each a five-pound note, they would have touched their hats, without a change of feature. In the warmth of this farewell, they forgot to touch their hats; but David had touched their hearts, which was better; and their love went with him, as he boarded the steamer.

This little episode was so characteristic of David. Diana thought it over, with tender amusement in her eyes, as she followed him up the gangway. Wherever he went he won the hearts of those who served him. He found out their names, their joys and sorrows, their hopes and histories, with astonishing rapidity. "I cannot stand the plan of calling people by their occupation," he used to say. "Like the crude British matron in the French hotel who addressed the first man she met in a green apron, as 'Bottines!'"

So "Boots," "Waiter," and "Ostler," became "Tom," "Dick," and "Harry," to David, where ever he went; and while other people were served by machines, for so much a day, he was hailed by men, and waited on with affection. And he, who never forgot a face, also had the knack of never forgetting the name appertaining to that face, nor the time and circumstance in which he had previously come in contact with it.

Diana soon had evidence of this as they boarded the liner, on which David had already traveled. On all sides, impassive faces suddenly brightened into smiles of welcome; and David's "Hullo, Jim!" or "Still on board, Harry?" would be met with: "Glad to see you looking better, Mr. Rivers"; or "We heard you was a-coming, sir" David, who had left love behind, found love awaiting him.

Opposite the purser's office, he hesitated, and turned to Diana.

"Where would you like to go?" he said, "We have nearly an hour."

"I want to see over the whole ship," said Diana. "But first of all, of course, your cabin." David looked pleased, and led the way down to a lower deck, and along a narrow passage, with doors on either side. At number 24 he stopped.

"Here we are," he said, cheerfully.

Diana entered a small cabin, already choked with luggage. It contained three berths. On two of them were deposited rugs, hand-bags, and men's cloth caps. A lower one was empty. Several portmanteaux blocked the middle of the small room. David followed her in, and looked around.

"Hullo!" he said. "Where is my baggage? Apparently it has not turned up. This is my bunk, right enough."

"What a squash!" exclaimed Diana.

Before David could reply, a steward put his head in at the door.

"Well, Martin," said David, "I'm back in my old quarters, you see. I am glad you are still on duty down this passage."

The man saluted, and came in with an air of importance.

"Glad to see you, sir, I'm sure; and looking a deal better than when you came home, sir. But I'm not to have the pleasure of waiting on you this time, Mr. Rivers. The purser gave orders that I was to hand you this, as soon as you arrived."

He handed David a letter, addressed to himself.

David tore it open, glanced at it; then turned to Diana, his face aglow with surprise and pleasure.

"I say!" he exclaimed. "They ask me to accept better accommodation, 'with the compliments of the company.' Well, I've heard of such a thing happening to actors, public singers, and authors; but this is the first time I have known it happen to a missionary! Where is number 74, Martin?"

"On the promenade deck, sir; nicely midship. Allow me to show you."

Martin led the way. David, full of excitement, pleasure, and surprise, followed, with Diana.

Diana took it very quietly—this astonishing attention of the company's. But her eyes shone like stars. Diana loved seeing people have surprises.

Number 74 proved to be a large airy stateroom for three; but only one lower berth was made up. David was in sole possession. It contained an easy chair, a wardrobe, a writing table, a movable electric lamp, and was so spacious, that David's baggage, standing in one corner, looked quite lost, and took up practically no room.

"A private bathroom is attached, sir," explained Martin, indicating a side door; "and a mate of mine is looking forward to waiting on you, sir I'm right sorry not to have you in 24, but glad to see you in more roomy quarters, Mr. Rivers."

"Oh, I say!" exclaimed David, boyishly, as Martin retired, closing the door. "They've actually given me an eighty guinea state-room all to myself! Heaven send there's no mistake! 'With the compliments of the company!' Think what that means!"

"Will it add very much to your comfort David?" asked Diana, innocently.

"Comfort?" cried David. "Why it's a palace! And just think of being to oneself—and an arm-chair! Four electric lights in the ceiling"—David turned them all on—"and this jolly little reading lamp to move about. I shall be able to read in my bunk. And two big windows; Oh, I say! I shall feel I ought to invite two other fellows in. It is too sumptuous for missionary!"

"No, you mustn't do that, David," said Diana. "It would be too disappointing to–to the company. Look upon it as an offering of gold and frankincense, and do not rob the giver of the privilege of having offered the gift. Promise me, David."

"Of course I promise," he said. "I am too absolutely thankfully grateful, to demur for a moment, about accepting it. Only, it *is* a bit overwhelming."

"Now trot me all over the ship," commanded Diana. "And then let us return here, to say good-bye."

CHAPTER XXI

"ALL ASHORE!"

IT had not taken long to see over the liner. Diana had flown about, from dining-saloon to hurricane-deck, in feverish haste to be back in number 74, in order to have a few quiet moments alone with David.

They were back there, now; and ten minutes remained before the sounding of the gong, warning friends to leave the ship.

"Sit in your easy chair, David," commanded Diana; "I shall like to be able to picture you there."

She moved about the room, examining every-thing; giving little touches here and there.

She paused at the berth. "What a queer: little place to sleep in!" she said; and laid her hand, for a moment, on the pillow.

Then she poured water into one of the tumblers placed it on the writing-table, took the Parma violets from her breast and from her muff, and arranged them in the tumbler.

"Put a little pinch of salt into the water David, when you come up from dinner, and the will soon revive; and serve, for a few days, to remind you of me! I am never without violets; as you may have noticed."

She hung up his coat and hat. "I wish I could unpack for you," she said. "This cosy little room makes me feel quite domesticated. I never felt domesticated, before; and I am doubtful whether the feeling would last many minutes. But how jolly it all is! I believe I should love a voyage on a liner. Don't be surprised if I turn up one day, and call on you in Ugonduma."

"You must not do that," said David.

"What fun it would be to arrive in the little garden, where the hippopotamuses dance their morning cake walk; pass up the path, between the oleanders; ring the bell—I suppose there is a bell?—and send in my card: *Mrs. David Rivers!* Tableau! Poor David! It would be so impossible to say: 'Not at home' in Ugonduma, especially to *Mrs. David Rivers!* The butler—are there butlers? —would be bound to show me in. It would be more astonishing than the hippopotamus! though less destructive to the oleanders! Oh, why am I so flippant!—David, I must see Martin's mate. I want to talk to him about taking proper care of you. Will he come if I ring this bell? . . . Oh, all right. But I am perfectly certain that while you are finding out how many children he has, and whether they have all had measles, he will fail to notice your most obvious wants."

Diana took off her hat, and laid it on the writing table. Then she came and knelt beside the arm of David's chair.

"David," she said, "before I go, will you give me your blessing, as you did on the night when you led me to the feet of the King?"

David stood up; but he did not lay his hands on that bowed head.

"Let us kneel together," he said, "and together let us ask, that our mistakes—if any—may be overruled; that our sins may be forgiven; that we may remain true to our highest ideals; and that—whether in life or by death—we may glorify our Kling, and be faithful followers of the Star."

.   .   .   .   .

The gong, following closely on the final words of David's prayer, crashed and clanged through the ship; booming out, to all concerned, the knell of inevitable parting.

Diana rose in silence, put on her hat, took a final look round the room; then, together, they passed out, and moved toward the gangway, down which the friends of passengers were already hurrying, calling back, as they went, final word of farewell.

Near the gangway Diana paused, and turned to David.

"You are sure all the dates and addresses you have given me are right?" she said.

David smiled. "Quite sure. I would not risk losing one of your letters."

"You do care that I should write?"

"I count on it," replied David.

"And you will write to me?"

"Undoubtedly I will."

"Quite soon?"

"I will begin a letter to-morrow, and tell you whether Martin's mate has any children; and if so, whether they have had the measles."

"It would be more to the point to tell me whether he takes proper care of you. David—I wish you were not going!"

A look leapt into David's eyes as of a drowning man sinking for the third and last time, who suddenly sees a rope dangling almost within his reach.

"Why?"

"I don't know. It seems so far. Are you sure you are quite well? Why are you so ghastly white?"

"Quite well," smiled David, We cannot all have Mrs. Vane's fine colour. Bid her good-bye for me."

All who were going, seemed to have gone. The gangway was empty. Passengers crowded to the side of the ship, waving in tearful silence, or gaily shouting last words, to friends lined up on the dock.

"All ashore!" shouted the sailor in charge of the gangway, looking at Diana.

She moved toward it, slowly; David at her side.

"Look here," said David, speaking hurriedly; "I should hate to watch you standing alone in that crowd, while we slowly pull out into midstream. Don't do it. Don't wait to see us go. I would so much rather you went straight to your car. It is just within sight. I shall see William arrange the rug, and shut you in. I shall be able to watch you actually safely on your way to Riverscourt; which will be much better than gradually losing sight of you in the midst of a crowd of strange faces. You don't know how long-drawn-out these dock partings are. Will you—will you do as I ask?"

"Why of course, I will, David," she said. "It is the only thing you have bidden me do since I promised to obey." Her lips trembled. "I hate saying good-bye, David. And you really look ill. I wish I had insisted on seeing Martin's mate."

"I'm all right," said David, with dry lips. "Don't you worry."

"All ashore!" remarked the sailor, confidentially, in their direction.

Diana placed one foot on the gangway; then turned and put her hand into David's.

"Good-bye, David," said Diana.

His deep eyes looked hungrily into her face—one last long earnest look.

Then he loosed her hand and bent over her, as she began to descend the gangway.

"Good-bye—*my wife!*" said David Rivera.

CHAPTER XXII

DIANA WINS

THE steady hum, and rapid onward rush, of the motor were a physical relief to Diana, after the continuous strain of the happenings of that eventful day.

She lay back, watching the flying houses, hedges, trees, and meadows—and allowed every nerve to relax.

She felt so thankful it was all over, and that she was going home—alone.

She felt very much as she had felt on her return to Riverscourt after Uncle Falcon's funeral. It had been such a relief then to be returning to a perfectly normal house, where everyday life could be resumed as usual. She had realized with thankfulness that the blinds would be up once more. There would be no hushed and silent room, which must be passed with reverent step, and bated breath, because of the awesome unnaturalness of the Thing which lay within. She had lost Uncle Falcon on the night of his death. The day of the funeral involved no further loss. It simply brought relief from a time of unnatural strain and tension.

This shrinking of Life from Death, is the strongest verification of the statement of Holy Scripture, that death came by sin. The redeemed soul in its pure radiance has gone on to fuller life.

"The body is dead, because of sin." All that is left behind is "sinful flesh." Death lays a relentless hand on this, claiming it as his due. Change and decay set in; and even the tenderest mourning heart has to welcome the coffin lid, grateful to kind Mother Earth for receiving and hiding that which—once so precious—has now become a burden. Happy they who, standing at the open grave, can appropriate and realize the great resurrection message: "He is not here! He is risen!"

Diana shifted her seat in the bounding car, drawing the rugs more closely around her.

Why was her mind dwelling thus on death and funerals, on the afternoon of her wedding-day?

How wonderful it was that this should actually be her wedding-day; and yet that she should still be Diana Rivers of Riverscourt, returning alone to her own domain, free and unfettered.

How well her plan had succeeded; and what an unexpected touch of pure romance had been added thereto, by the fact that, after all, she had, at the last, done for David's sake, that which he though he was doing for hers. There was a selflessness about the motives of both, in this marriage, which made it fragrant with the sublimest essence of frankincense. Surely only good and blessing could ensue.

Diana contemplated with satisfaction the additional prestige and assurance given to her position in the neighbourhood, by the fact that she could now take her place in society as a married woman.

How much hateful gossip would be silence for ever; how many insolent expectations would be disappointed; how many prudish criticisms and censorious remarks would have to whisper themselves into shamefaced silence.

Diana looked forward with gleeful amusement to answering the astonished questions of her many friends. How perfectly she had vindicated the line she had always taken up. Here she was, safely established, with all a married woman's privileges, and none of her odious obligations.

The old frumps, whom it was amusing to shock, would be more shocked than ever; while the younger spirits, who acclaimed her already, would hail her more loudly than ever: "Diana! Victress! Queen!"

And all this she undoubtedly owed to David, who had made her his—

Then suddenly she found herself confronted by that which, ever since the motor started, she had been fighting resolutely into her mental background; a quiet retrospection of the moment of her parting with David.

Brought face to face with it, by the chance mention of one word, Diana at once—giving up fencing with side issues, past and future—turned and faced this problem of the present. Brave at all times, she was not a coward when alone.

She took off her hat, rested her head against the soft springiness of the padded back of her motor; closed her eyes, and pressed both hands tightly against her breast,

David had said: "Good-bye, my wife." It was the name he meant to use in all his letters. "Good-bye, *my wife.*"

It now seemed to Diana that the happenings of that whole day had been moving toward that culminating moment, when David's deep tender voice should call her his wife; yet he had not done so, until only a narrow shifting plank, on which her feet already stood, lay between them, and a last earthly farewell.

Diana had sped down the gangway; and when her feet touched the wharf she had fled to her car without looking back; knowing that if she looked back, and saw David's earnest eyes watching her from the top, his boyish figure standing, slim and erect—she would have turned and rushed back up the gangway, caught his hand to her breast, and asked him to say those words again. And, if David had called her his wife again—in that tone which made all things sway and reel around her and fortune, home, friends, position seem a nothing to the fact that she was *that* to him—she could never have let go his hand again. The; must have remained for ever on the same side of the gangway; either she sailing with David to Central Africa, or David returning with her to Riverscourt.

Yet she did not want to go to Africa; and she certainly did not want David at Riverscourt! Her whole plan of life was to reign supreme in her own possessions, mistress of her home, mistress of her time, and, most important of all, mistress of herself.

Then what was the meaning of this Strange disturbance in the hitherto unruffled calm of her inner being? What angel had come down, on lightning wing, to trouble the still waters of her deepest self?

Diana was confronted by that most illusive of psychological problems, the solving of the mystery of a woman's heart—and she possessed no key thereto. Her knowledge of the world, her advanced ideas, her indiscriminate reading, had not supplied her with the golden key, which lies in the fact of the utter surrender of a noble woman, to the mighty love, and the infinite need, of a strong, good man.

She had chosen to go home alone. She had preferred this parting of the ways. Then why was it so desperately sweet to recall David's voice saying: "Good-bye, *my wife*"? Why did nothing still this strange aching at her breast, save the remembrance of the touch of his hand, as she had pressed it against her?

She would have stopped the motor and bidden her man race back to the wharf, on the chance of having a last sight of David, standing on the deck of the liner, had he not bidden her go at once, without delay; so that, in thus going, she was rendering him the one act of obedience possible, in their brief wedded life.

   .   .   .   .   .

The wintry sun soon set behind the Hampshire hills.

The primrose of the sky faded into purple twilight: twilight was quickly merged in chilly darkness.

The car paused a moment for the kindling of its huge acetylene lamps; then rushed onward, more rapidly than before.

Diana sat on in shadow. One touch of a button would have flooded the interior of her motor with light; but she preferred the quiet darkness. In it she could better hear her husband's voice, and see the gleam of his deep earnest eyes.

"Good-bye, my wife—my wife—my wife—.Good-bye, my wife!"

   .   .   .   .

Diana must have fallen asleep. The opening of the door of the motor roused her.

William had turned on the lights, lifted out the rug, and stood with it flung over his arm, waiting for her to step out.

Half dazed, she took up her hat and smoothed her tumbled hair.

She glanced at the seat beside her, almost expecting to see David.

Then she remembered, and quickly stepped out of the motor.

The great doors of Riverscourt stood wide. A ruddy light from the blazing log fire in the hall, streamed out over the newly fallen snow.

Old Rodgers, deferential, yet very consciously paternal, his hands shaking with suppressed excitement, stood just within.

The housekeeper, expectant and alert, a bow of white satin ribbon in a prominent position in her cap, waited at the foot of the wide oak staircase.

The poodle, his tufts tied up with white ribbon, moved forward to greet his mistress; then advanced gravely into the portico, and inspected the empty motor. The poodle's heart was in the grave of Uncle Falcon. Weddings did not interest him. But the non-arrival of the bridegroom— who had once, with a lack of discrimination quite remarkable, even in a human being, mistaken him for Mrs. Marmaduke Vane—seemed a fact which required verification and investigation. The poodle returned, smiling, from his inspection of the empty interior of the motor. He had not paid much attention to the lengthy discussions in the servants' hall. But this much he knew. Old Rodgers had won his bet. The housekeeper would have to pay. This pleased the poodle, who resented the fact that the housekeeper had first trimmed her own cap, and then tied him up with the remnants;—adding to this obvious slight, a callous disregard of his known preference for green or crimson, where the colour of his bows was concerned.

As Diana entered the house, the old clock in the hall began to strike six; distant Westminster chimes sounded from an upper landing; an unseen cuckoo jerked out its note six times, then slammed its door; while the old clock, measured and sonorous, refusing to be either hurried or interrupted, slowly finished its six strokes.

Diana flung her cloak to Rodgers, and ordered tea in the library. Then, with a greeting to her housekeeper, she passed upstairs to her own room.

Mrs. David Rivers had come home.

CHAPTER XXIII

UNCLE FALCON WINS

DIANA dined alone at the little round table in the big dining-room. She wore the white satin gown she had worn on the evening of Christmas Day, when David dined with her. The table decoration was lilies of the valley and Parma violets.

After dinner she went to the library, restless and lonely, yet glad to be alone; thankful she had postponed to the morrow, the return of Mrs. Marmaduke Vane.

On her writing-table, in a silver frame, stood the photograph of a special chum of hers, a man with whom she frequently played tennis in summer, and rode in winter; a good-looking fellow, with the appearance of an all-round sportsman. His gay friendly eyes looked out at her with an air of easy comradeship, as she paused for a moment beside the table.

Diana was fond of this portrait of Ronald Ingram. It always stood on her writing-table. But, this evening, she suddenly took it up, and put it, face downwards, into a drawer. It had served to remind her that she possessed no photograph of David.

She moved over to the fireplace, tall and lovely, perfectly gowned, surrounded by all the luxury she loved—yet indescribably desolate.

She stood, wrapped in thought, warming her hands at the fire; then sank into Uncle Falcon's armchair, in which she had sat while she and David discussed their intended marriage.

Did she need a portrait of David?

Hardly. He was so vividly pictured in her mental vision.

She could see him in the pulpit of the little church at Brambledene— keen, eager, inspired; full of his subject; the dark eyes shining in his thin worn face.

She could see him in the vestry, seated on the high stool; boyish, shy; very much taken aback by her unexpected entry.

She could see him at the piano in the drawing-room, completely unconscious of his surroundings; enveloped in the music he himself was making.

She could see him seated opposite to her in the chair now empty, a look of strange detachment upon his tired face, as with infinite tact and gentleness he explained to her why he felt able, after all, to accede to her request; never departing from his own standpoint in the matter; yet making the thing as easy for her as possible.

She could see him in the church of St. Botolph, as he had stood that morning—was it really only that morning?—awaiting her. How strange had been the summons in his eyes, which drew her to his side. Ah, if there had but been *love* between them, how wonderful a memory would have been that look in David's eyes!

She could see him in the railway train—in boyishly high spirits, because nothing now stood between him and his departure for his beloved sphere of work—seated opposite to her at the little table in the dining-car, rubbing the mist off the windows with his table napkin, and exclaiming over the beauties of the Hampshire hills and villages.

"Lord, *now* lettest Thou Thy servant depart in peace." Poor David! She had certainly interfered with his peace of mind during the fortnight which had preceded their strange wedding. Well, he had departed in peace, and was undoubtedly gone "to be a light to lighten the Gentiles." And what a difference her money would make to the success of his work.

And then—she could see him as he bent *down* to her from the top of the gangway, his dark eyes gazing into hers, and said: "Good-bye, my wife." Surely, for the moment, it had meant something to David to call her his wife? She had never before seen quite such a look in any man's eyes. Was it fancy, or was there a hunger in them, which seemed to match the ache at her own breast? Sentimental fancy on her own part, no doubt; for had not David said of their wedding service: "It meant no more than we intended it should mean"?

How odious and impossible a state of things, if she—Diana Rivers—who had proposed this marriage, as a mere business transaction—should now be imagining into it sentiment which she had expressly stipulated should never enter therein. If David knew of it, would she not be forced to bow her head in shame, before his clear honest eyes?

No; certainly she needed no photograph of David!

She glanced at the portrait of Uncle Falcon hanging over the mantelpiece; then looked away at once. She was rather afraid of Uncle Falcon to-night. David had said she was to flaunt her victory in Uncle Falcon's face. She had replied that she might have done so, if *he* had been going to be with her. David had made no reply; but she had felt him shrink into himself. He had been too honest to express regret to his bride, that his engagements took him elsewhere on his wedding evening; and too kind, to show relief. When she had said: "David, I shall be quite alone at Riverscourt to-night," David had remarked: "Oh, look at the undulating line of those distant hills!"

A little gleam of amusement illumined the sad face, resting against the dark leather of Uncle Falcon's big chair; and, as the firelight played upon it, dimples peeped out. Had she looked up, she would have seen a corresponding twinkle in Uncle Falcon's amber eyes.

It really was rather funny. David and his table napkin! She knew she had not behaved quite well towards David, who was such a very faithful and very proper person. She felt she should always hate the distant line of undulating hills! If only he had tried to kiss her, and she could have boxed his ears, she would have enjoyed that journey better.

But, the next moment, a rush of tears drowned the gleam of fun in those sweet eyes. She had remembered David's face, as he said: "Good-bye, my wife." It seemed sacrilege even to *think* of boxing his ears! How ill he had looked, during those final minutes on the boat. It made it so terribly easy to picture David's face as it would look when he lay dying—dead.

Diana's tears fell silently. She, who scarcely ever wept, now found herself weeping without restraint, in a vague, helpless sort of way; and about nothing—that was the foolish part of it—she was crying about absolutely nothing!

"This will never do!" said Diana. "I am being as silly as an *ordinary* married woman. I must find something sensible to think about."

She rose from her chair, stretched her beautiful arms over her head; then walked across to a table to look for a book. Her eye fell upon a concordance, lying where she had left it on that evening of indecision and perplexity.

Suddenly she remembered words of David's in his sermon on Christmas Eve. They came back to her as clearly as if they had that moment been spoken.

"Myrrh, in the Bible," David had said, "stands for other things besides death. We must not pause to do so now; but some time, at your leisure, look out each mention of myrrh. You will find it stands for love—love, of the sweetest, tenderest kind; love so complete, that it must bring with it self-abnegation, and a mingling of pain with its bliss."

Yes, David had said this. How suitable that to-night—of all nights—she should do as he had wished.

But, first, she went to the window, drew aside the curtains, and looked out.

Snow had ceased to fall. The sky was clear and cloudless. There was no moon ; but, low on the horizon, shone one brilliant star.

It seemed to Diana, that at that very moment, from somewhere out on the ocean, David's eyes were also on that star. It brought him very near. It made his last prayer very real.

She leaned her head against the window frame, and watched it silently.

"Whether in life or in death," said David's quiet voice, "may we glorify our King, and be faithful followers of the star."

Then she drew the curtain close once more found a Bible, took up the concordance, and went back to Uncle Falcon's chair to do as David had suggested.

The first reference to which she turned, chanced to be the thirteenth verse of the first chapter of the Book of Canticles—divinest love-poem ever written.

Bending over it, in the firelight, Diana read the opening words.

"*A bundle of myrrh is my well-belovèd unto me— —*"

Then, suddenly, her eyes dilated. She pressed her hands against her breast.

Then she bent over, and finished the verse; reading each word slowly, to the very last.

.   .   .   .   .

"David! David! David!"

A bundle of myrrh is my well-beloved unto me! Oh, David, speeding each moment farther and farther away, on fife's relentless ocean; hastening to that distant land "that is very far off," from which there is no return!

She lay back in the chair; opened her arms wide ; then closed them— on nothingness.

"David! David!"

She understood now.

This pain at her breast, this ache of her heart, would never be stilled, until David's dear head rested here where his hand had been pressed. And David had gone from her—for ever.

"Good-bye, my wife . . . It meant no more than we intended it should mean. . . . Good-bye, my wife."

She held her hands clasped to her bosom. She looked, wide-eyed, at the empty chair, opposite.

"David," she whispered, "David, come back to me!"

It seemed, to her, that David must hear, and must return. This agony of awful loneliness could not endure. . . . David! . . . David! . . . David! . . .

At last she rose, leaned her arms upon the marble mantelpiece, and looked up into the searching eyes of the portrait.

"Uncle Falcon," she whispered, bravely; "Uncle Falcon—*you have won.*"

The eyes of the old man who had loved her, seemed to look down sadly, sorrowfully, into hers. She had won; and he had won; but there was no triumph in either victory.

The only undisputed victor, in that hour, was Love who is lord of all; and even Love fled, with drooping wings, from a desolation which had been brought about by sacrilege at the altar.

Diana laid her golden head upon her arms. Its coronet of pride fell from it. She was shaken from head to foot by desperate weeping.

David had said: "A love so complete that it must bring with it self-abnegation, and a mingling of pain with its bliss." She had had one glimpse of what the bliss might have been. She was tasting the pain to the full.

Self stepped for ever off the throne of her woman's heart; and Love, undisputed, held full sway.

She turned from the fireplace, sank upon the floor beside the chair in which David had sat; then laid her head upon it, clasping her arms around its unresponsive emptiness.

"David! . . . David! . . . David!"

But the distant liner was ploughing steadily through the dark waters. Each moment took him farther from her; nearer to the land from which there is no return.

"Good-bye, my wife."

After a while, Diana ceased to call him.

She lay very still. No sound broke the silence of the room, save the low shuddering sobs of a breaking heart.

But the star in the sky still shone, though heavy curtains veiled it.

And David, pacing the hurricane deck, where were no curtains, lifted his eyes to its clear shining; and, in the midst of his own desperate pain, saw in it an emblem of hope, a promise of guidance, a beacon light in this vast desert of utter desolation.

.   .   .   .   .

And midnight brought merciful sleep to both.

Here endeth GOLD

FRANKINCENSE

CHAPTER XXIV

THE HIDDEN LEAVEN

CHRISTMAS Eve had come round again. The successive changes of each season had passed over Riverscourt;—the awakening of early spring, when earth threw off her pall of snow, and budding life won its annual triumph over the darkening chill of winter;—the bloom and blossom of summer, when all nature lifted up its voice and sang to the sunshine, amid fragrance of flowers and shade of soft green foliage;—the rich fulfilment of autumn, when blossom ripened into fruit, and trees turned to crimson and gold, emblem of the royal wealth of yielded harvest.

All this had come, and gone; and now, once more, earth slept 'neath leaden skies; and bare branches forked out, hopeless, over the sodden turf.

"Is this the end?" rasped the dead leaves, as the north wind swept them in unresisting herds down the avenue of beeches. "The end! The end!" wailed the north wind. "*The grass withereth, the flower fadeth—*" Then Hope, born of Faith and Experience, cried: "*But the word of our God shall stand for ever! While the earth remaineth, seedtime and harvest, and cold and heat, and summer and winter, and day and night shall not cease.* This is not death, but sleep. When spring sounds the reveillé, life will stir and move again beneath the sod; all nature will respond, and there shall come once more the great awakening; the dismal sentries of darkness and of death may cease to challenge; the troops of light and life march on their way. Again the victory will be with spring."

During the year, now nearly over, Diana's inner life had reflected each of these transitions, going on around her, in her own park and gardens.

In the lonely despairing weeks following her wedding-day, her heart seemed numb and dead; her empty arms stiffened like leafless branches. Her love had awakened, only to find itself entombed.

But, with the arrival of David's first letter, there burst upon her winter the glad promise of spring.

"My dear wife," wrote David; and, as she read the words, strong possessive arms seemed to enfold her. Though distance divided, she was, unalterably, *that* to him: "My dear wife."

The letter proceeded, in calm friendliness, to give her a full account of his voyage; nothing more; yet with an intimacy of detail, an assurance of her interest, which came as balm to Diana's sore heart. And the letter ended: "Yours ever, David Rivers."

Then followed a sweet summer-time of wonderful promise. David's letters reached her by every mail They always began: "My dear wife"; they always ended: "Yours ever, David Rivers"; they held no word of anything closer or more intimate in their tie, than was in the bond; yet, as Diana shared his hopes and expectations, his difficulties, and their surmounting; as she followed with him along each step in the new development of his work, the materializing of his ideas, the fulfilment of his plans, by means of her gift of gold—it seemed to her that all this was but the promise of spring; that a glad summer must soon come when David's heart should awaken to a need—not only of her sympathy and of her help, but of *herself*; that, at no distant date, the mail would bring a letter, saying: "My wife, I want you. Come to me!"

She forgot that, owing to their unnatural marriage, she was, of all women, the one whom David could not, however much he might desire to do so, attempt to woo and win. She realized her side of the question; yet, womanlike, forgot his. No hint of her need of him was allowed to creep into her letters, even between the lines; yet she eagerly searched David's for some indication that his heart was beginning to turn toward her, in more than friendliness. It seemed to her, that her growing love for him must awaken in him a corresponding love for her.

But David's letters continued calm and friendly; and, as his work became more absorbing, they held even less of personal detail, or of intimate allusion to her life at home.

Yet this summer-time was one of growth and bloom to Diana, for there blossomed up, between him and herself, by means of constant letters, a wonderful friendship.

Their position, the one toward the other, was so unique; and, having no one else with whom to share their inner lives and closest interests, they turned to one another with a completeness which made a diary of their correspondence.

The one subject upon which neither dared to be frank, was their love the one for the other. Each was the very soul of honour, and each felt bound by their mutual compact to hide from the other how infinitely more their marriage had meant than they had ever dreamed it could, or intended it should, mean.

With the awakening of her love for David, Diana passed through agonies of shame at the recollection of the crude, calm way in which she had asked him to marry her.

During the long days before the arrival of his first letter, she used, almost every evening, to stand as she had stood that afternoon, facing the empty chair which had then held David; and, whispering the fateful words, recall his face of protest; his look of horrified dismay. This was the penance she imposed on her proud spirit; and she would creep upstairs afterwards, her fair head bowed in shame; a beautiful Godiva, who had ridden forth, not to save her townspeople, but to gain her own desired ends.

Poor David! How he had leapt up in instant protest: "I cannot do this thing!" Her suggestion to him had not even partaken of the nature of a royal proposal of marriage, when the young man knows that the choice has fallen upon himself, and stands waiting, with ready penknife, to slit the breast of his tightly buttoned tunic, and insert therein the fair white rose of a maiden's proffered love. David's uniform of amazed manhood, had provided no improvised buttonhole for Diana's undesired flower. He had stood before her, dismayed but implacable: "I cannot do this thing!" Poor David, in his shabby jacket, with his thin, worn face, and eyes ablaze. Diana cowered before the Peeping Tom of her own vivid remembrance.

But, with the reading of his first letter, the words "my dear wife," stole around her as protective arm?, shielding her from shame, and comforting her in her loneliness, with the fact of how much she had, after all, been able to give him. Yet never—never—must word from her reveal to David that she had given him, unasked, the whole love of her woman's heart. Should he come to need it, and ask for it, he would find it had all along been his.

At first, Diana's life had moved along its accustomed lines; with David, and all he was to her, as a sweet central secret, hidden deeply in her heart of hearts.

But, before long, she began to experience that which has been beautifully described as "the expulsive power of a new affection." David—like the little leaven, which a woman took and hid in three measures of meal—David, working outward from that inner shrine, leavened her whole life."

He had not asked her to give up hunting, or dancing, or any of the gaiety in which she delighted. Yet the more she lived in touch with his strenuous life of earnest self-sacrifice, the less these things attracted her.

Diana's friends never found her dull; but they gradually grew to realize that her horizon had widened immeasurably beyond their own; that the focusing points in her field of vision were things totally unseen by themselves; that, in some subtle way, she had developed and grown beyond their comprehension. They loved her still, but they left her. Diana Rivers, of Riverscourt, ceased to be the centre of an admiring crowd.

They left her; but she was not conscious of their going.

She stood alone; yet did not know that she was lonely.

The only leaving of which she was aware, was that David had left her on their wedding-day; the only loneliness, that David never intended to return.

Truly, the little leaven had leavened the whole lump.

The glitter and the glamour of the kingdoms of this world had passed away. The kingdom of heaven held sway in Diana's heart.

But the King of that kingdom at this period of Diana's life was David.

CHAPTER XXV

THE PROPERTY OF THE CROWN

THE summer passed in perpetual expectation; which, when autumn arrived, seemed ripe for fulfilment.

Diana's mind was so absorbed by her love for David, that she scarcely realized how completely she kept it out of her letters; or that his reticence might merely have been a reflection of her own. Also she every now and then relieved her feelings by writing him a complete outpouring. This, often written side by side with her letter for the mail, she would seal up in an envelope addressed to David, and place in a compartment of the sandal-wood box in which she kept all his letters, with a vague idea that some day she herself would be able to place in his hands these unposted missives.

One afternoon, just as she was closing both envelopes, callers arrived. They stayed to tea, leaving only a few minutes before Rodgers came in with the post-bag,

Diana stamped her letter, and placed it in the bag. Then spent half an hour looking through some of David's before locking them up with the one she had just written. This was especially full of tenderness and longing; and, though the quick blood mantled her cheek at the recollection of words it contained, her heart felt lightened and relieved.

"How foolish I am," she thought; "no wiser than the ordinary married women, whom I used to despise."

She took up a little pile of these letters, lying safely in their own compartment in the sandalwood casket.

"They all belong to David," she whispered. "Some day—he will see them."

Then something about the dress of the one she had just placed with the rest, caught her eye. The writing was hurried, and more like that which she had rapidly finished for posting, while Rodgers waited.

She tore it open.

My dear David.

She glanced at the end. Then she sprang up and pealed the bell.

Yours affectionately, Diana Rivers, was in her hand. *Your wife, who loves you and longs for you,* had gone to David!

Rodgers reported, in an unmoved undertone, that the man with the post-bag had started for Riversmead, on his bicycle, twenty minutes ago.

"Order the motor," commanded Diana. "Tell Knox to come round as quickly as possible. I must overtake the post-bag."

She placed her letter in a fresh envelope, rapidly addressed, sealed, and stamped it; flew up for a hat and coat, and was downstairs, ready to start, within five minutes of her discovery of the mistake.

She paced the hall like a caged lion. Every word she had written stood out in letters of fire. Oh folly, folly, to have let the two letters lie side by side!

"It meant no more than we intended it should mean". . . *Your wife, who loves you and longs for you.*

At last the motor hummed up to the portico. Diana was in it before it drew up.

"Overtake Jarvis," she said, and sat back, palpitating.

They flew down the avenue, and along the high road. But Jarvis had had nearly half an hour's start, and was a dependable man. A little way from the lodge gates they met him returning.

"On! To the post-office!" cried Diana.

It so happened that a smart, new post-office had lately been opened, in the centre of the little town—a stone building, very official in appearance, Its workings were carried out with great precision and authority. The old postmaster was living up to the grandeur of his new building.

Diana walked in, letting the door swing behind her.

"Has the Riverscourt bag been emptied yet?" she inquired. "If not, bring it to me unopened."

A clerk went into the sorting-room, and returnee in a few minutes with the letter-bag, open and empty.

"Has the mail gone?" demanded Diana.

No, the mail had not gone. It was due out, it a few minutes,

The letters were being sorted. She could hear the double bang-bang of the postmarking.

"I wish to see the Postmaster," said Diana.

The Postmaster was summoned, and, hurrying out, bowed low before the mistress of Riverscourt She did not often come, in person, even to the *new* post-office.

Diana knew she had a difficult matter to broach, and realized that she must not be imperious.

DR. might reign at Riverscourt; but E.R. was sovereign of the realm! Her love-letter to David had now become the property of the King; and this courteous little person, bowing before her, was, very consciously, the King's official in Riversmead. Was not E.R. carved with many flourishes on a stone escutcheon on the face of the new post-office?

Diana, curbing her impatience, smiled graciously at the Postmaster.

"May I have a few words with you, in your private room, Mr. Holdsworth?" she said.

Full of pleased importance, the little great man ushered her into his private sanctum, adjoining the sorting-room.

A bright fire burned in the grate. The room was new, and not yet papered; and the autumn evening was chill. Diana walked up to the fire, drew off her gloves and, stooping, warmed her hands at the blaze.

Then she turned and faced the Postmaster.

"Mr. Holdsworth, I want you to do me a great kindness. An hour ago, I put by mistake into our post-bag, a letter addressed to my husband which it is most important that be should not receive. It was a mistake. Here is the letter I intended for him. I want you to find the other in the sorting-room, and to get it back for me."

The little man stiffened visibly. E.R. seemed writ large all over him.

"That is impossible, madam," he said, "absolutely impossible. Once posted, a letter becomes the property of the Crown until it reaches the hands of the addressee. I, as a servant of the king, have to see that all Crown property is safeguarded. I could not, under any circumstances whatever, return a letter once posted,"

"But it is my own letter!" exclaimed Diana. "An hour ago it lay on my writing-table, side by "side with this one for which it was mistaken It is my own property; and I *must* have it back."

"It ceased to be your property, Mrs. Rivers, when it was taken from your private post-bag and placed among other posted letters. Neither you nor I have any further control over it."

Diana's imperious temper flashed from her eyes, and flamed into her cheeks. Her first impulse was to fling this little person aside, stride into the sorting-room, and retrieve her letter to David, at any cost.

Then a wiser mood prevailed. She came a step nearer, looking down upon him with soft pleading eyes.

"Mr. Holdsworth," she said, "you are an official of the Crown, and a faithful one ; but, even before that, you are a man. Listen! I shall suffer days and nights of unspeakable anguish of mind, if that letter goes. My husband is out in the far wilds of Central Africa. That letter would mean endless worry and perplexity to him, in the midst of his important work; and also the wrecking of a thing very dear to us both. So strongly do I feel about it, that, if it goes, I shall sail on the same boat travelling night and day by the fastest route, in order to intercept it at his very gate! See how I trust you, when I tell you all this!"

The Postmaster hesitated. "You could cable him to return it to you unopened," he said.

"I could," replied Diana; "but that would involve a mystery and a worry; and I would give my life to shield him from worry. See! Here is the letter intended for this mail, ready stamped and sealed. All I ask you to do, is to substitute this one for the other."

She held out the letter, and looked at the Postmaster.

His eyes fell before the pleading in hers.

He was a Crown official and an Englishman. Had she offered him a hundred pounds to do this thing, he would have shown her out of his office with scant ceremony. But the haughty young lady of Riverscourt, in all her fearless beauty, had looked at him with tears in her grey eyes, and had said: "See how I trust you."

He hesitated: his hand moved in the direction of the letter, his fingers working nervously.

Diana laid her hand upon his arm, bending towards him.

"*Please,*" she said.

He took the letter.

"I will see whether the other is already gone," he mumbled, and disappeared through a side door, into the sorting-room.

In a few moments he returned, still holding Diana's letter. His plump face was rather pale, and his hand shook. He laid Diana's letter on the table between them.

"I am very sorry, Mrs. Rivers," he said. "I cannot possibly give you back a letter once posted. Were I known to have done such a thing, I should at once be dismissed."

Diana paled, and stood very still, considering her next move.

"I cannot *give* you back the letter," said the Postmaster. His eyes met hers; then dropped to the letter lying on the table between them.

Then the stars in their courses fought against David, for suddenly Diana understood. This was the letter she wanted, placed within her reach.

With a rapid movement she pounced upon it. verified it at a glance, tore it to fragments, and flung them into the flames.

"There!" she said. "You did not give it to me, and I have not taken it. It is simply gone—as if it had never been either written or posted."

Then she turned to the little fat man near the door, and impulsively held out her hand. "God bless you, my friend!" she said. "I shall never forget what you have done for me this day."

"We had best both forget it," whispered the Postmaster, thickly. "If a word of it gets about I lose my place."

"Never you fear!" cried Diana, her buoyancy returning, in her relief and thankfulness. "I trusted you, and you may safely trust me."

"Hush," cautioned Mr. Holdsworth, as he opened the door; "we had best both forget." Then, as she passed out: "Your letter was just in time, m'am," he remarked aloud, for the benefit of the clerks in the office. "I placed it in the bag myself."

"Thank you," said Diana. "It would have troubled me greatly to have missed this evening's mail. I am much obliged to you, Mr. Holdsworth."

Leaning back in the motor, on her homeward way, her heart felt sick at the suspense through which she had passed.

A reaction set in. The chill of a second winter nipped the bloom of her summer, and the rich fulfilment promised by her golden autumn. The fact that it seemed such an impossible horror that one of her tender love-letters should really reach David, proved to her the fallacy of the consolation she had found in writing them.

It placed him far away—and far away for ever He would never know; he would never care; he would never come. . . . *It meant no more than we intended it should mean. . . . Good-bye, my wife.*

Tears stole from beneath Diana's closed and rolled silently down her cheeks.

Your wife, who loves you and longs for you! But David would never know. It was so true—oh, so true! But David would never know.

．　　　．　　　．　　　．　　　．

And, away in the African swamps, at that very hour, David, lying in his wooden hut, recovering from one of the short bouts of fever, now becoming so frequent, leaned upon his elbow and drew from beneath his pillow Diana's last letter, which he had been too ill to read when the mail came in; scanned it through eagerly, seeking for some word which might breathe more than mere friendliness; pressed his hot lips against the signature, *yours affectionately, Diana Rivers;* then lay back and fought the hopeless consuming longing which grew as the months passed by, strengthening as he weakened.

"I promised it should never mean more than she intended," he said. "She chose me, because she trusted me. I should be a hound, to go back! But oh, my wife—my wife—my wife!"

．　　　．　　　．　　　．　　　．

"You can serve dinner for me in the library to-night, Rodgers," said Diana. "Tell Mrs. Mallory I shall dine there alone. I am tired. Yes, thank you; I caught the mail."

She shivered. "Order fixes everywhere, please. The place is like an ice-house. Winter has taken us unawares."

She moved wearily across the great silent hall, and slowly mounted the staircase.

No light shone through the stained-glass window at the bend of the staircase; the stem outline of Rivers knights stood unrelieved by glow of colour. The knight with the dark bared head, his helmet beneath his arm, more than ever seemed to resemble David; not David in his usual quid gentleness; but David, standing white and rigid protesting, in startled dismay: "Why not? Why, because even if I wished—even if you wished—even if we both wished for each other—in that way. Central Africa is no place for a woman I would never take a woman there."

As she looked at the young knight with the close-cropped dark head, and white face, she remembered her sudden gust of fury against David; and the mighty effort with which she had surmounted it. Her answer came back to her with merciless accuracy; and, turning half-way up the second flight of stairs, she faced the shadowy knighy and repeated it in low tones.

"My dear Cousin David, you absolutely mistake my meaning. I gave you credit for more perspicacity. I have not the smallest intention of going to Central Africa, or of ever inflicting my presence or my companionship upon you. . . . And you yourself have told me, over and over, that you never expect to return to England."

Diana's hand tightened upon the balustrade, as she stood looking across at the big window. These were the words she had spoken to David,

The bareheaded knight remained immovable; but his face seemed to whiten, and his outline to become more uncompromisingly mail-clad.

"David," came the low tender voice from the staircase, "oh, David, I *do* want you—'in that way'! I would go to Central Africa or anywhere else in the wide world to be with you, David. Send for me, David, or come to me—oh, David come to me!"

The tall slim figure on the staircase leaned towards the shadowy window, holding out appealing arms.

A bitter smile seemed to gather on the white face of the steel-clad knight. "*I* am to provide the myrrh," said David's voice.

Diana turned and moved slowly upward.

She could hear the log fire in the hall beginning to hiss and crackle.

She shivered. "Yes, it is winter," she said; "it is winter again; and it has taken us unawares."

CHAPTER XXVI

A PILGRIMAGE

ON the afternoon of Christmas Eve, Diana sat in the library writing to David. She had drawn up a small table close to the fire. The room was cosy, and perfectly quiet, excepting for the leap and crackle of flames among the huge pine logs.

Diana dated her letter; then laid aside her pen, and, resting her chin in her hand, read over once again David's Christmas letter, which had reached her that morning.

It was very full of the consecration of the Church of the Holy Star, which was to take place before the Feast of Epiphany.

It held no allusions to the anniversaries, so soon coming round; the days which, a year age had been fraught with happenings of such deep importance to them both.

Long after she had reached *Yours ever, David Rivers,* Diana sat with bent head, pondering over the closely written sheets, so pregnant with omissions trying to make up her mind as to whether she should take her cue from David, and ignore the significance of these days; or whether she should act upon her first instinctive impulse, and write freely of them.

The firelight flickered on her coils of golden hair, and revealed the fact that her face had lost the rounded contour of that perfect buoyancy of health, which had been hers a year ago. Its thinness, and the purple shadows beneath the eyes, made her look older; but, as she lifted her eyes from the closely written sheets of foreign paper, and gazed, with a wistful little smile, into the fire, there was in them such a depth of chastened tenderness, and in her whole expression so gentle a look of quiet patience—as of a heart keeping long vigil, and not yet within sight of dawn—that the mellowing and softening of the spirit looking forth from it, fully compensated for the thinning and ageing of the lovely face. Diana, in her independent radiance, was there no longer; but David's wife took up her pen to write to David, with a look upon her face, which would have brought David to his knees at her feet could he but have seen it.

Uncle Falcon's amber eyes gleamed down upon her. They had never twinkled since her wedding night; but they often shone with a strangely comprehending light. Sometimes they said: "We have both won, Diana"; at other times: "We have both lost"; according to her mood. But always they were kindly, and always they gave her sympathy, and, unfailingly, they understood.

The old house rang with the merry voices of children. Notwithstanding the solemn protestations of old Rodgers, they were apparently playing hide-and-seek up and down the oak staircase, along the upper corridors, and in and out of the deep hall cupboards.

Diana was not fond of children. An extra loud whoop or bang in her vicinity did not call up an indulgent smile upon her face; and, at last, when the whole party apparently fell headlong down the stairs together, Diana, with a frown of annoyance, rang the bell and told Rodgers to request Mrs. Mallory *to* see that there was less roughness in the games.

Certainly Diana was not naturally fond of children. Yet during these years in which she was striving to let her whole life be a perpetual offering of frankincense, she filled her house with them, at Christmas, Easter, and midsummer.

They were the children of missionaries; boys and girls at school in England, whose parents in far distant parts of the world, could give them no welcome home in holiday-time. They would have had a sad travesty of holidays, at school, had not Diana invited them to Riverscourt, giving them a right royal time under the gentle supervision of Mrs. Mallory, the young widow of a missionary killed in China, who now lived with Diana as her companion and secretary Mrs. Marmaduke Vane had wedded Mr. Inglestry, within three months of Diana's own marriage.

As the house grew more quiet, Diana again took up her pen. She could hear Mrs. Mallory shepherding the children along the upper corridors into a play-room at the farther end of the house

For a moment she felt a pang of compunction a having so peremptorily stopped the hide-and-seek; but salved her conscience by the remembrance of the magnificent Christmas-tree, loaded with gifts, standing ready in the ante-room, for the morrow's festivities.

Poor little forsaken girls and boys! She had no mother-love to give them. But she gave them what she could—gold, frankincense; in many cases the climate in which their parents lived provided the myrrh, when they had to be told at school of the death, in a far-off land, of a passionately loved and longed-for mother, whose possible home-coming before long, had been the one gleam of light on the grey horizon of a lonely little heart's school-life.

Poor desolate little children; orphaned, yet not orphans!

Diana laid down her pen. and stretched her hand towards the bell, to send word that the hide-and-seek might go on. Then smiled at her own weakness. Why, even their mothers would have been obliged sometimes to say: "Hush! "If only Diana had known it, their own mothers would have said "Hush!" far more often than she did!

She took up her pen, and her surroundings were completely forgotten, as she talked to David.

"RIVERSCOURT, Christmas Eve.

"MY DEAR DAVID,—How well you timed your Christmas letter. It reached me this morning. So I have it for Christmas Eve, Christmas Day, and Boxing Day—all three important anniversaries to us. Had I but thought of it in time, I might have kept a sheet for each day. Instead of which, in my eagerness for news concerning the Church of the Holy Star, I read your whole long letter through, the very moment I received it. However, it will bear reading twice, or even three times; It is so full of interest.

"Indeed I shall be with you in thought at the opening ceremony. I intend to motor over to Winchester, and spend the time in prayer and meditation in your little Chapel of the Epiphany.

"It will not by any means be my first pilgrimage there, David. It is the place of all others where I find I can most easily pray for your work. I kneel where you knelt, and look up at the stained glass representation of the Wise Men. It brings back every word of the sermon you preached this day last year.

"When you were there, did you happen to notice the window on the left, as you kneel at the rail? It represents the Virgin bending over the Baby Christ. She is holding both His little feet in one of her hands. I can't understand why; but that action seems so extraordinarily to depict the tenderness of her mother-love. I dislike babies myself, exceedingly; yet, ever since I saw that window, I have been pursued by the desire to hold a baby's two little feet in my hand that way, jus to see how it feels! I am certain your mother often held your feet so, when you were a wee baby, David; and I am equally certain my mother never held mine. Don't you think tenderness, shown to little children, before they are old enough to know what tenderness means, makes a difference to the whole lives? I am sure I grew up hard-hearted simply because no demonstration of affection was ever poured out upon me in my infancy. You grew up so sweet and affectionate to every one simply because your mother lavished love upon you, kissed your curls, and held both your baby feet in one of her tender hands, when you were a tiny wee little kiddie, and knew nothing at all about it! There! Now you have one of my theories of life, thought out as I knelt in your little chapel, meaning to spend the whole time in prayer for your work.

"Last time I was there, just as I left the chapel, Evensong was beginning. I slipped quietly down the cathedral and sat at the very bottom of the vast nave. The service was going on away up in the choir, through distant gates. The music seemed to come floating down from heaven. They sang the 'Nunc Dimittis' to Garrett in F. 'Lord, whispered the angel voices, on gently floating harmony, 'Lord, now lettest Thou Thy servant depart in peace.' 'Depart in peace,' repeated the silvery trebles, soaring back to heaven! I thought of you; and of how you quoted it, looking up at the picture of Simeon in the temple, as we walked down old St. Botolph's Church. How relieved you were to be off, David; and how glad to go.

"I still make pilgrimages to St. Botolph's, when spending any time in town; or when I take a panic over your health, or your many African perils, snakes, poisoned darts, and such like things—not to mention an early hippopotamus, dancing a cake-walk in your front-garden, before breakfast.

"The verger is becoming accustomed to my visits. At first she watched me with suspicion, evidently fearing lest I had designs on the cherubs of the lectern, or purposed carving my name upon the altar-rail. When she found my prayer and meditation covered no such sinister intentions, she gave up prowling round, and merely kept an eye on me from her seat at the bottom of the church, Last time I went, I had quite a long talk with her, and found her a most interesting and well-informed person; well up in the history of the old church, and taking a touching pride and delight in it; evidently fulfilling her duties with reverent love and care, not in the perfunctory spirit-one finds only too often among church officials.

"But, oh David, what a contrast between this refined, well-educated woman, and the extraordinary old caretaker at that church to which you went when you were first ordained! Did I tell you I made a pilgrimage there? I thought it a beautiful church, and took a quite particular interest in seeing the pulpit, and all the other places in which you performed, for the first time, the sacred functions of your holy office.

"But I can't return there, David, or remember it with pleasure, because of the appalling old gnome who haunts it, and calls herself the 'curtiker.' I never saw anything quite so terrifyingly dirty, or so weirdly coming to pieces in every possible place and yet keeping together. And there was no avoiding her. She appeared to be ubiquitous.

"When I first entered the church, she was on her knees in the aisle, flopping a very grimy piece of: house-flannel in and out of a zinc pail, containing what looked like an unpleasant compound of ink and soapsuds. Our acquaintance began by her exhorting me, in a very loud voice, to keep out of the 'pile.' The pail was the very last place into which one would desire to go. So, carefully keeping out of it, and avoiding the flops of the flannel which landed each time in quite unexpected places I fled up the church. A moment later, as I walked round the pulpit examining the panels, she popped up in it triumphant, waving a black rag, which I suppose did duty for a duster. Her sudden appearance, in the place where I was picturing you giving out your first text, made me jump nearly out of my skin. Whereupon she said: 'Garn! and came chuckling down the steps, flapping he black rag on the balustrade. I hadn't a notion what 'garn' meant; but concluded it was Cockney for 'go on,' and hurriedly went.

"But it was no good dodging round pillars or taking circuitous routes down one aisle and up another, in attempts to avoid her. Wherever I went she was there before me, always brandishing some fresh implement connected with the process which, in any other hands, might have been church cleaning. So at last I gave up trying to avoid her, and stood my ground bravely, in the hopes of gleaning information from her very remarkable conversation. I say 'bravely,' because she became much more terrifying when she talked She held her left eye shut, with her left hand, put her face very close to mine, and looked at me out of the right eye. She didn't seem able to talk without looking at me; or to look at me, without holding one eye shut.

"I was dining at the Brands' that evening, and happened to say to the man who took me in: 'Do you know how terrifying it is to talk to a person who holds one eye shut, and looks at you with the other?' He wanted to know what I meant; so I showed how my old lady had done it, with head pushed forward, and elbow well up. Everybody else went into fits; but my man turned out to be a rising oculist, and took it quite seriously; declared it must be a bad case of astigmatism; asked the name of the church, and is going off there to examine her eyes and prescribe glasses!

"I tell you all this, in case she was a protégé of yours; for she remembers you, David.

"I am doubtful as to what manner of reception she will give to my friend the oculist. I felt bound to tell him she would most probably say 'Garn!' and his convulsive amusement seemed to me disproportionate to the mildness of the joke. Her incomprehensible remarks, and her astonishing Cockney make rational conversation with her very difficult. While I was in the church, a mild-looking curate came in, and tried to explain something which was wanted. I could not hear the conversation, but I saw her, at the bottom of the church, holding her eye, and glaring at him. She came back to me, brandishing a dustpan. "Ear that?' she said. 'Garn! As I always say to 'em: "A nod's as good as a wink to a blind 'orse!"'

"Now that sounded like a proverb, and she said it as if it were a very deep pronouncement, which might settle all ecclesiastical difficulties, and solve all parochial problems. But, when one comes to think of it, what on earth does it mean?

"Well David, she remembers you; so I have no doubt whatever that you know all about her; when she became a widow—all caretakers *are* widows, aren't they? how, and from what cause; the exact number of her children; how many she has buried, and how many are out in the world; what 'carried off' the former, and what are the various occupations of the latter. Not possessing your wonderful faculty for unearthing the family history and inner life of caretakers, I only know that her favourite conviction is: that a nod's as good as a wink to a blind horse; and—that she remembers you.

"I felt shy about mentioning you, while I was examining all the places of special interest; but when I reached the door, to which she accompanied me, gaily twirling a moulting feather broom, I turned, and ventured to ask whether she remembered you. She instantly clapped her hand over her eye; but the other gleamed at me, with a concentrated scorn, for asking so needless a question; and with ill-disguised mistrust, as if I were a person who had no business to have ever a nodding acquaintance with you.

"'It would taike a lot of furgittin' ter furgit *'im!'* she observed, her face threateningly near mine; the whirling feather broom moulting freely over both of us. ''E's the sort of gent as maikes a body remember!'

"So now, my dear David, we know why I never forget to write to you by each mail. You are the sort of gent who makes a body remember!

"I asked her what she chiefly recollected about you. She stared at me for a minute, with chill disapproval. Then her face illumined, suddenly ''Is smoile,' she said.

"I fled to my motor. I felt suddenly hysterical She had such quaint black grapes in her bonnet and you *have* rather a nice smile you know, David.

"Not many smiles come my way, nowadays, excepting Mrs. Mallory's; and they are so very ready-made. You feel you could buy them in Houndsditch, at so much a gross. I know about Houndsditch, because it is exactly opposite St. Botolph's, out of Bishopsgate Street. I tried to have a little friendly conversation with the people who stand in the gutter all along there, selling extraordinary little toys for a penny; also studs and buttonhooks, and bootlaces. They told me they bought them in Houndsditch by the gross. One man very kindly offered to take me to Houndsditch, and show me where they bought them. It was close by, so I went. He walked beside me, talking volubly all the way. He called me 'Lidy,' all the time. It sounded uncomfortably like a sort of pet-name, such as' Liza or 'Tilda; but I believe it was Bishopsgate for 'Lady,' and intended to be very respectful.

"The wholesale shop was a marvellous place; so full of little toys, and beads, and scent-bottles, and bootlaces, that you just crowded in amongst them, and wondered whether you would ever get out again.

"My very dirty friend was also very eager, and pushed our way through to the counter. He explained to a salesman that I was a 'lidy' who wanted to 'buoy.' The salesman looked amused; but there seemed no let or hindrance in the way of my 'buoying,' so I bought heaps of queer things, kept samples of each, and gave all the rest to my friend for his stock-in-trade. He was so vociferous in his thanks and praises, and indiscriminate mention of both future states, that I dreaded the walk back to Bishopsgate. But, fortunately, Knox, having seen me cross the road, had had the gumption to follow; so there stood the motor blocking the way in Houndsditch. Into it I fled, and was whirled westward, followed by a final: 'Gawd bless yur, lidy!' from my grateful guide,

"These people alarm me so, because I am never sure what they may not be going to say next. When *you* talk to them, David, you always seem able to hold the conversation. But if *I* talk to them, almost immediately it is they who are talking to me ; while I am nervously trying to find a way to escape from what I fear they are about to say.

"But I was telling you of Mrs. Mallory's smiles— —

.   .   .   .   .

"Just as I wrote that, my dear David, Mrs. Mallory appeared at the door, wearing one of them, and inquired whether I was aware that it was nearly eleven o'clock; all the children were asleep, and she was waiting to help me 'do Santa Claus'?

"So I had to leave off writing, then and there, and 'do Santa Claus' for my large family, with Mrs. Mallory's help. I began my letter early in the afternoon; and, with only short breaks for tea and dinner, have been writing ever since. Time seems to fly while I sit scribbling to you of all my foolish doings. I only hope they do not bore you, David. If the reading of them amuses you, as much as the writing amuses me, we ought both to be fairly well entertained.

"Now I am back in the library, having been round to all the beds, leaving behind at each a fat, mysterious, lumpy, rustling stocking! Oh, do you remember the feel of it, as one sat up in the dark? One had fallen asleep, after a final fingering of its limp emptiness. One woke— remembered!—sat up—reached out a breathless hand—and lo! it was plump and full—filled to overflowing. Santa Claus had come!

"I wish Santa Claus would come to empty hearts!

"David, you don't know how hard it is to go the round of those little beds upstairs, and see the curly tumbled heads on the pillows; feeling so little oneself about each individual head, yet knowing that each one represents a poor mother, thousands of miles away, who has gone to bed aching for a sight of the tumbled curls on which I look unmoved; who would give anything—anything—to be in my shoes just for that five minutes.

"There is a tiny girl here now, we call her 'Little Fairy,' whose mother died eight weeks ago, just as the parents were preparing to return to England. The little one is not to be told until the father arrives, and tells her himself. She thinks both are on the way. She talks very little of the father, who appears to be a somewhat austere man; but every day she says: 'Mummie's tumming home! Mummie's tumming home!' When her little feet begin to dance as she trips across the hall, I know they are dancing to the tune of 'Mummie's tumming home!' Each evening she gives me a soft little cheek to kiss, saying anxiously: 'Not my mouf, Mrs. Rivers; I's keeping that for mummie!' It's breaking me, David. If it goes on much longer I shall have to gather her into my arms, and tell her the truth, myself.

"Oh, why—why—why do people do these things in the name of religion; on account of so-called Christian work.

"I wish I loved children! Do you think there is something radically wrong with one's whole nature, when one isn't naturally fond of children?

"Hark! I hear chimes! David, it is Christmas morning! This day last year, you dined with me. Where shall we be this time next year, I wonder? What shall we be doing?

"I wish you a happy Christmas, David.

"Do you remember Sarah's Christmas card? Yes, of course you do. You never forget such things. Sarah retailed to me the conversation in St. Botolph's about it; all you said to her; all she said to you. So you and I were the turtledoves! No wonder you 'fair shook with laughin'!' Good old Sarah! I wonder whether she has 'gone to a chicken' for godpapa. Oh, no! I believe I sent him a turkey.

"There are the 'waits' under the portico. '*Hark the herald angels sing!*'

"I hope they won't wake my sleeping family, or there will be a premature feeling in stockings. These selfsame 'waits' woke me at midnight when I was six years old. I felt in my stocking, though I knew I ought not to do so until morning. I drew out something which rattled deliciously in the darkness. A little round box, filled with 'hundreds and thousands.' Do you know those tiny, coloured goodies? I poured them into my eager little palm. I clapped it to my mouth, as I sat up in my cot, in the dark. I shall never forget that first scrunch. They were mixed beads!

"Moral. . . .

"No, you will draw a better moral than I. My morals usually work out the wrong way.

"I must finish this letter on Boxing Day. Christmas Day will be very full, with a Christmas-tree and all sorts of plans for these little children of other people.

"Well the mail does not go until the 26th, and I shall like to have written to you on *our* three special days—Christmas Eve, Christmas Day, and Boxing Day. Good night, David."

CHAPTER XXVII

A QUESTION OF CONSCIENCE

"Boxing Day.

"WELL, my dear David, all our festivities are over, and having piloted our party safely into the calm waters of Boxing Day afternoon, I am free to retire to the library, and resume my talk with you.

"What a wonderful season is Christmas! It seems to represent words entirely delightful. Light, warmth, gifts, open hearts, open hands, goodwill—and, I suppose the children would add, turkey, mince-pies, and plum-pudding. Well, why not? I am by no means ashamed of looking forward to my Christmas turkey; in fact I once mentioned it in a vestry as an alluring prospect, to a stern young man in a cassock! I must have had the courage of my convictions!

"No, the fact of the matter is, I was very young then, David; very crude; altogether inexperienced. You would find me older now; mellowed, J hope; matured. Family cares have aged me.

"Yesterday, however, being Christmas Day, I threw off my maturity, just as one gleefully leaves off wearing kid gloves at the seaside, and became an infant with the infants. How we romped, and how delightfully silly we were! After the midday Christmas dinner, as we all sat round at dessert, I could see Mrs. Mallory eyeing me with amazed contempt, because I wore the contents of my cracker—a fine guardsman's helmet, and an eyeglass, which I jerked out and screwed in again, at intervals, to amuse the children. When I surprised Mrs. Mallory's gaze of pitying scorn, I screwed in the eyeglass for her especial benefit, and looked at her through it, saying: 'Don't I wear it as if to the manner born, Mrs. Mallory?' 'Oh, quite,' said Mrs. Mallory, with an appreciative smile. 'Quite, my dear Mrs. Rivers; quite.' Which was so very 'quite quite,' that nothing remained but for me to fix on my guardsman's helmet more firmly, and salute.

"Mrs. Mallory's cracker had produced a jockey cap, in green and yellow, and it would have delighted the children if she had worn it jauntily on her elaborately crimped coiffure. But she insisted upon an exchange with a dear little girl seated next her, who was feeling delightfully grown-up, in a white frilled Marie Antoinette cap, with pink ribbons. This, on Mrs. Mallory's head, except that it was made of paper, was exactly what she might have bought for herself in Bond Street; so she had achieved the conventional, and successfully avoided amusing us by the grotesque The jockey cap was exactly the same shape as the black velvet one I keep for the little girls to wear when they ride the pony in the park. The disappointment on the face of the small owner of the pretty mob-cap passed quite unnoticed by Mrs. Mallory. Yet she *adores* children. I, who only tolerate them, saw it. So did the oldest of the boys-such a nice little fellow. 'I say, Mrs. Rivers,' he said, 'swapping shouldn't be allowed.' 'Quite right, Rodney,' said I. 'Kiddies, there is to be no swapping!' 'Surely,' remarked Mrs. Mallory in her shocked voice, 'no one present here would think of *swapping?*' Rodney said, 'Crikey!' under his breath; and I haven't a notion, to this hour, what meaning the elegant verb 'to swap' holds for Mrs. Mallory.

"But here I go again, telling you of all sorts of happenings in our home life, which must seem to you so trivial. I wish I could write a more interesting letter; especially this afternoon, David. This time last year you and I were having our momentous talk. There was certainly nothing trivial about that! I sometimes wish you could know—oh, no matter what! It is useless to dwell perpetually on vain regrets. And as we *are* on the subject of Mrs. Mallory, David, I want to ask your opinion on a question of conscience which came up between her and myself.

"Oh, David, how often I wish you were here to tackle her for me, as you used to tackle poor old Chappie; only the difficulties caused by Chappie's sins were as nothing, compared with the complications caused by Lucy Mallory's virtues.

"She is such a gentle-looking little woman, in trailing widow's weeds; a pink and white complexion, china blue eyes, and masses of flaxen hair elaborately puffed and crimped. She never knows her own mind for five minutes at a time, is never quite sure on any point, or able to give you a straightforward yes or no. And yet, in some respects, she is the most obstinate person I ever came across. My old donkey, Jeshurun, isn't in it with Mrs. Mallory, when once she puts her dainty foot down, and refuses to budge. Jeshurun waxed fat and kicked, and did everything he shouldn't, but always yielded to the seduction of a carrot. But it is no good waving carrots at Mrs. Mallory. She won't look at them! She reminds me of the deaf adder who stoppeth her ears, lest she should hear the voice of the charmer. And always about such silly little things that they are not worth a battle.

"But the greatest trial of all is, that she has a morbid conscience.

"Oh, David! Did you ever have to live with a person who had a morbid conscience?

"Now—if it won't bore you—may I just give you an instance of the working of Mrs. Mallory's morbid conscience, and perhaps you will help me, by making a clear pronouncement on the matter. Remember, I only have her here because she is a missionary's widow, left badly off, and not strong enough to undertake school teaching, or any arduous post involving long hours. I have tried to make her feel at home here, and she seems happy. Sometimes she is a really charming companion.

"The first evening she was here, she told me she had always been 'a great Bible student.' She spends much time over a very large Bible, which she marks in various coloured inks, and with extraordinary criss-cross lines, which she calls 'railways.' She explained the system to me one day, and showed me a new 'line' she had just made. You started at the top of a page at the word *little*. Then you followed down a blue line, which brought you to a second mention of the word *little*. From there you zigzagged off, still on blue, right across to the opposite page; and there found *little* again This was a junction! If you started down a further blue line you arrived at yet a fourth *little*, but if you adventured along a red line, you found *less*.

"I had hoped to learn a lot from Mrs. Mallory when she said she was a *great* Bible student, because I am so new at Bible study, and have no one to help me. But I confess these railway excursions from *little* to *little*, and from *little* to *less*, appear to me somewhat futile! None of the *littles* had any connexion with one another; that is, until Mrs. Mallory's blue railway connected them. She is now making a study of all the Marys of the Bible. She has a system by which she is going to prove that they were all one and the same person. I suggested that this would be an infinite pity; as they all have such beautiful individual characters, and such beautiful individual histories.

"'Truth before beauty, my dear Mrs. Rivers,' said Mrs. Mallory.

"'Cannot truth and beauty go together?' I inquired.

"'No, indeed,' pronounced Mrs. Mallory, firmly. 'Truth is a narrow line; beauty is a snare.'

"According to which method of reasoning, my dear David, I ought to have serious misgivings as to whether your Christmas Eve sermon, which changed my whole outlook on life, was true—seeing that it most certainly was beautiful!

"Now listen to my little story.

"One morning, during this last autumn, Mrs. Mallory received a business letter at breakfast, necessitating an immediate journey to town, for a trying interview. After much weighing of pros and cons, she decided upon a train; and I sent her to the station in the motor.

"A sadly worried and distressed little face looked out and bowed a tearful farewell to me, as she departed. I knew she had hoped I should offer to go with her; but it was a lovely October day, and I wanted a morning in the garden, and a ride in the afternoon. It happened to be a very free day for me; and I did not feel at all like wasting the golden sunshine over a day in town, in and out of shops with Mrs. Mallory;

watching her examine all the things which she, after all, could not 'feel it *quite* right to buy.' She never appears to question the rightness of giving tired shop people endless unnecessary labour. I knew she intended combining hours of this kind of negative enjoyment, with her trying interview.

"So I turned back into the house, sat down in the sunny bay window of the breakfast-room, and took up the *Times,* thankful that the dear lady had departed by the earliest of the three trains which had been under discussion during the greater part of breakfast.

"But my conscience would not let me enjoy my morning paper in peace. I had not read five lines before I knew that it would have been kind to have gone with Mrs. Mallory; I had not read ten before I knew that it was unkind to have let the poor little soul go alone. She was a widow and worried; and she had mentioned the departed Philip, as a bitterly regretted shield, prop, and mainstay, many times during breakfast.

"I looked at the clock. The motor was, of course, gone; and the quarter of an hour it would take to send down to the stables and put in a horse would lose me the train. I could just do it on my bicycle if I got off in four minutes, and rode hard.

"Rodgers trotted out my machine, while I rushed up for a hat and gloves. I was wearing the short tweed skirt, Norfolk coat, and stout boots, in which I had intended to tramp about the park and gardens; but there was not time to change I caught up the first hat I could lay hands on slipped on a pair of reindeer gloves as I ran down stairs, jumped on to my bicycle, and was half-way down the avenue before old Rodgers had recovered his breath, temporarily taken by the haste with which he had answered my pealing bell.

"By dint of hard riding, I got into the station just in time to fling my bicycle to a porter, and leap into the guard's van of the already moving train.

"At the first stop, I went along and found Mrs. Mallory, alone and melancholy, in an empty compartment. Her surprise and pleasure at sight of me, seemed ample reward. She pressed my hand, in genuine delight and gratitude.

"'I couldn't let you go alone,' I said. Then, as I sat down opposite to her, something—it may have been her own dainty best attire—made me suddenly conscious of the shortness of my serviceable skirt, and the roughness of my tweed. 'So I am coming with you after all,' I added; 'unless you think me too countrified, in this get-up; and will be ashamed to be seen with me in town!'

"Mrs. Mallory enveloped me, thick boots and all, in grateful smiles.

"'Oh, of *course not'* she said. '*Dear* Mrs. Rivers! Of course not! You are quite *too* kind!'

"Now, win you believe it, David? Weeks afterwards she came to me and said there was something she *must* tell me, as it was hindering her in her prayers, and she could not enjoy 'fully restored communion,' until she had confessed it, and thus relieved her mind.

"I thought the dear lady must, at the very least, have forged my signature to a cheque, I sat tight, and told her to proceed. She thereupon reminded me of that October morning, and said that she *had* thought my clothes countrified, and *had* felt ashamed to be seen with me in town.

"Oh, David, can you understand how it hurt? When one had given up the day, and raced to the station, and done it all to help her in her trouble. It was not so much that she had noticed that which was an obvious fact. It was the pettiness of mind which could dwell on it for weeks, and then wound the friend who had tried to be kind to her, by bringing it up and explaining it.

"I looked at her for a moment absolutely at a loss what to reply. At last I said: 'I am very sorry, Mrs. Mallory. But had I stopped, on that morning, to change into town clothes, I could not have caught your train.'

"'Oh, I know!' she cried, with protesting hands. 'It did not matter at all. It is only that I felt I had not been absolutely truthful.'

"Now, David—you, who are by profession a guide of doubting souls, an expounder of problems of casuistry, a discerner of the thoughts and intents of the heart—will you give me a pronouncement on this question? In itself it may be a small matter; but it serves to illustrate a larger problem.

"Which was the greater sin in Mrs. Mallory: to have lapsed for a moment from absolute truthfulness ; or, to wound deliberately a friend who had tried to be kind to her? Am I right in saying that such an episode is the outcome of the workings of a morbid conscience? It is but one of many.

"I am often tempted to regret my good old Chappie, though she was not a Bible student, had not a halo of fluffy flaxen hair, and never talked, with clasped hands, of the perfections of departed Philips. I am afraid Chappie used to lie with amazing readiness; but always in order to please one, or to say what she considered the right thing.

"By they way, Chappie and Mr. Inglestry dined here the other night. Whenever I see them, David, I am reminded of how we laughed in the luncheon-car, on our wedding-day, over having left Chappie at the church, with two strings to her bow. I remember you said: 'Two beaux to her string' more exactly described the situation; a pun for which I should have pinched you, had my spirits on that morning been as exuberant as yours. Poor old Inglestry does not look as well as he used to do. There may be a chance for godpapa, yet!

"What an epistle! And it seems so full of trivialities, as compared with the deep interest of yours. But it is not given unto us all to build churches. Some of us can only build cottages—humble little four-roomed places, with thatched roof and anxious windows. I try to cultivate a little garden in front of mine, full of fragrant gifts and graces. But, just as I think I have obtained some promise of bloom and beauty, Mrs. Mallory annoys me, or something else goes wrong, and my quick temper, like your early hippopotamus, dances a devastating cake-walk in the garden of my best intentions, and tramples down my oleanders.

"Mrs. Mallory spends most of her time building a mausoleum to the memory of the Rev. Philip. Just now, she is gilding the dome. I get so tired of hearing of Philip's perfections. It almost tempts me to retaliate by suddenly beginning to talk about you. It would be good for Mrs. Mallory to realize that she is not the only person in the world who has married a missionary, and lost him. However, in that case, my elaborate parrying of many questions would all be so much time wasted. Besides, she would never understand you and me, and our—friendship.

"When the late Philip proposed to her, he held her hand for an hour in blissful silence, after she had murmured 'yes'; then bent over her and asked whether she took sugar in her tea; because, if she did, they must take some out with them; it was difficult to obtain in the place to which they were going! Philip was evidently a domesticated man. I should have *screamed*, long before the hour of silence was up; and flatly refused to go to any country where I could not buy sugar at a moment's notice!

"Oh, David, I must stop! You will consider this flippant. But Uncle Falcon enjoys the joke. He is looking more amused than I have seen him look for many months. He would have liked to see Philip trying to hold my hand. Uncle Falcon's amber eyes are twinkling.

"Talking of cottages, I was inspecting the schools the other day, and the children recited' po-tray' for my benefit. They all remarked together, in a sing-song nasal chant: 'The cottage *was* a thatched one,' with many additional emphatic though unimportant facts. I suggested, when it was over, that' The cottage was a *thatched* one,' might better render the meaning of the poet. But the schoolmaster and his wife regarded me doubtfully; saying that in the whole of their long experience it had always been: 'The cottage *was* a thatched one.' I hastily agreed that undoubtedly a long-established precedent must never be disregarded; and what *has been* should ever—in this good conservative land of ours—for that reason, if for no other, continue to be. Then I turned my attention to the drawing and needlework.

"How my old set would laugh if they knew how often I spend a morning inspecting the schools. But many things in my daily life now would be incomprehensible to them and, therefore, amusing.

"How much depends upon one's point of view. I jumped upon a little lady in the train the other day, travelling up to town for a day's shopping, for saying with a weary sigh and dismal countenance, that she was 'facing Christmas'! Fancy approaching the time of gifts and gladness and thought for others, in such a spirit! I told her the best 'facing' for her to do, would be to 'right about face' and go home to bed, and remain there until Christmas festivities were over! She pulled her furs more closely around her, and tapped my arm with the jewelled pencilcase with which she was writing her list of gifts. 'My dear Diana,' she said, 'you have always been so fatiguingly energetic' This gave me food for thought. I suppose even the sight of the energy of others is a weariness to easily exhausted people. A favourite remark of Chappie's used to be, that the way I came down to breakfast tired her out for the day.

"Well, as I remarked before, I must close this long epistle. I am becoming quite Pauline in my postscripts. As I think of it on its way to you, I shall have cause to recite with compunction: 'The letter *was*—a long one!'

"Good-bye, my dear David.

"May all best blessings rest upon the Church of the Holy Star, and upon your ministry therein.

"Affectionately yours,
"DIANA RIVERS.

"P.S. Don't you think you might relieve my natural wifely anxiety, by giving me a few details as to your general health? And please remember to answer my question about Mrs. Mallory's conscience"

CHAPTER XXVIII

DAVID'S PRONOUNCEMENT

WHEN David's reply arrived, in due course, he went straight to the point in this matter of Mrs. Mallory's conscience, with a directness which fully satisfied Diana.

"It is impossible," wrote David, "to give an opinion as to which was the greater or lesser wrong, when your friend had already advanced so far down a crooked way. Undoubtedly it was a difficult moment for her in the railway carriage, as in all probability her own critical thought gave you the mental suggestion of not being suitably got up for town. But you, in similar circumstances, would have said: 'Why, what does the fact of your clothes being countrified matter, compared to the immense comfort of having you with me. And if all the people we meet, could know how kind you have been and how you raced to the train, they would not give a second thought to what you happen to be wearing.'

"But a straightforward answer, such as you would have given, would not be a natural instinct to a mind habitually fencing and hedging, and shifting away from facing facts.

"Personally, on the difficult question of confession of wrongdoing, I hold this: that if confession rights a wrong, and is clearly to the advantage of the person to whom it is made, then confession is indeed an obvious duty, which should be faced and performed without delay.

"But—if confession is merely the method adopted by a stricken and convicted conscience, for shifting the burden of its own wrongdoing by imparting to another the knowledge of that wrong, especially if that knowledge will cause pain, disappointment, or perplexity to an innocent heart—then I hold it to be both morbid and useless.

"Mrs. Mallory did not undo the fact of her lapse from absolute truthfulness by telling you of it, in a way which she must have known would cause you both mortification and pain. She simply added to the sin of untruthfulness, the sins of ingratitude, and of inconsideration for the feelings of another. Had she forged your signature to a cheque, she would have been right to confess it, because confession would have been a necessary step toward restitution. All confession which rights a wrong, is legitimate and essential. Confession which merely lays a burden upon another is morbid and selfish. The loneliness of a conscience under conviction, bearing in solitude the burden of acute remembrance of past sins, is a part of the punishment those sins deserve. Then—into that loneliness—there comes the comfort of the thought: 'He Who knows all, understands all; and He Who knows and understands already, may be fully told all.' And, no sooner is that complete confession made, than there breaks the radiance of the promise, shining star-like in the darkness of despair: 'If we confess our sins, He is faithful and just to forgive us our sins, and to cleanse us from all unrighteousness.' Mrs. Mallory could thus have got back into the light of restored communion, without ever mentioning the matter to you.

"But this kind of mind is so difficult to help, because its lapses are due to a lack of straightforward directness, which would be, to another mind, not an effort, but an instinct.

"Such people stand in a chronic state of indecision, at perpetual cross-roads, and are just as likely to take the wrong road as the right; then, after having travelled far along that road, are pulled up by complications arising, not so much from the predicament of the moment, as from the fact that they vacillated into the wrong path at the crucial time when they stood hesitating. They need Elijah's clarion call to the people of Israel: 'How long halt ye between two opinions? If the Lord be God, follow Him; but, if Baal, then follow him'—honest idolatry being better than vacillating indecision.

"This species of mental lameness reminds me of a man I knew at college, who had one leg longer than the other. He was no good at all at racing on the straight; but round the grass plot in the centre of one of our courts, no one could beat him. He used to put his short leg inside, and his long leg out, and round and round he would sprint, like a lamplighter. People who halt between two opinions always argue in a circle, but never arrive at any definite conclusion. They are no good on the straight. They find themselves back where they originally started. They get no farther.

"Mrs. Mallory should take her place in the Pool of Bethesda among the blind, and the halt, and the withered. She should get her eyes opened to a larger outlook on life; her crooked walk made straight, and her withered sensibilities quickened into fresh life. Then she would soon cease to try you with her morbid conscience.

"Mrs. Mallory should give up defacing her Bible with the ink of her own ideas or the ideas of others. Human conceptions, however helpful, should not find a permanent place, even in your own individual copy of the Word of God. The particular line of truth they emphasized may have been the teaching intended for that particular hour of study. But, every time you turn to a passage, you may expect fresh light and a newly revealed line of thought. If your eye is at once arrested by notes and comments, or even by the underlining of special words, your mind slips into the groove of a past meditation; thus the liberty of fresh light, and the free course of fresh revelation, are checked and impeded. Do not crowd into the sacred *sanctuary* of the Word, ideas which may most helpfully be garnered in the *classroom* of your notebook. Remember that the Bible differs from all human literature in this: that it is a living, vital thing—ever new, ever replete with fresh surprises. The living Spirit illumines its every line, the living Word meets you in its pages. As in the glades of Eden, when the mysterious evening wind *(ruach)* stirred the leaves of the trees, making of that hour 'the cool of the day'—you can say, as the wind of the Spirit breathes upon your passage through the Word: 'I hear the voice of the Lord God walking in the garden in the cool of the day.' Then, passing down its quiet glades, straightway, face to face, you meet your Lord. No unconfessed sin can remain hidden in the light of that meeting. No conscience can continue morbid if illumined, cleansed, adjusted, by habitual study of the Word.

"There! I have calmly given my view of the matter, as being 'by profession, a guide of doubting souls, an expounder of problems of casuistry,' and all the other excellent things it pleased you to cal me.

"Now—as a man—allow me the relief of simply stating, that I should dearly like to pound Mrs. Mallory to pulp, for her utter ingratitude to you."

This sudden explosion on David's part brought out delighted dimples in Diana's cheeks; and, thereafter, whenever Mrs. Mallory proved trying, she found consolation in whispering to herself: "David—my good, saintly David—would dearly like to pound her to pulp!"

CHAPTER XXIX

WHAT DAVID WONDERED

ONE more episode, culled from the year's correspondence, shows the intimacy, constantly bordering on the personal, which grew up between David and Diana.

He had mentioned in one of his letters, that among a package of illustrated papers which had reached his station, he had found one in which was an excellent photograph of Diana, passing down the steps of the Town Hall to her motor, after opening a bazaar at Eversleigh.

David had written with so much pleasure of this that Diana, realizing he had no portrait of her, and knowing how her heart yearned for one of him, went up to town, and was photographed especially for him.

When the portrait arrived, and her own face looked out at her from the silver wrappings, she was startled by its expression. It was not a look she ever saw in her mirror. The depth of tenderness in the eyes, the soft wistfulness of the mouth, were a revelation of her own heart to Diana. She had been thinking of her husband when the camera unexpectedly opened its eye upon her. The clever artist had sacrificed minor details of arrangement, in order to take her unawares before a photographic expression closed the gates upon the luminous beauty of her soul.

Diana hurried the picture back into its wrappings. It had been taken for David. To David it must go; and go immediately, if it were to go at all. If it did not go at once to David, it would go into the fire.

It went to David.

With it went a letter.

"MY DEAR DAVID,—I am much amused that you should have come across a picture of me in an illustrated paper. I did not see it myself; but I gather from your description, that it must have been taken as I was leaving the Town Hall after the function of which I told you in September. Fancy you being able to recognize the motor and the men. I remember having to stand for a minute at the top of the long flight of steps, while some of the members of the committee, who had organized the bazaar, made their adieus. I always hate all the hand-shaking on these occasions. I suppose you would enjoy it, David. To you, each hand would mean an interesting personality behind it. I am afraid to me it only means something unpleasantly hot, and unnecessarily literal in the meaning it gives to 'handshake.' Don't you know a certain style of story which says, in crucial moments between the hero and the heroine: 'He wrung her hand and left her'? They always wring your hand—a most painful process—when you open bazaars, but they don't leave you! You are constrained at last to flee to your motor.

"'The fellow in the topper'"—Diana paused here to refer to David's letter, then continued writing, a little smile of amusement curving the corners of her mouth—"The 'good-looking fellow in the topper' who was being' so very attentive' to me, and 'apparently enjoying himself on the steps,' is our Member. His wife, a charming woman, is a great friend of mine. She should appear just behind us. The mayoress had presented me with the bouquet he was holding for me. I foisted it upon the poor man because, personally, I hate carrying bouquets. I dare say it had the effect in the snapshot of making him look 'a festive chap.' But he was not enjoying himself, any more than I was. We had both just shaken hands with the Mayor!

"It seems so funny to think that a reproduction of this scene should have found its way to you in Central Africa ; and I am much gratified that you considered it worth framing and hanging up in your hut.

"I am glad you thought me looking so like myself. I don't think I am much given to looking like other people! Unlike a little lady in this neighbourhood who is never herself, but always some one else, and not the same person for many weeks together. It is one of our mild amusements to wonder who she will be next. She had a phase of being me once, with a bunch of *artificial* violets on her muff!

"But to return to the picture. It has occurred to me that, as you were so pleased with it, you might like a better. It is not right, my dear David, that the only likeness you possess of your wife, should be a snapshot in a penny paper. So, by this mail, I send a proper photograph, taken the other day on purpose for you. Are you not flattered, sir?"

The letter then went on to speak of other things; but, before signing her name, Diana drew the photograph once more from its wrappings, and looked at it, shyly, wistfully. She could not help seeing that it was very beautiful. She could not help knowing that her heart was in her eyes. What would they say to David—those tender, yearning eyes? What might they not lead David to say to her?

At last his answer came.

"How kind of you to send me this beautiful large photograph, and very good of you to have had it taken expressly for me. I fear you will think me an ungrateful fellow, if I confess that I still prefer the snapshot, and cannot bring myself to take it from its frame.

"This is lovely beyond words, of course, and immensely artistic, but it gives me more the feeling of an extremely beautiful fancy picture. You see, I never saw you look as you are looking in this portrait, whereas the Town Hall picture is you, exactly as I remember you always; tall and gay, and immensely enjoying life, and life's best gifts.

"Conscious of ingratitude. I put the portrait up on the wall of my hut; but I could not leave it there, and it is now safely locked away in my desk.

"I could not leave it there for two reasons; its effect on myself, and its effect on the natives.

"Reason No. 1.Its effect on myself: I could not work, while it was where I could see it. It set me wondering; and a fellow is lost if he once starts wondering, out in the wilds of Central Africa.

"Reason No. 2. Its effect on the natives: They all began worshipping it. It became a second goddess fallen from heaven, like unto your namesake at Ephesus. They had seen a Madonna, brought here by an artist travelling through. They took this for a Madonna—and well they might. They asked: Where was the little child? I said: There was no little child. Yet still they worshipped. So I placed it under lock and key."

Diana laid her head down on the letter, after reading these words. When she lifted it, the page was blotted with her tears. Sometimes her punishment seemed heavier than she could bear.

She took up her pen, and added a postscript to the letter she was just mailing.

"Dear David, what did you wonder? Tell me".

And David, with white set face, wrote in answer: "I wondered who— — " then started up, and tore the sheet to fragments; threw prudence to the winds; went out and beat his way for hours through the swampy jungle, fighting the long grasses, and the evil clinging tendrils of poisonous growths.

When he regained his hut, worn out and exhausted, the stars were pricking in golden pin-points through the sky; one planet hung luminous and low on the horizon.

David stood in his doorway, trying to gain a little refreshment from the night wind, blowing up from the river.

Suddenly he laughed, long and wildly; then caught his breath, in a short dry sob.

"My God," he said, "I have so little! Let me keep to the end the one thing in my wife which I possess: my faith in her."

Then he passed into the hut, closing the door; groped his way to the rough wooden table; lighted a lamp, and sitting down at his desk, drew Diana's portrait from its silver wrappings, placed it in front of him, and sat long, locking at it intently, his head in his hands.

At last he laid his hot mouth on those sweet pictured lips, parted in wistful tenderness, as if offering much to one at whom the grey eyes looked with love unmistakable.

Then he laid it away, out of sight, and rewrote his letter.

"I wondered," he said, "at the great kindness which took so much trouble, only for me."

CHAPTER XXX

RESURGAM

"RIVERSCOURT, Feast of Epiphany.

"MY DEAR DAVID,—A wonderful thing has happened, and I am so glad it happened on the Feast of the Star, which is also—as you will remember—our wedding-day.

"I want to tell you of it, David, because it is one of those utterly unexpected, beautiful happenings, which, on the rare occasions when they do occur, make one feel that, after all, nothing is irrevocably hopeless, even in this poor world of ours, where mistakes usually appear to be irretrievable, and where wisdom, bought too dearly and learned too late, can bring forth no fruit save in the mournful land of might-have-beens.

"Last year, this day was one of frost and sunshine. This year, the little Hampshire farms and homesteads, all along the railway, cannot have looked either cosy or picturesque; and the distant line of undulating hills must have been completely hidden by fog and mist. It has sleeted, off and on, during the whole morning—a seasonable attempt at snow somewhere up above, frustrated by the unseasonable murky dampness of the earth, below, I wonder how often God's purposes for us, of pure white beauty, are prevented by the murk and mist of our own mental atmosphere.

This sounds like moralizing, and so it is! I thought it out, in Brambledene church this morning, while godpapa was enjoying himself in the pulpit.

"He took for his text: 'They departed into their own country another way.' He displayed a vast amount of geographical information, concerning the various ways by which the three Wise Men—oh, David, there were *three* all through the sermon; and I felt so wrathful, because Mrs. Smith's back view—I mean *my* back view of Mrs. Smith—was so smugly complacent, and she nodded her head in approval, every time godpapa said 'three.' I could have hurled my Bible, open at Matthew ii., at godpapa; and an agèd and mouldy copy of Hymns Ancient and Modem at Mrs. Smith; a performance which would have carried on, in a less helpful way, your particular faculty for making that congregation sit up. This desire on my part will possibly lead you to conclude, my dear David, that your wife was giving way to an unchristian temper. But she was not. She was simply experiencing a wifely pride in your sermons, and a quite justifiable desire that every word they contained should be understood and corroborated. Other ladies have hurled stools in defence of the faith, and thereby taken their place in the annals of history. Why should not your wife hurl a very, *very* old copy of Ancient and Modern Hymns and Tunes, and thus become famous?

"Well, as I was saying, godpapa was being very learned as to the probable route by which the Wise Men returned home, though he had already told us it was impossible to be at all certain as to the locality from which they started. This struck me as being so very like the good people who tell us with authoritative detail where we are going, although they know not whence we came.

"This thought unhitched my mind from god-papa's rolling chariot of eloquence, which went lumbering on along a high road of Eastern lore and geographical research, regardless of the fact that my little mental wheel had trundled gaily off on its own down a side alley.

"This tempting glade, my dear David, alluring to a mind perplexed by the dust of godpapa's highway, was an imaginary sermon, preached by *you*, on this selfsame text.

"I seemed to know just how you would explain all the different routes by which souls reach home; and how sometimes that 'other way' along which they are led is a way other than they would have chosen, and difficult to be understood, until the end makes all things clear. In the course of this eloquent and really helpful sermon of yours, occurred that idea about the snow, which caused me to digress at the beginning of my letter, in order to tell you I had been to Brambledene.

"The little church looked very much as it did last year; heavy with evergreen, and gay with flock texts, and banners. The font looked like a stout person suffering from sore throat. It was carefully swathed in cotton-wool and red flannel. The camphorated oil one took for granted. I sat in my old corner against the pillar. Sarah was in church. I had a feeling that, somehow, you were connected with the fact of her presence there. We gave each other a smile of sympathy. We both owe much to you, David.

"But you will think I am never coming to the point of my letter—the wonderful thing which has happened. I believe I keep postponing it, because it means so much to me; I hardly know how to write it, and yet I am longing to tell you.

"Well—after luncheon I felt moved, notwithstanding the weather, to go for a tramp in the park. There are days when I cannot possibly remain within doors. My holiday children were having a romp upstairs, in charge of Mrs. Mallory.

"I happened to go out through the hall; and, just as I opened the door, a station fly drove up, and the solitary occupant hurriedly alighted. I should have made good my retreat, leaving this unexpected visitor to be dealt with by Rodgers, had I not caught sight of her face, and been thereby arrested on the spot. It was the sweetest, saddest, most gently lovely face; and she was a young widow, in very deep mourning.

"'Is this Riverscourt,' she asked, as I came forward, 'and can I speak, at once, to Mrs. Rivers?'

"I brought her in. There was something strangely familiar about the soft eyes and winning smile, though I felt quite sure I had never seen her before.

"I placed her on the couch in the drawing-room, where you first saw Chappie; and turned my attention to the fire, while she battled with an almost overwhelming emotion.

"Then she said: 'Mrs. Rivers, I am a missionary, I have just returned from abroad. I only reached London this morning. My little girl had to be sent on, nearly a year ago. I have just been living for the hour when I should see her again. They tell me, you, in your great kindness, have had her here for the Christmas holidays, and that she is here still. So I came straight on. I hope you will pardon the intrusion.'

"'Intrusion!' I cried. 'Why, how could it be an intrusion? If you knew what it means to me when I hear of any of these bereft little boys and girls finding their parents again! But we have at least a dozen children here just now. What is the name of your little girl?'

"'Her name is Eileen,' said the gentle voice, 'but we always call her "Little Fairy."'

"David, my heart seemed to bound into my throat and stop there!

"'Who—who are you?' I exclaimed.

"The young widow on the sofa opened her arms with an unconscious gesture of love and longing.

"'I am Little Fairy's mummie,' she said simply.

"'But– –' I cried; and stopped. I suppose my face completed the unfinished sentence.

"'Oh, yes,' she said, 'I had forgotten you would know of the telegram. In some inexplicable way it got changed in transit. It was my husband's death it should have announced, not mine. I lost him very suddenly, just as we were almost due to leave for home. I did not wish my children to be told until my return. I wanted to tell them myself.'

"I rang the bell, and sent a message to Mrs. Mallory to send Little Fairy at once to the drawing-room. Then I knelt down in front of Fairy's mummie, and took both her trembling hands in mine. It does not come easy to me to be demonstrative, David, but I know the tears were running down my cheeks.

"'Oh, you don't know what it has been!' I said. 'To think of you as dead and buried, thousands of miles away; and to hear that baby voice, singing in joyous confidence: "Mummie's tumming home!" And the little mouth kept its kisses so loyally for you. I was told each evening: "Not my mouf,—that's only for Mummie!" I used to think I *must* tell her. Thank God, I didn't! And now— –'

"I broke off. Little Fairy's mummie was sobbing on my shoulder. We held each other, and cried together.

"'You won't leave her again?' I said.

"'Oh, no,' she whispered, 'never, never! I also have two little sons at school in England. *I* never could feel it right to be parted from the children. It was my husband—who— –'

"Then we heard a little voice, singing on the stairs.

"I ran out to the hall.

"That sweet baby, in a white frock and blue sash, was tripping down the staircase. Mrs. Mallory's middle-class instincts had rapidly made her tidy. She looked a little picture as she came' holding by the dark oak banisters.

"'Mummie's—tumming—home!' proclaimed the joyous voice—a word to each step. She saw me, waiting at the bottom, and threw me a golden smile.

"I caught her in my arms. I couldn't kiss her; she was not mine to kiss. But I looked into her little face and said: 'Mummie's *come* home, darling! Mummie's *come* home!'

"Then I ran to the drawing-room. I had meant to put her down at the door. But, David, I couldn't! I carried her in and put her straight into her mother's arms. I saw the little mouth, so carefully guarded, meet the living, loving lips. which I had pictured as cold and dead.

"Then I walked over to the window, and stood looking out at the sleet and drizzle, the leafless branches, the sodden turf, the dank cold deadness of all things without. Ah, what did they matter, with such love, such bliss, such resurrection within!

"David, I have always said I did not like children. For years I have derided the sacred obligation of motherhood. I have often declared that nothing would induce me, under any circumstances to undertake it. At last, by my own act, I have put myself into a position which makes it impossible that that love, that tie, that sweet responsibility, should ever be mine. I don't say, by any means, that I wish for it, but I have felt lately that my former attitude of mind in the matter was wrong, ignorant, sinful.

"And—oh, how can I make my meaning plain—it seemed to me that in that moment, when I put that little child into those waiting arms, without kissing her myself—I expiated that mental sin. I shall always have a hungry ache at my heart, because I gave Little Fairy up without kissing her, but that very hunger means conviction, confession, and penance. I shall never have a little child of my own; but I have experienced something of the rapture of motherhood, in sharing in this meeting between my little baby-girl and the mother I had thought dead.

"And now, David, I will tell you a secret. Had the father arrived home with the awful news, I had meant to ask leave to adopt Little Fairy. But you see I am not intended even to have other people's children for my own.

"After a while, as I stood at the window, I heard the mother say: 'Darling, dear father has not come home.'

"'Oh,' said Fairy's contented little voice, asking no questions.

"'Darling,' insisted the quiet tones of the mother, 'dear father has gone to be with Jesus.'

"I looked round. The baby-face was earnest and thoughtful. She lifted great questioning eyes to her mother.

"'Oh,' she said. 'Did Jesus want him?'

"'Yes,' said the sweet voice, controlling a sudden tremor. 'Jesus wanted him. So we have lost dear father, darling.'

"Then Fairy knelt up on her mother's knee, and put both little arms round her mother's neck, with a movement of unspeakable tenderness.

"'But we've gotted each uvver, Mummie,' she said.

"Oh, David, *we've gotted each other!* It seemed just everything to that little heart. And I believe it was everything to the mother, too.

"Now, do you wonder that this has made me feel as if none of earth's happenings, however sad, need be altogether hopeless; no mistake, however great, is wholly irretrievable.

"Our own sad hearts may say: 'He has lain in the grave four days already.' But the voice of the Christ can answer: 'Lazarus, come forth!'

"Are you not glad this wonderful thing took place on the Feast of the Star?

"Affectionately yours, Diana Rivers."

.   .   .   .   .

It so happened that David had a sharp bout of fever soon after the arrival of this letter. His colleague wondered why, in his delirium, he kept on repeating: "When I am dead, she can have a Fairy of her own! She can have a little Fairy, when I am dead!"

CHAPTER XXXI
"I CAN STAND ALONE"

In the early summer following the first anniversary of their wedding-day, Diana's anxiety about David increased.

His letters became less regular. Sometimes they were written in pencil, with more or less incoherent apologies for not using ink. The writing was larger than David's usual neat small handwriting; the letters less firmly formed.

After receiving one of these, Diana experimented. She lay upon a couch, raised herself on her left elbow, and wrote a few lines upon paper lying beside her. This produced in her own writing exactly the same variation as she saw in David's.

She felt certain that David was having frequent and severe attacks of fever, but he still ignored all questions concerning his own health, or merely answered: "All is well, thank you"; and Diana had cause to fear that this answer was given in the spirit of the Shunammite woman who, when Elisha questioned: "Is it well with the child?" answered: "It is well"; yet her little son lay dead at home.

In June, Diana wrote to David's colleague, asking him privately for an exact account of her husband's health. But the colleague was loyal. David answered the letter As usual, all was well; but it was *not* well that Diana had tried to learn from some one else a thing which she had reason to suppose David himself did not wish to tell her. He wrote very sternly, and did not veil his displeasure.

Womanlike, Diana loved him for it.

"Oh, my Boy!" she said, smiling through her tears; "my David, with his thin, white face, tumbled hair, and boyish figure! Sick or well, absent or present, he would always be master. I must try Sir Deryck."

But she got nothing out of her friend the doctor, beyond a somewhat stiff reminder that he had told her on her wedding-day that her husband ought to return from Central Africa within the year. Had she really allowed him to go, without exacting a promise that he would do so? He might live through two years of that climate; but his constitution could not possibly stand a third.

Her question, as to whether Sir Deryck had received recent news of David's health, remained unanswered.

Diana felt annoyed and indignant. A naturally sympathetic man is expected to be unfailingly sympathetic. But the doctor was strong as well as kind. He had been perplexed by the suddenly arranged marriage; surprised at David's reticence over it; and when he realized that David was sailing, without his bride, on the afternoon of his wedding-day, he had been inclined to disapprove altogether.

Diana sensed this disapproval in the doctor's letter. It hurt her; but it also stimulated her pride toward him and, in a lesser degree, toward David. That which they did not choose to tell her, she would no longer ask.

She was acquainted with at least half a dozen women who, under similar circumstances, would have telegraphed for an appointment, rushed up to town, and poured out the whole story to Sit Deryck in his consulting-room.

But Diana was not that kind of woman. Her pain made her silent. Her stricken heart called in pride, lest courage should fail. The tragic situation was of her own creating. That which resulted therefrom she would bear alone.

She could not see herself a penitent, in the green leather armchair, in Sir Deryck's consulting-room. A grander woman than she had sat there once, humbled to the very dust, that she might win the crown of love. But Diana's strength was of a weaker calibre. Her escutcheon was also the pure true heart, but its supporters were Courage on the one side, and Pride on the other; her motto: "I can stand alone."

So she lived on, calmly, through the summer months, while David's letters grew less and less frequent; and, at last, in October, the blow fell.

CHAPTER XXXII

THE BLOW FALLS

IN October, during the second autumn of their married life, the blow fell.

A letter came from David; very clear, very concise, very much to the point; written in ink, in his small neat writing.

"MY DEAR WIFE,—" wrote David, "I hope you will try to understand what I am about to write and not think, for a moment, that I undervalue the pleasure and help I have received from our correspondence, during the year and nine months which have elapsed since my departure from England. Your letters have been a greater cheer and blessing than you can possibly know. Also it has been an untold help to be able to write and share with you, all the little details of my interests out here.

"I am afraid these undeniable facts will make it seem even stranger to you, that I am now writing to ask that our correspondence should cease.

"I dare say you have noticed that my letters lately have been irregular, and often, I am afraid, short and unsatisfactory. The fact is—I have required all my remaining energy for the completion of my work out here.

"I want to bid you farewell, my wife, while I still have strength to write hopefully of my present work, and joyously of the future. I will not, now, hide from you, Diana, that my time here is nearly over. Do you remember how I said: 'I cannot *promise* to die, you know'? I might have promised, with a good grace, after all.

"This will be the last letter I shall write; and when you have answered it, *do not write again.* I may be moved from here, any day; and can give you no address.

"You must not suppose, my wife, that owing to the ceasing of our correspondence, you will be left in any uncertainty as to when the merely nominal bond which has bound us together is severed, leaving you completely free.

"I have written you a letter, which I carry, sealed and addressed, in the breast pocket of my coat. It bears full instructions that it is to be forwarded to you immediately after my death. A copy of it is also in my dispatch-box, so that—in case of anything unforeseen happening to my clothes—the letter would without fail be sent to you, so soon as my belongings came into the hands of our Society.

"This letter is not, therefore, my final farewell; so I do not make it anything of a good-bye, though it puts an end to our regular correspondence. And may I ask you to believe that there is a reason for this breaking off of our correspondence, a reason which I cannot feel free to tell you now; but which I have explained fully, in the letter you will receive after my death? If you now find this step somewhat difficult to understand, believe me, that when you have read my other letter, you will at once admit that I could not do otherwise. I would not give your generous heart a moment's pain; even through a misunderstanding.

"And now, from the bottom of my heart, may I thank you for all you have done for me and for my work? Any little service I was able to render you, was as nothing compared with all you have so generously done for me, and been to me, since the Feast of Epiphany, nearly two years ago.

"Your help has meant simply everything to the work out here. I am able to feel that I shall leave behind me a fully established, flourishing, growing, eager young Church. My colleague is a splendid fellow, keen, earnest, and a good Churchman. If you feel able to continue your support, he will be most grateful, and I can vouch for him as did the Jews of old, for the Roman centurion: 'He is worthy, for whom thou shouldest do this thing.'

"And, oh, if some day, Diana, you yourself could visit the Church of the Holy Star! Some day; but not yet.

"For this brings me to the closing request of my letter.

"I cannot but suspect that your kind and generous heart may incline you—as soon as you receive this letter, and know that I am dying—to come out here at once, in order to bid a personal farewell to your friend.

"*Do not do so.* Do not leave England until you receive word of my death. I have a reason, which you will understand by and by, for laying special stress upon this request; in fact, it is my last wish and command, my wife. (I have not had much opportunity for tyranny, have I?)

"How much your sympathy, and gay bright friendship, have meant to me, in this somewhat lonely life, no words can say.

"Just now I wrote of the time, so soon coming, when the nominal bond between us would be severed leaving you completely free. You must not even feel yourself a widow, Diana; because you will not really be one. I have called you my 'wife' I know; but it has just been a courtesy title. Hasn't it?

"Yet—may 1 say it?–I trust and believe the very perfect friendship between us will be a lasting link, which even death cannot sever. And there is a yet closer bond: One Lord, one Faith one Baptism. This is eternal.

"So—I say again as I said, with my hands on your bowed head, on that Christmas night so long ago. before we knew all that was to be between us:

"The Lord bless thee, and keep thee;
The Lord make His face shine upon thee, and
be gracious unto thee;

The Lord lift up His countenance upon thee, and give thee peace."

"Good-bye, my wife.

"Yours ever,

"DAVID RIVERS."

CHAPTER XXXIII

REQUIESCAT IN PACE

DIANA sat perfectly still, when she had finished reading David's letter.

A year ago she would have flung herself upon her knees, sobbing: "David, David!" But the time for weeping and calling him had long gone by. These deeper depths of anguish neither moaned nor cried out. They just silently turned her to stone.

Every vestige of colour had left her face, yet she did not know she was pale. She sat, looking straight before her, and—realizing.

David was dying, and David did not want her.

David was dying in Central Africa; yet his last request was that she should stay in England until she heard of his death.

Every now and then her lips moved. She was repeating, quietly: "The merely nominal bond which has bound us together." And then, with a ghastly face, and eyes which widened with anguish: "I have called you my 'wife,' I know; but it has just been a courtesy title. Hasn't it?"

Hasn't it! Oh, David, has it? Was it a courtesy title at the top of the gangway? *Good-bye, my wife.* Was it a courtesy title, when that deep possessive yearning voice rang in her ears for hours afterwards; teaching her at last what love, marriage, and wifehood might really have meant?

Was it a courtesy title when his first letter arrived, and the words *my dear wife* came round her in her shame, like strong protective arms?

All this time, had it meant even less to David than she had thought?

Often her punishment had seemed greater than she could bear. Often the branding-iron of vain regret had seared her quivering heart.

But this—this was indeed the cruel pincers of the Roman torture-chamber at her very breasts!

It had been just a courtesy title; and she had hugged it to her, as the one thing which proved that—however little it might ever mean—at least she was more to David than any one else on earth.

On earth! How much longer would he be on earth? David, with his boyish figure, and little short coat. Ah! In the pocket of that coat was a letter for her—one more letter; his farewell. And she was not to receive it until it would be too late to send any answer.

Oh, David, David! Is all this mere accident, or are you deliberately punishing your wife for the slight she put upon your manhood? She did it in ignorance, David. She mounted the platform of her own ignorance, and spoke out of the depths of her absolute inexperience.

Too late to send any answer! Yes; but there was time to answer this one. If she caught to-night's mail, David might yet receive her reply, and learn the truth before he died.

Pride and Courage stepped away, leaving, unsupported, the escutcheon of the pure true heart.

She took pen and paper and wrote her last letter to David.

Even had that letter been sent, so wonderful an outpouring of a woman's pent-up love and longing, so desperate a laying bare of her heart's life, could only have been for the eye of the man for whom it was intended. To read it would have been desecration; to print it, sacrilege.

But the letter was not sent. Half-way through Diana suddenly remembered that when it reached David he would be ill and weak, perhaps actually dying. She must not trouble his last moments with such an outpouring of grief and remorse, of longing and of loneliness.

And here we see the mother in Diana, coming to the fore in tender thought for David, even in the midst of her own desperate need to tell him all. Nothing must trouble his peace at the last.

The passionate outpouring was flung into a drawer.

Diana took fresh paper, and drew it toward her.

Courage came back to his place at the right of the escutcheon. Pride stayed away, for ever slain. But, in his stead, there stepped to the left, the Madonna with eyes of love, the Infant in her arms.

Then Diana—thrusting back her own fierce agony, that David might die in peace—began her final letter.

"RIVERSCOURT.

"MY DEAR, DEAR DAVID,—I do not need to tell you how deeply I feel your letter, bringing the news it does about yourself. But of course I understand it perfectly, and you must not worry at all over trying to make any further explanations. I will do exactly as you wish, in every detail.

"Of course, I should have come out directly your letter reached me, if you had not asked me not to do so. I long to be with you, David. If you should change your mind, and wish for me, a cable would bring me, by the next boat, and quickest overland route. Otherwise I will remain in England, until I receive your letter,

"I cannot stay at Riverscourt. It would be too lonely without any prospect of letters from you. But you remember the Hospital of the Holy Star of which I told you, where I was training when Uncle Falcon wrote for me? I have been there often lately, going up once a week for a day in the out-patients' department; and last week my friend, the matron, told me that the sister in one of the largest wards—my old ward—must, unexpectedly, return home for an indefinite time. This was placing them in somewhat of a difficulty.

"I shall now offer to take her place, and go there for three months or so; anyway until after Christmas. But Riverscourt will remain open, and all my letters will be immediately forwarded.

"You must not mind my going to the hospital. I shall find it easier to bear my sorrow, while working day and night for others. For, David—oh, David, it *is* a terrible sorrow!

"I must not worry you now, with tales of my own poor heart; but ever since I lost you, David, ever since our wedding-day evening, I have loved you, and longed for you, more, and more, and more. When you called me your wife on the gangway, it revealed to me, suddenly, what it really meant to be your wife.

"Oh, my Boy, my Darling, when I lose you, I shall be a widow indeed! But you must not let the thought of my sorrow disturb your last moments. Perhaps, when you reach the Land that is very far off. I shall feel you less far away" than in Central Africa. Be near me, sometimes, if you can, David.

"I shall go on striving to offer my gifts, though the gold and the frankincense will be overwhelmed by the myrrh. But the Star we have followed together, will still lead me on. And perhaps it will guide me at last to the foot of the shining throne, where my Darling will sit in splendour. And I shall see his look call me to him, as it called in old St. Botolph's; and I shall pass up the aisle of glory, and hear him say: 'Come, my wife.' Then I shall kneel at his feet, and lay my head on his knees. Oh, David, David!

"Your own wife, who loves you and longs for you,

"DIANA RIVERS."

There was much she would have expressed otherwise; there were some things she would have left unsaid; but there was no time to rewrite her letter. So Diana let it go as it was; and it caught the evening mail.

But even so, David never saw it, for it arrived, alas, just twenty-four hours too late.

Here endeth FRANKINCENSE

MYRRH

CHAPTER XXXIV

IN THE HOSPITAL OF THE HOLY STAR

ONCE again it was Christmas Eve; but, in the midst of the strenuous life of a busy London hospital, Diana scarcely had leisure to realize the season, or to allow herself the private luxury of dwelling in thought upon the anniversaries which were upon her once more; the three important dates, coming round for the third time.

She had fled from a brooding leisure—a leisure in which she dared not await the news of David's death, or the coming of his farewell letter—and she had fled successfully.

The Sister of Saint Angela's ward, in the Hospital of the Holy Star, had no time for brooding, and very few moments in which to give a thought to herself or her own sorrows. The needs of others were too all-absorbing.

Diana, in the severe simplicity of her uncompromising uniform; Diana, with a stiffly starched white cap, almost concealing her coronet of soft golden hair, bore little outward resemblance to David's sweet Lady of Mystery, who had stood in an attitude of hesitancy at the far end of Brambledene Church, on that winter's night two years before.

And yet the grey eyes held a gentleness, and the firm white hands a tenderness of touch, unknown to them then.

During the two months of her strong, just rule in the ward of Saint Angela, the only people who feared her were those who sought to evade duty, disobey regulations, or feign complaints.

The genuine sufferer looked with eager eyes for the approach towards his bed of that tall, gracious figure; the passing soul strained back from the Dark Valley to hear the words of hope and cheer spoken, unfalteringly, by that kind voice; the dying hand clung to those strong fingers, while the first black waves passed over, engulfing the outer world.

Christmas Eve had been a strenuous day in the ward of Saint Angela. Two ambulance calls, and an operation of great severity, had added to the usual routine of the day's work.

It was Diana's last day in charge. The Sister, whose place she had temporarily filled, returned to the hospital at noon, and came on duty at four o'clock.

Diana went to her own room at five, with a pleasant sense of freedom from responsibility, and with more leisure to think over her own plans and concerns than she had known for many weeks. At seven o'clock Sir

Deryck was due, for an important consultation over an obscure brain case which interested him. Until then, she was free. On the following day she intended to return to Riverscourt.

Her little room seemed cosy and homelike as she entered it. The curtains were drawn, shutting out the murky fog of the December night. The ceaseless roar of London's busy traffic reached her as a muffled hum. too subdued and continuous to attract immediate notice. A lighted lamp stood on the little writing-table, A bright fire burned in the grate; a kettle sang on the hob. A tea-tray stood in readiness beside her easy chair.

Within the circle of the lamplight lay a small pile of letters, just arrived. At sight of these Diana moved quickly forward, glancing through them with swift tension of anxiety.

No, it was not among them.

Several times each day she passed through this moment of acute suspense.

But, not yet had David's letter reached her.

Yet, somehow, she had long felt certain that it would come on Christmas Eve: the letter, at sight of which she would know that her husband had reached at last "the Land that is very far off."

Moving to the fireplace, she made herself some tea, in the little brown pot which, from constant use, by day and by night, had become a humble yet unfailing friend.

Then she lay back in her chair, with a delightful sense of liberty and leisure, and gave herself up to a quiet hour of retrospective thought.

It seemed years since that October morning when David's letter had reached her and she had had to face the fact that he was dying, yet did not want her; indeed begged, commanded her, to stay away.

In that hour she lost David; lost him more completely than she could ever lose him by death. A loved one lost in life, is lost indeed. She had never been worthy of David. She had tried hard, by a life of perpetual frankincense, to become worthy. But no effort in the present could undo the great wrong of the past.

Before the relentless hand of death actually widowed her, her sad heart was widowed by the fact that her husband was dying, yet did not want her with him; that his last weeks were to be undisturbed by letters to, or from, her. Her one joy in the present, her sole hope for the immediate future, had died at that decision.

Nothing remained for her but submissive acquiescence, a waiting in stony patience for the final news, and a wistful yearning desire that, while yet in life, David might learn, from her letter, the truth as to her love for himself. If it had reached him in time, it might bring her the consolation of an understanding postscript to that final farewell which was to come to her at last from the breast-pocket of David's coat.

Her departure from Riverscourt had been quickly and easily arranged.

For once, Mrs. Mallory's plans had worked in conveniently with other people's. On the very evening of the arrival of David's letter, she had sought Diana in the library, and had announced, amid tears and smiles and many incoherent remarks about Philip, her engagement to the curate of a neighbouring parish.

For the moment, Diana's astonishment ousted her ready tact. Whatever else Mrs. Mallory might or might not be, Diana had certainly looked upon her as being what Saint Paul described as a "widow indeed." And when Mrs. Mallory went on to explain that, though her own feelings were still uncertain and vague to a degree, dear Philip was so touchingly pleased and happy, Diana rose and stood, with bent brows, on the hearth-rug, until Mrs. Mallory finally made it clear that by one of those exceedingly wonderful coincidences in which we may surely trace the finger of an All-wise Providence, the curate's Christian name was also Philip! So the Philip who was so touchingly pleased and happy, was Philip number two!

This was enough for Diana. It was the final straw which broke the back of her much-enduring sympathy.

She unbent her level brows, smiled her congratulations, and, from that moment, swept Mrs. Mallory completely out of her mind and out of her life. She subsequently signed the cheque for a substantial wedding-present as impersonally as, a moment later, she signed another in payment of her coal merchant's account. Her own widowed spirit rendered it impossible to her ever to give another conscious thought to Mrs. Mallory.

At first, life in the hospital, with its incessant interest and constant round of important duties, roused her mind to a new line of thought, and wearied her body into sound and dreamless slumber, whenever sleep was to be had.

But, before long, the work became routine; her physique adjusted itself to the "on duty" and "off duty" arrangements.

Then a terrible loneliness, as regards the present, and blank despair in regard to the future, laid hold of Diana. She seemed to have lost all. She cared no longer for her stately home, her position in the county, all the many advantages for which she had ventured so bold a stake. She had now voluntarily surrendered them; and here she was, back in the hospital, in nurse's uniform, in her small simply furnished room, working hard, in order to escape from leisure. Here she was, in the very position to avoid which she had married David, and here she was, having married David, learnt to love him, and then—lost him.

Her gift of gold seemed worth little or nothing.

Her gift of frankincense had ended in heart broken failure.

What was left now, save myrrh—David's gift of myrrh, and her anguish in the fact that he offered it?

During this period of blank despair, Diana went one afternoon to a service in a place where many earnest hearts gathered each week for praise, prayer, and Bible study. She went to please a friend, without having personally any special expectation of profit or of enjoyment.

The proceedings opened with a hymn—a very short hymn of three verses, which Diana had never before heard. Yet those words, in their inspired simplicity, were to mean more to her than anything had ever as yet meant in her whole life. Before the audience rose to sing, she had time to read the three verses through.

> Jesus, stand among ns,
>   In Thy risen power;
> Let this time of worship
>   Be a hallowed boar.
>
> Breathe Thy Holy Spirit
>   Into every heart;
> Bid the fears and sorrows,
>   From each soul depart.
>
> Thus, with quickened footsteps,
>   We'll pursne our way;
> Watching for the dawning
>   Of the eternal day.

Who can gauge the power of an inspired hymn of prayer? As the simple melody rose and fell, sung by hundreds of believing, expectant hearts, Diana became conscious of an unseen Presence in the midst, overshadowing the personality of the minister, just as in the noble monument to Phillips Brooks, outside his church in the beautiful city of Boston, the mighty tender figure of his Master, standing behind him, overshadows the sculptured form of the great preacher.

The presence of the risen Christ was there; the Power of the risen Christ, then and there, laid hold upon Diana.

> Jesus, stand among us,
>   In Thy risen power—

pleaded a great assemblage of believing hearts; and, in very deed. He stood among them; and He drew near in tenderness to the one lonely soul who, more than all others, needed Him.

None other human words reached Diana during that "hour of worship." He, Who stood in the midst, dealt with her Himself, in the secret of her own spirit-chamber.

She saw the happenings of the past in a new light.

First of all, Self had reigned supreme.

Then—when the great earthly love had ousted Self—she had placed David upon the throne.

Now the true and only King of Love drew near in risen power; and she realized that He was come, in deepest tenderness, to claim the place which should all along have been His own.

> Bid the fears and sorrows
> From each soul depart.

"Fear not; I am the First and the Last, and the Living One."

Her whole life just now had seemed to be made up of fears and sorrows; but they all vanished in the light of this new revelation: "Christ is all, and in all."

Her broken heart arose, and crowned Him King.

Her love for David, her anguish over David, were not lessened; but her heart's chief love was given to Him unto Whom it rightfully belonged; and her soul found, at last, its deepest rest and peace.

> Thus, with quickened footsteps,
>   We'll pursue our way;
> Watching for the dawning
>   Of the eternal day.

Diana went out, when that hour was over, with footsteps quickened indeed. Hitherto she had been watching, in hopeless foreboding, for news of David's death. Now she was watching, in glad certainty, for the eternal dawn, which should bring her belovèd and herself to kneel together at the foot of the throne. For He Who sat thereon was no longer David, but David's Lord.

At last she realized that she too could bring her offering of myrrh. She remembered David's words in that Christmas Eve sermon, so long ago: "Your present offering of myrrh is the death of self, the daily crucifying of the self-life. 'For the love of Christ constraineth us, because we thus judge: that if one died for all, then were all dead; and that He died for all, that they which live, should not henceforth live unto themselves, but unto Him, Who died for them, and rose again.' Your response to that constraining love; your acceptance of that atoning death; your acquiescence in that crucifixion of self, constitute your offering of myrrh."

She understood it now; and she felt strangely, sweetly, one with David. He, in the wilds of Central Africa; she, in a hospital in the heart of London's busy life, were each presenting their offering of myrrh; and God, Who alone can make all things work together for good, had overruled their great mistake, and was guiding them, across life's lonely desert, to the feet of the King.

From that hour, Diana's life was one of calm strength and beauty. Her heart still momentarily ceased beating at the arrival of each mail; she still yearned for the assurance that David had received her letter; but the risen power which had touched her life had bestowed upon it a deep inward calm, which nothing could ruffle or remove.

Yet this Christmas Eve, so full of recollections, brought with it an almost overwhelming longing for David.

As she lay back in her chair, the scene in the vestry rose so clearly before her. She could see him seated on the high stool, little piles of money and the open book in front of him, two wax candles on the table. She could see David's luminous eyes as he said: "I cannot stand for my King. I am but His messenger, the voice in the wilderness crying: Prepare ye the way of the Lord; make His paths straight."

Poor David! AH unbeknown to himself, she had made him stand for his King. Yet truly he had prepared the way; and now, at last, the King was on the throne.

   .   .   .   .   .

Diana roused herself and looked at the clock: five minutes to seven.

She rose, and going to the window drew aside the curtain. The fog had partially lifted; the sky was clearing. Through a forest of chimneys there shone, clear and distinct, one brilliant star.

"And when they saw the star they rejoiced," quoted Diana. "Oh, my Boy, are you now beyond the stars, or do you still lift dear tired eyes to watch their shining?"

Then she dropped the curtain, left her room, and passed down the flight of stone stairs to meet Sir Deryck.

CHAPTER XXXV

THE LETTER COMES

As Diana and the great specialist passed through the lower hall the ambulance bell sounded, sharply.

They mounted the stairs together.

"Ambulance call from Euston Station," shouted the porter, from below.

Diana sighed. "That will most likely mean another bad operation to-night," she remarked to Sir Deryck. "These fogs work pitiless havoc among poor fellows on the line. We had a double amputation this afternoon—a plate-layer, with both legs crushed. The worst case I have ever seen. Yet we hope to save him. How little the outside world knows of the awful sights we are suddenly called upon to face, in these places, at all hours of the day and night!"

"Does it try your nerve?" asked the doctor, as they paused a moment at the entrance to the ward.

Diana smiled, meeting his clear eyes with the steadfast courage of her own.

"No," she said. "My hunting-field experiences stand me in good stead. Also, when one is responsible for every preparation which is to ensure success for the surgeon's skill, one has no time to encourage or to contemplate one's own squeamishness."

The doctor smiled, comprehendingly.

"Hospital life eliminates self," he said.

"All life worth living does that," rejoined Diana, and they entered the ward.

Half an hour later they stood together near the top of the staircase, talking in low voices over the case in which Sir Deryck was interested. They heard, below, the measured tread on the stone floor, of the ambulance men returning with their burden. It was the "call" from Euston Station.

The little procession slowly mounted the stairs: two men carrying a stretcher, a nurse preceding, the house-surgeon following.

Diana rested her hand on the rail, and bent over to look.

A slight, unconscious figure lay on the stretcher. The light fell full on the deathly pallor of the worn face. The head moved from side to side, as the bearers mounted the steps. One arm slipped down, and hung limp and helpless.

"Steady!" called the house-surgeon, from below.

The nurse turned, gently lifted the nerveless hand, and laid it across the breast.

Diana, clutching the rail, gazed down speechless at the face, on which lay already the unmistakable shadow of death.

Then she turned, seized Sir Deryck's arm, and shook it.

"It is David," she said. "Do you hear? Oh, my God, it is David!"

The doctor did not answer; but, as the little procession reached the top of the staircase, he stepped forward.

"Found unconscious in the Liverpool train," said the house-surgeon. "Seems a bad case; but still alive."

The bearers moved towards the ward; but Diana, white and rigid, barred the way.

"Not here," she said, and her voice seemed to her to come from miles away. "Not here. Into the private ward."

They turned to the left and entered a small quiet room.

"It is David," repeated Diana, mechanically. "It is David."

They placed the stretcher near the bed, which the nurse was quickly making ready.

As if conscious of some unexpected development, all stood away from it, in silence.

Diana and the doctor drew near. Their eyes met across the stretcher.

"It is David," said Diana. "He has come back to me. Dear God, he has come back to me!"

Her grey eyes widened. She gazed at the doctor, in startled unseeing anguish,

"Just help me a moment, Mrs. Rivers, will you?" said Sir Deryck's quiet, steady voice. "You and I will place him on the bed, and then, with Dr. Walters's help, we can soon see what to do next. Put you hands so. . . . That is right. Now, lift carefully. Do not shake him."

Together they lifted David's wasted form, and laid it gently on the bed.

"Go and open the window," whispered Sir Deryck to Diana. "Stand there a moment or two; then close it again Do as I tell you, my dear girl. Do it, *for David's sake.*"

Mechanically, Diana obeyed. She knew that if she wished to keep control over herself, she must not look just yet on that dear dying face; she must not see the thin travel-stained figure.

She stood at the open window, and the breath of night air seemed to restore her powers of thought and action. She steadied herself against the window frame, and lifted her eyes. Above the forest of chimney stacks, shone one brilliant star.

Her Boy was going quickly—beyond the stars. But he had come back to her first.

Suddenly she understood why he had stopped the correspondence. He was on the eve of his brave struggle to reach home. And why he had begged her to remain in England—oh, God, of course! Not because he did not want her, but because he himself was coming home. Oh, David, David!

She turned back into the room.

Skilful hands were undressing David.

Something lay on the floor. Mechanically Diana stooped and picked it up. It was his little short black jacket; the rather threadbare "old friend"

Diana gave one loud sudden cry, and put her hand to her throat.

Sir Deryck stepped quickly between her and the bed; then led her firmly to the door.

"Go to your room," he said. "It is so far better that you should not be here just now. Everything possible shall be done. You know you can confidently leave him to us. David himself would wish you to leave him to us. Sit down and face the situation calmly. He may regain consciousness, and if he does, you must be ready, and you must have yourself well in hand."

The doctor put her gently out, through the half-open door.

Diana turned, hesitating.

"You would call me—if?"

"Yes," said the doctor; "I will call you—then."

Diana still held David's jacket. She slipped her hand into the breast-pocket, and drew out a sealed envelope.

"Sir Deryck," she said. "this is a letter from David to me, which I was to receive after his death. Do you think I may read it now?"

The doctor glanced back at the bed. A nurse stood waiting with the hypodermic and the strychnine for which he had asked. The house-surgeon, on one knee, had his fingers on David's wrist. He met the question in the doctor's eyes, and shook his head.

"Yes, I think you may read it now," said Sir Deryck gently; and closed the door.

CHAPTER XXXVI

DIANA LEARNS THE TRUTH

DIANA passed to her room, with the sense of all around her being dream-like and unreal.

When the unexpected, beyond all imagining, suddenly takes place in a life, its everyday setting loses reality; its commonplace surroundings become intangible and vague. There seemed no solidity about the stone floors and passages of the hospital; no reality about the ceaseless roar of London traffic without.

The only real things to Diana, as she sank into her armchair, were that she held David's coat clasped in her arms; that David's sealed letter was in her hand; that David himself lay, hovering between life and death, just down the corridor.

At first she could only clasp his coat to her breast, whispering brokenly: "He has come back to me! David, David! He has come back to me!"

Then she realized how all-important it was, in case he suddenly recovered consciousness, that she should know at once what he had said to her in his farewell letter.

With an effort she opened it, drew out the closely written sheets, and read it; holding the worn and dusty coat still clasped closely to her.

"MY DEAR WIFE,—When you read these Lines, I shall have reached the Land from whence there is no return—'the Land that is very far off.'

"Very far off, yet not so far as Central Africa. Perhaps, as you are reading, Diana, I shall be nearer to you than we think; nearer, in spirit, than now seems possible. So do not let this farewell letter bring you a sense of loneliness, my wife. If spirits can draw near, and hover round their best beloved, mine will bend over you, as you read.

"Does it startle you, that I should call you this? Be brave, dear heart, and read on; because —as I shall be at last in the Land from whence there is no return—I am going to tell you the whole truth; trusting you to understand, and to forgive.

"Oh, my wife, my beloved! I have loved you from the very first; loved you with my whole being; as any man who loved *you*, would be bound to love.

"I did not know it, myself, until after I had made up my mind to do as you wished about our marriage. I had sat up all night, pondering the problem; and at dawn, after I had realized that without transgressing against the Divine Will I could marry you, I suddenly knew—in one revealing flash—that I loved you, my beloved—*I loved you.*

"How I carried the thing through, without letting it be more than you wished, I scarcely know now. It seems to me, looking back upon those days from this great solitude, that it was a task beyond the strength of mortal man.

"And it was, Diana. But not beyond the strength of my love for you. If, as you look back upon our wedding, and the hours which followed, and—and the parting, my wife, it seems to you that I pulled it through all right, gauge, by that, the strength of my love.

"Oh, that evening of our wedding-day! May I tell you? It is such a relief to be able to tell you, at last. It cannot harm you to learn how deeply you have been loved. It need not sadden you, Diana, because every man is the better for having given his best.

"The longing for you, during those first hours, was so terrible. I went down to my cabin—you remember that jolly big cabin, 'with the compliments of the company'—but your violets stood on the table, everything spoke of you; yet your sweet presence was not there, and each revolution of the screw widened the distance between us—the distance which was never to be recrossed.

"I tried to pray, but could only groan. I took off my coat; but when I turned to hang it up, I saw my hat, hanging where you had placed it. I slipped on my coat again. I could not stay in this fragrance of violets, and in the desperate sense of loneliness they caused.

"I mounted to the hurricane deck, and paced up and down, up and down. For one wild moment I thought I would go off, when the pilot left; hurry back to you, confess all, and throw myself on your mercy—my wife, my wife!

"Then I knew I could never be such a hound as to do that. You had chosen me, because you trusted me. You had wedded me, on the distinct understanding that it was to mean nothing of what marriage usually means. I had agreed to this; therefore you were the one woman on the face of God's earth, whom I was bound in honour not to seek to win.

"Yet, I wanted you, my wife; and the hunger of that need was such fierce agony.

"I went to the side of the ship. Beating my clenched fists on the woodwork, seemed to help a little. Then—I looked over.

"We were surging along through the darkness. I could see the white foam on the waves, far down below.

"Then—Diana, dare I tell you all?—then the black waters tempted me. I was alone up there. It would mean only one headlong plunge—then silence and oblivion. God forgive me, that in the agony of that moment of Time, I forgot Eternity.

"But lifting my eyes, I looked away from those black waters to where—clear on the horizon—shone a star.

"Somehow that star brought you nearer. It was a thing you might be seeing also, on this our wedding-night. I stood very still and watched it, and it seemed to speak of hope. I prayed to be forgiven the sin of having harboured, even for a moment, that black, cowardly temptation.

"Then, all at once, I remembered something May I tell you, my wife, my wife? It cannot harm you, after I am dead, that I should tell you. I remembered that you had laid your hand for one moment on the pillow in my bunk. At once, I seemed rich beyond compare. *your* hand—your own dear hand!

"I ran down quickly, and in five minutes I was lying in the dark, the scent of violets all me, and my head where your dear hand had rested. And then—God gave me sleep.

"My wife, I have often had hard times since then, but never so bad as that first night. And, though I have longed for you always, I would not have had less suffering; because to have suffered less would have been to have loved you less; and to have loved you less would have been unworthy of you, Diana;—of you and of myself.

"But what an outpouring! And I meant to write entirely of bigger and more vital things, in this last letter. Yet I suppose *I love you* is the most vital thing of all to me; and, when it came to being able to tell you fully, I felt like writing it all down, exactly as it happened. I think you will understand.

"And now about the present.

"I can't die, miles away from you! Since death has been coming nearer, a grave out here seems to hold such a horror of loneliness. It would be rest, to lie beneath the ground on which your dear feet tread. Also, I am possessed by a yearning so unutterable to see your face once more, that I doubt if I *can* die, until I have seen it.

"So I am coming back to England, by the quickest route; and, if I live through the journey, I shall get down into the vicinity of Riverscourt somehow, and just once see you drive by. You will not see me, or know that I am near; so I don't break our compact, Diana, It may be a sick man's fancy, to think that I can do it, yet I believe I shall pull it through. So, if this comes into your hands, from an English address, you will know that, most likely, before I died I had my heart's desire—one sight of your sweet face; and having had it, I died content.

"Ah, what a difference love—the real thing—makes in a man's life! God forgive me, I can't think or write of my work. Everything has now slipped away, save thoughts of you. However, you know all the rest.

"I am writing to ask you not to write again, as I shall be coming home—only I daren't give you that, as the reason! And also to beg of you not to leave England. Think what it would be, if I reached there, only to find you gone!

"And now about the future, my belovèd; *your* future.

"Oh, that picture! You know—the big one? I can't put on paper all I thought about it; but—it showed me—I knew at once—that somehow, some one had been teaching you—what love means.

"Diana, don't misunderstand me! I trust you always, utterly. But we both made a horrible mistake. Our marriage was an unnatural, unlawful thing. It is no fault of yours, if some one —before you knew what was happening—has made you care, in something the way I suddenly found I cared for you.

"And I want to say, that this possibility makes me glad to leave you free—absolutely free, my wife.

"You must always remember that I want you to have the best, and to know the best. And if some happy man who loves you and is worthy can win you, and fill your dear life with the golden joy of loving—why, God knows, I wouldn't be such a dog in the manger as to begrudge you that joy, or to wish to stand between.

"So don't give me a thought, if it makes you happier to forget me. Only—if you do remember me sometimes—remember that I have loved you, always, from the very first, with a love which would have gladly lived for you, had that been possible; but, not being possible, gladly dies for you, that you—at last—may have the best.

"And so, good-bye, my wife,
"Yours ever,
"DAVID RIVERS."

CHAPTER XXXVII

"GOOD-NIGHT, DAVID"

WHEN Diana had finished reading David's letter, she folded it, replaced it in the envelope; rose, laid aside her uniform, slipping on a grey cashmere wrapper, with soft white silk frills at neck and wrists.

Then she passed down the stone corridor, and quietly entered the darkened room where David was lying.

A screen was drawn partly round the bed.

A nurse sat, silent and watchful, her eyes upon the pillow.

She rose, as Diana entered, and came forward quickly.

"I am left in charge, Mrs. Rivers," she whispered. "I was to call you at once when I saw the change. The doctors have been gone ten minutes. Sir Deryck expects to return in an hour. He is fetching an antitoxin which he proposes trying, if the patient lives until his return. Dr. Walters thinks it useless to attempt anything further. No more strychnine is to be used."

"Thank you," said Diana, gently. "Now you can go into the ward, nurse. I will take charge here. If I want help, I will call. Close the door softly behind you. I wish to be alone."

She stood quite still, while the nurse, after a moment's hesitation, left the room.

Then she came round to the right side of the bed, knelt down, and drew David into her arms, pillowing his head against her breast. She held him close, resting her cheek upon his tumbled hair, and waited.

At length David sighed, and stirred feebly. Then he opened his eyes.

"Where—am I?" he asked, in a bewildered voice.

"In your wife's arms," said Diana, slowly and clearly.

"In—my wife's—arms? "The weak voice, incredulous in its amazed wonder, tore her heart; but she answered, unfaltering:

"Yes, David. In your wife's arms. Don't you feel them round you? Don't you feel her heart beating beneath your cheek'? You were found unconscious in the train, and they brought you to the Hospital of the Holy Star, where, thank God, I chanced to be. My darling, can you understand what I am saying? Oh, David, try to listen! Don't go, until I have told you. David—I have read your letter; the letter you carried in your breast-pocket. But, oh darling, it has been the same with me as with you! I have loved you and longed for you all the time. Ever since you called me your wife on the boat, ever since our wedding-evening, I have loved you, my Boy, my darling—loved you, and wanted you. David, can you understand?"

"Loved—loved *me?*" he said. Then he lay quite still, as if striving to take in so unbelievable a thing. Then he laughed—a little low laugh, half laugh, half sob—a sound unutterably happy, yet piteously weak. And, lifting his wasted hand, he touched her lips; then, for very weakness, let it fall upon her breast.

"Tell me—again," whispered David.

She told him again; low and tenderly, as a mother might croon to her sick child, Diana told again the story of her love; and, bending over, she saw the radiance of the smile upon that dying face. She knew he understood.

"Darling, it was love for you which brought the look you saw in the photograph. There was no other man. There never will be, David."

"I want you—to have—the best," whispered David, with effort.

"This *is* the best, my dearest, my own," she answered, firmly. "To hold you in my arms, at last—at last. David, David; they would have been hungry always, if you had not come back. Now they will try to be content."

"I wish—" gasped the weak voice, "I wish—I need not— –"

"Thine eyes shall see the King in His beauty," said Diana, bravely.

She felt the responsive thrill in him. She knew he was smiling again.

"Ah yes," he said. "Yes. In the Land that is very far off. Not so far as—as– –"

"No, darling. Not so far as Central Africa."

"But—no—return," whispered David.

"Yet always near, my own, if I keep close to Him. You will be in His presence; and He will keep me close to Him. So we cannot be far apart."

He put up his hand again, and touched her lips. She kissed the cold fingers before they dropped, once more, to her breast.

"Has our love—helped?" asked David.

"Yes," she said. "It brought me to the King. It was the guiding Star."

"The King of Love." murmured David. "The King of Love—my Shepherd is. Can you—say it?"

Then, controlling her voice for David's sake, Diana repeated, softly:

> The King of Lore, my Shepherd is,
>   Whose goodness faileth never,
> I nothing lack, if I am His,
>   And He is mine for ever.
>
> In death's dark vale I fear no ill,
>   With Thee, dear Lord, beside me;
> Thy rod and staff, my comfort still,
>   Thy Cross before, to guide me.

And so, through all the length of days,
Thy goodness faileth never;
Good Shepherd, may I sing Thy praise,
Within Thy house for ever.

"For ever!" said David. "For ever! It is not death, but life—everlasting life! This is life eternal—to know Him."

After that he lay very still. He seemed sinking gently into unconsciousness. She could hardly hear him breathing.

Suddenly he said: "I don't know what it is! It seems to come from your arms, and the pillow—you did put your hand on the pillow, didn't you, Diana?—I feel so rested, and I feel a thing I haven't felt for months. I feel sleepy. Am I going to sleep?"

"Yes, darling," sue answered, bravely. "You are going to sleep."

"Don't let's say 'Good-bye,'" whispered David. "Let's say 'Good-night.'"

For a moment Diana could not speak. Her tears fell silently. She prayed he might not feel the heaving of her breast.

Then the utter tenderness of her love for him came to the rescue of her breaking heart.

"Good-night, David," said Diana, calmly.

He did not answer. She feared her response had been made too late.

Her arms tightened around him.

"Good-night—good-night, my Boy, my own!"

"Oh—good-night, my wife," said David. "I thought I was slipping down into the long grasses in the jungle. They ought to cut them. I wish you could see my oleanders."

Then he turned in her arms, moving his head restlessly to and fro against her breast, like a very tired little child seeking the softest place on its pillow; then settled down, with a sigh of complete content.

Thus David fell asleep.

CHAPTER XXXVIII

THE BUNDLE OF MYRRH

"'IF he sleep, he shall do well,'" quoted the doctor, quietly. "Nothing but this could give him a chance of pulling through."

Diana looked up, dazed.

Sir Deryck was bending over her, scrutinizing closely, in the dim light, the quiet face upon her breast.

"Is he alive?" she whispered.

The doctor's fingers had found David's pulse.

"Alive? Why, yes," he said; "and better than merely alive. He has fallen into a natural sleep. His pulse is steadying and strengthening every moment. If he can but sleep on like this for a couple of hours, we shall be able to give him nourishment when he wakes. Don't move! I can do what has to be done, without disturbing him. . . . So! that will do. Now tell me. Can you remain as you are for another hour or two?"

"All night, if necessary," she whispered.

"Good! Then I will place a chair behind the screen, and either a nurse, or Walters, or myself will be there, without fail; so that you can call softly, if you need help or relief."

He bent, and looked again closely at the sleeping face.

"Poor boy," he whispered, gently. "It seems to me he has, in God's providence, reached, just in time, the only thing that could save him. Keep up heart, Mrs. Rivers. Remember that every moment of contact with your vital force is vitalizing him. It is like pouring blood into empty veins; only a more subtle and mysterious process, and more wonderful in its results. Let your muscles relax, as much as possible. We can prop you with pillows, presently."

The doctor went softly out.

"All night, if necessary," repeated Diana's happy heart, in an ecstasy of hope and thankfulness. "A bundle of myrrh is my well-belovèd unto me; he shall lie all night—all night—Oh, God, send me strength to kneel on, and hold him!"

She could feel the intense life and love which filled her, enveloping him, in his deathly weakness. She bent her whole mind upon imparting to him the outflow of her vitality.

The room was very still.

Distant clocks struck the hour of midnight.

It was Christmas Day!

From an old church, just behind the hospital, where a midnight carol service was being held, came the sound of an organ, in deep tones of rolling harmony. Then, softened by intervening windows, into the

semblance of angelic music, rose the voices of the choristers, in the great
Christmas hymn:

> Hark, the herald angels sing.
> Glory to the new-born King!

And kneeling there, in those first moments of Christmas morning;
kneeling in deepest reverence of praise and adoration, Diana's
womanhood awoke at last, in full perfection.

> Glory to the new born King.

the helpless Babe of Bethlehem, pillowed upon a maiden's gentle
breast, clasped in a virgin mother's arms; the Babe Whose advent should
hallow the birth of mortal infants, for all time;

> Born to raise the sons of earth;
> Born to give them second birth.

Diana hardly knew, as she knelt on, listening to the quiet breathing at
her bosom, whether the rapture which enfolded her was mostly mother-
love, or wifely tenderness.

But she knew that her heart beat in unison with the heart of the Virgin
Mother in Bethlehem's starlit stable.

She had seen, in one revealing ray of eternal light, the true vocation of
her womanhood.

And again the organ pealed forth triumphant chords; while the voices
of the distant choir carolled:

> Hark, the herald angels sing,
> Glory to the new-born King

CHAPTER XXXIX

HOME, BY ANOTHER WAY

EACH Feast of Epiphany, Mr. Goldsworthy makes a point of asking David to preach the Epiphany sermon in Brambledene Church,

The offertory, on these occasions, is always devoted to the work of the Church of the Holy Star, in Ugonduma. The offertory is always the largest in the whole year, but that may possibly be accounted for by the fact that Diana invariably puts a sovereign into the plate. David smiles as he sees it lying on the vestry table. It calls up many memories. He knows it was dropped into the plate by the hand which has given thousands to the work in Central Africa. He wears on his watch-chain the golden coin which, on that Christmas Eve so long ago, was Diana's first offering to his work in Ugonduma.

When David mounts the pulpit stairs, and appears behind the red velvet cushion, he looks down upon his wife, sitting in the corner near the stout whitewashed pillar, its shape accentuated, as is the annual custom, by heavy wreathings of evergreens.

She has become his Lady of Mystery once more; for the love of a noble-hearted woman is a perpetual cause of wonderment to the man upon whom its richness is outpoured nor does he ever cease to marvel, in his secret heart, that he should be the object upon which such an abandonment of tenderness is lavished.

And before the second Epiphany came round, that most wonderful of all moments in a man's life had come to David—the moment when he first sees a small replica of himself, held tenderly in the arms of the woman he loves; when the spirit of a man new-born, looks out at him from baby eyes; when he shares his wife's love with another; yet loves to share it.

Thus, more than ever, on that occasion, was the gracious woman, wrapped in soft furs, seated beside the old stone pillar, his Lady of Mystery. Yet, as she lifted her sweet eyes to his, expectant, they were the faithful, comprehending eyes of his wife, Diana; and they seemed to say: "I am waiting. I have come for this."

Instantly the sense of inspiration filled him. With glad assurance, he gave out his text, and read the passage, conscious, as he read it, that he knew more of its full meaning than he had known when he preached upon it from that pulpit, four years before:

"When they saw the star, they rejoiced with exceeding great joy. . . . And when they had opened their treasures, they presented unto Him gifts—gold, and frankincense, and myrrh."

* * * * *

Diana, in her motor, awaited David outside the old lich-gate.

As he sprang in beside her, and the car glided off swiftly over the snow, she turned to him, her grey eyes soft with tender memories.

"And when they had offered their gifts, David," she said, "when the gold, and the frankincense, and the myrrh had each been accepted—what then?"

"What then?" he answered, as his hand found hers upon her muff, while into his face came the look of complete content she so loved to see: "Why then—they went home, by another way."

Here endeth MYRRH

Echo Library
www.echo-library.com

Echo Library uses advanced digital print-on-demand technology to build and preserve an exciting world class collection of rare and out-of-print books, making them readily available for everyone to enjoy.

Situated just yards from Teddington Lock on the River Thames, Echo Library was founded in 2005 by Tom Cherrington, a specialist dealer in rare and antiquarian books with a passion for literature.

Please visit our website for a complete catalogue of our books, which includes foreign language titles.

The Right to Read
Echo Library actively supports the Royal National Institute of the Blind's Right to Read initiative by publishing a comprehensive range of large print and clear print titles.

Large Print titles are in 16 point Tiresias font as recommended by the RNIB.

Clear Print titles are in 13 point Tiresias font and designed for those who find standard print difficult to read.

Customer Service
If there is a serious error in the text or layout please send details to feedback@echo-library.com and we will supply a corrected copy. If there is a printing fault or the book is damaged please refer to your supplier.

Printed in the United States
109873LV00004B/7/A